As Lenardo's troops surged
through the streets toward
the approaching enemy,
a roaring wall of flame consumed them.

Lenardo grabbed Wulfston. "You've got to knock out their Reader!"

Wulfston nodded and concentrated. Mortar crumbled. Bricks shifted. The building wall swayed and fell, crushing at least twenty Adepts to death. In retaliation, a hurled thunderbolt flung Wulfston across the street.

Sheets of flame lighted the air. Thunderbolts shook the ground. Lenardo leaped back as the man next to him convulsed, a bolt searing through the body as it fell blasted, dead at Lenardo's feet.

The voice of the renegade Reader rang in Lenardo's head. //This time you won't escape. This time I'll kill you!//

Also by
Jean Lorrah

SAVAGE EMPIRE

By Jean Lorrah and Jacqueline Lichtenberg

FIRST CHANNEL

DRAGON LORD OF THE SAVAGE EMPIRE

JEAN LORRAH

PLAYBOY
PAPERBACKS

DRAGON LORD OF THE SAVAGE EMPIRE

Copyright © 1982 by Jean Lorrah

Cover illustration copyright © 1982 by PBJ Books, Inc., formerly PEI Books, Inc.

Published simultaneously in the United States and Canada by PBJ Books, Inc., formerly PEI Books, Inc. 200 Madison Avenue, New York, New York 10016. Printed in the United States of America. Library of Congress Catalog Card Number: 82-82000.

ISBN: 0-867-21221-7

First printing December 1982.

The entire *Savage Empire* series is dedicated to the person who got me into professional sf writing and then encouraged me to start my own series:

Jacqueline Lichtenberg

My thanks also go to Sharon Jarvis, my editor at Playboy Paperbacks, for her help and encouragement.

I would also like to thank the many readers who sent comments about *Savage Empire*. Here is the book you asked for, the further adventures of Lenardo and Aradia. As this book is published, I am completing the third book in the series, *Captives of the Savage Empire*.

If there are readers who would like to comment on this book, my publisher will forward letters to me. If you prefer, you may write to me at Box 625, Murray, KY 42071. If your letter requires an answer, please enclose a self-addressed stamped envelope.

All comments are welcome. I came to professional sf writing through fan writing and publishing, where there is close and constant communication between writers and readers. Thus I shall always be grateful for the existence of sf fandom, which has provided me with many exciting experiences and through which I have met so many wonderful people.

Jean Lorrah
Murray, Kentucky

Chapter One

The full moon lighted the land with ghostly luminescence. Lenardo, a dread fear constricting his heart, sought out Castle Nerius. He found the hills, the road, the forest. In a nearby field, the flat rock where they built the funeral pyres lay empty, cold in the pale moonlight.

As he approached the castle, his anxiety increased . . . and then he saw it, its walls and towers fallen, smoke rising from the remains of the houses that had clustered about its gate. There was no sign of life.

She's dead! By all the gods—I deserted her, and now she's dead, and our child with her.

Lenardo jolted out of his waking dream, the same dream that had haunted his sleep the past two nights. He had put it down to anxiety at being forced into a position of leadership, a role he was not born or trained to. But now, when the vision rose again in broad daylight, he wondered whether it was true—one of his precognitive flashes. He had never before had one so long or so detailed—or so persistent.

He was riding away from Castle Nerius, away from the events that had turned a Master Reader of the Aventine Empire into a Lord of the Land among the savages. Away from Aradia.

It was too far now to Read back to Castle Nerius. They had come a day's journey and another morning's ride. Within a few hours, Lenardo and his followers would reach the city of Zendi—his city now, the capital of the land he ruled. His land for as long as he could hold it.

It won't have to be long, he thought, reassuring himself.

I'll soon be able to begin peace negotiations between the savages and the Aventine Empire.

From some distance away, fear impinged on his consciousness. Someone else must have spotted the new Lord of the Land at the head of his army. He had been Reading that apprehension sporadically ever since they had crossed the no-man's-land scarred by the battle of Adepts and entered the lands Aradia had awarded to Lenardo.

This time, though, the fear was not the numb anxiety of conquered people pondering their fate. It rose to sharp terror and sparked with hatred, and Lenardo deliberately concentrated on the distant scene, trying to Read the cause of the raw emotions. . . .

A boy ran in terror, with a group of people chasing him in almost equal fear. All were peasants in rags, starvation-thin, but their fear on this early-summer morning spurred them on. The boy was in his midteens, long-legged and driven by panic, darting into the hedgerows in hope of finding a hiding place. His thoughts were incoherent: *I'm not! I'm not! I didn't do anything!*

Whatever crime the peasants thought the boy had committed, Lenardo Read that he was innocent. He spurred his horse, shouting, "Helmuth, Arkus! Follow me!"

The two men did not question his order but followed as Lenardo left the road, galloping cross-country in the direction of the manhunt.

The breathless quarry turned, seeking a way out. It was too far to the rocky outcroppings near the road. The muscles in his legs twitched; his heart thudded in his ears. Every way he looked there was open farmland, and the newly sprouted crops were not yet high enough to offer shelter.

As the boy hesitated in panic, the others rushed upon him, pulling him down, beating him, kicking him while he screamed, "I'm not, I'm not! It was my granther said it." Then one of the men kicked him in the jaw, and the words died into moans.

Lenardo flinched at every blow, with the boy's pain attacking him more and more strongly as he decreased the distance between them.

"Stop," he shouted, long before the peasants could possibly hear him over their own mad cries. "The boy is innocent."

But it was too late. A kick to the temple mercifully rendered the peasant boy unconscious, and as his pain cut off, Lenardo Read the others clubbing him with fists and farm tools, kicking him, aiming always at his head until they had beaten it to a bloody pulp—well after the boy was dead.

The three horsemen came pounding up, Helmuth and Arkus ahead of Lenardo, who had stopped spurring his horse in sick despair when the boy died. The peasants turned, their savage satisfaction changed once more to terror. They didn't know who these horsemen were, but any horsemen were people in authority who might do to the peasants whatever they pleased. Like the boy before them, they looked for somewhere to hide and found themselves trapped.

Helmuth and Arkus were armed, but their shields bore no device, as Lenardo had not yet chosen a symbol.

Arkus demanded with the voice of authority, "What have you done? How dare you murder one of my lord's people?"

Panicked eyes looked from one to the other of the two soldiers, but no one dared speak.

Helmuth said, "Tell us why you have done this." He was an old man, his voice gentler than Arkus'.

One of the peasants stepped forward, half bowing, and looking furtively toward Lenardo, who sat numbly staring at the blood-spattered tableau.

The peasant took in Lenardo's fine clothes and the wolf's-head pendant hanging on his breast. Then he stared at the sword Lenardo wore and asked hesitantly, "My lord?"

Lenardo understood his confusion. If a Lord Adept could not use his magical powers, neither could he then use a sword. *But I'm not a Lord Adept. I'm not fit to be a lord at all.*

Before Lenardo could answer, Arkus said, "Bow to

your new lord. And then speak, before his first act in this land is to punish you."

The peasants fell to their knees, and their spokesman babbled, "Oh, my lord—be welcome! The boy was a Reader, my lord—your enemy. We only killed one with the witch-sight—"

"Enough," Lenardo got out past the lump in his throat. He knew that they killed Readers here, had known the danger he faced when he left the empire on his quest into the savage lands—but that would change now. "I am—" he began, but Helmuth cut him off.

"This is Lenardo, your ruler. Never again will you take the law into your hands this way. You will take your problems to the magistrate Lord Lenardo appoints or to my lord himself."

The peasants were astonished, Lenardo Read. Drakonius, the Adept who had ruled this land for many years, had taken no interest in the problems of the common people, except to punish them if they did not provide enough men and food for his armies.

"Listen well to Helmuth's words," Lenardo said. "There will be a system of justice in this land." He could not yet bring himself to say "my land." "Never again will you kill someone without a proper hearing."

"But he was a Reader, my lord."

"He was not—"

Again Helmuth cut him off, this time recalling that he could communicate directly with Lenardo without the peasants' knowing. //They are terrified enough, my lord. Do not let rumor destroy you before you prove you can rule.// "He was not given a hearing," the old man said aloud. "You cannot be certain he was a Reader at all."

Lenardo was sweating after the hard ride, the pain, and his own nervous tension. He flung back the light cloak he had put on against the early-morning chill, exposing his right forearm, where the dragon's head, mark of the Aventine Exile, was burnt deep and permanently into his flesh. It was long-healed now, and he had grown accustomed to it, but when the peasants saw it, they gasped.

Lenardo felt their eyes devouring him in a strange combination of hope and fear. Then the man who spoke for them cried, "The white wolf and the red dragon! The boy was right. And he *was* a Reader, my lord, to have seen ye so."

No, the boy had not been a Reader. Lenardo knew that but accepted Helmuth's caution and didn't say it. Instead, he said, "Should you suspect anyone else of Reading, you will do him no harm. He is to be brought to me in Zendi. Is that clear?"

"Yes, my lord."

The peasants continued to grovel, waiting anxiously, and Lenardo Read that they expected to be punished for breaking a law he hadn't made yet. It was what Drakonius would have done.

Looking at the battered corpse, he asked, "Does this boy have a family?"

"Yes, my lord. A mother and a sister in the village. His father and granther died in the battle at Adigia."

"And you have destroyed the last man in that family," said Lenardo. "There can be no recompense for such a loss, but I charge all of you: Whatever needs those women have—plowing land, cutting wood, anything their men would have done for them—you are to do it. Do not think you can neglect this charge without my knowing. Arkus, ride back to the village with these men and extend my sympathy to the boy's family. Give them a measure of silver. It will not compensate, but perhaps it will ease their lives a bit."

The utter astonishment of the peasants followed Lenardo as he and Helmuth rode back toward their train. The old man said, "That was a very good move, my lord. It is exactly what the Lady Aradia would have done."

"Aradia could have stopped them before the boy was murdered," Lenardo replied bitterly.

"But she wouldn't have known it was happening at all," Helmuth pointed out.

That was true. Readers and Adepts had individual powers, but when they worked together. . . .

How life has changed in just a few short weeks!

Lenardo had been a teacher in the Academy at Adigia,

expecting to spend the rest of his life there, until Adigia was attacked by savage Adepts under the direction of a Reader: Galen, a boy Lenardo had trained but who had turned traitor to the empire. The only person who could hope to take Galen from the enemy was another Reader. Lenardo, who had taught Galen the techniques he had turned upon his own people, volunteered to go, speaking the same traitorous words Galen had in order to be condemned to exile: "We cannot fight the savages off. They are defeating us with their Adept powers. We must offer to share our Readers' abilities with them in order to gain peace."

The words were a lie at the time he spoke them. *But now I believe them*, he thought as he rode beside Helmuth, angling back toward the road.

Arkus joined them, reporting, "You really surprised those men, my lord. Drakonius would have destroyed their whole village if they'd gone against his will."

"Even if they didn't *know* his will?"

"That way, people got to know it very quickly." The young officer grinned, and Lenardo felt a moment's disgust at his callousness.

"Arkus, the destruction of people's lives is never amusing."

Arkus sobered. "My lord, I have not forgotten that you spared my life. Whatever your will, I shall serve you."

But Arkus did not really understand. Years of teaching had given Lenardo patience. Only time and exposure to a different way of thinking would change Arkus's attitude. *Just as leaving the empire changed mine.*

Leaving the empire in total ignorance, only by good fortune did Lenardo escape being taken by Drakonius. Fortune or fate—he was not certain what to term the sequence of events that had led him to wander, delirious with fever from an infection in his branded arm, into Aradia's lands. There his wolf's-head pendant—a gift from an old friend on his day of exile—was identified as the sign of the Lady Aradia, leader of an alliance of Adepts seeking to halt the spread of Drakonius' power and cruelty.

Aradia's father, Nerius, the one Adept with powers to equal Drakonius', was dying of a tumorous growth in his brain. With Lenardo's Reading to guide them, Aradia and her foster brother, Wulfston, had been able to dissolve the growth—and the old Adept had recovered in time to lead them in battle when Drakonius attacked.

In that battle, Nerius had been struck through by one of the thunderbolts that were the Adepts' most powerful weapon. But Drakonius had also died, and all his Adept henchmen with him. And Galen. *My student*, Lenardo reminded himself. *My fault his life was blighted. How can I take responsibility for other lives after Galen?*

The battle in which Galen died had taken place only a week ago. By savage custom, Aradia had divided the land they had won, awarding part of it to her brother Wulfston, part to the Lady Lilith, the only ally who had remained faithful in the face of Drakonius' attack. Then, to Lenardo's shock, she had announced, "The portion of land southward from the border of Lilith's land, east from Wulfston's, and west from mine I give to Lenardo."

Lenardo had asked her to cede those lands to the Aventine Empire as part of a peace treaty he hoped to negotiate as her emissary. Instead, she had given them to him, telling him that if he chose, he could return the lands to the Aventine Emperor. "He will take them, I guarantee it. And after that he will listen to nothing you have to say; I guarantee that, too."

Lenardo was forced to agree. The empire allowed Readers no power; they were the only citizens without the right to be elected to office. Only when he looked at his homeland from a new perspective did Lenardo question the customs that had taught him not to want money or property—tokens given to failed Readers who must leave the Academies to live among nonReaders.

But if his own empire had kept control over him, had not Aradia done so as well? The land she had given him was surrounded on three sides by Aradia, her brother, and their closest ally. True, Lenardo had asked her for Zendi . . . but she need not have divided the conquered lands in precisely that fashion.

On the other hand, she had left him with no border unprotected, except the southern border, which met the walls of the empire. No rival Lord Adept could attack Lenardo without first taking one of the three powerful Adepts whose alliance had defeated Drakonius.

Lenardo could not be certain of Aradia's motivations, for Adepts were the only people he could not Read. She was a possessive ruler, and yet she wanted him to learn to rule: "It is the only way you will make what you want of the world."

Lenardo fingered the wolf's-head pendant, symbol of his allegiance to Aradia. It was alabaster, carved so that a vein of violet beneath the translucent surface formed the eyes—Aradia's violet eyes, her pale skin, pale hair, perfect embodiment of the symbol. He recalled her smile, at once animal-innocent and wolf-cunning. He and Aradia shared a dream: an Academy at Zendi where Adepts and Readers would learn to work together. As long as they shared that dream, she would not be his enemy.

Most of Lenardo's train had kept on along the road toward Zendi, Lenardo's new home. It was also an old home to him; he had been born there, when it was still part of the Aventine Empire. Now he planned to restore its beauty as he remembered it from childhood.

But not all of his followers had kept on along the road. Eight men from the old Zendi garrison under Arkus' command had followed when Lenardo left the road—had followed part way and were now waiting . . . Lenardo Read them and realized that it was an ambush. *A Reader. Should have known better. Crazy, running off that way.*

One move that seemed erratic to them, and they were ready not just to abandon him but to kill him.

"Arkus—Helmuth—ambush ahead! Our own men."

"What?" from Arkus. "My lord, they wouldn't—"

"Spread out. They're just beyond the rocks. They intend to kill Helmuth and me—and you, Arkus, if you don't join them."

"My lord, I wouldn't!" The young commander paled in fear. His loyalty was firm, but would Lenardo believe it?

"I can Read you, Arkus, as easily as I Read them. They think to take us by surprise. We'll take them instead."

Arkus was first through the passageway, with Lenardo and Helmuth close behind. The soldiers didn't have to Read to know that they were caught. Realizing that Lenardo had Read them, they attacked.

The passageway between the rocks was narrow enough here so that all eight could not attack at once. Lenardo and his men turned their horses and took the attack of the first three easily: Helmuth was experienced, Arkus was young and strong and eager, and Lenardo's Reading told him his opponent's every move before it was made. In moments, three traitors were dead, and their horses were churning to escape while the other five attackers strove to reach their quarry.

"Get the Reader!" shouted one of the soldiers, and all five tried to converge on Lenardo.

One crossed swords with him while another maneuvered behind him. He Read the man but could not turn until he had dispatched the one before him. Jerking on his horse's reins, he made the animal rear; the sword of the man before him cut the horse's chest, while that of the attacker behind went harmlessly under Lenardo's arm, tangling in his cloak. He clasped his arm to his side, pinning the weapon as his horse plunged, screaming in pain, attacking man and horse before him in its momentary madness. The other horse caught the excitement and also reared, unseating its rider, and plunged through the melee, knocking other fighters out of its way. Lenardo ran his sword through the man scrambling to his feet and then twisted to disarm the man whose sword he still held pinned. Too late! He had drawn his dagger, and even as Lenardo was bringing his sword around and trying to control his horse, he flung the knife straight at Lenardo's heart, from not five paces away.

Lenardo's attempt to duck was useless; he was a dead man—until the dagger swerved to one side and dropped harmlessly to the ground. *Arkus*. He had that one Adept skill to influence the motion of small objects. Breathing a prayer of thanks to all the gods, Lenardo skewered his now-terrified assailant and turned to help Helmuth and Arkus. They needed no help. Two of the last three attackers were already dead, and the last one, now fighting afoot with Helmuth, was disarmed even as he watched.

Helmuth backed the man against the rock wall, sword at his middle, saying, "Now you will tell us the meaning of this attack. Who sent you? Who dares attack my lord?"

"Helmuth—no!" Lenardo shouted, but it was too late. The man's mind filled with horrified images of the tortures a Lord Adept could inflict, and he threw himself forward onto Helmuth's sword. The old man could not backstep quickly enough. He gasped, withdrawing the sword, and knelt by the fallen man, but there was nothing he could do.

"My lord, forgive me," said Helmuth. "We should have been able to question him, find out how many traitors there are among your army." As he said it, he looked at Arkus, holding his bloody sword at the ready.

"My lord, I knew nothing of their plot," Arkus said, pleading.

"I know," Lenardo tried to reassure him. "Helmuth, there was no plot."

"Those men swore loyalty to you," the old man said.

"True, nor did they begin this journey with the intent to turn on me. They were simply afraid and uncertain of how well a Reader could rule. When I went dashing off the road for no apparent reason, their worst doubts were confirmed, and *that* is when they decided they'd be better off without me. I *Read* them, Helmuth. Believe me—and believe Arkus. He didn't have to save my life just now, you know."

"I *did* have to, my lord," Arkus said firmly. "It was my duty as your sworn man."

Helmuth wiped off his sword and sheathed it. "I'm sorry I doubted you, lad. My lord, your horse is injured. You'd best ride one of these others. Arkus, help me put the bodies up on horses. We'll show the others what happens to those who think they can betray my lord."

When they rejoined their followers, shock went through the soldiers at seeing their fellows dead. Although Arkus and Helmuth told exactly what had happened, Lenardo

Read the rumors that immediately started to spread. Before they had gone five miles, he had become a brilliant leader who had set a trap to test the loyalty of his followers. There was no resentment. Those who had had no part in the plot against him felt themselves that much safer in having so clever a lord.

Lenardo sighed to himself. The logic of savages. What if they knew his intention to make an alliance with the empire? Would he ever be able to? If he earned the trust of these people, would he lose the trust of the Readers at home?

The problem weighed heavily. It might be months before he could go home, and by then Masters Portia and Clement, who had sent him on his mission into the savage lands, might not be willing or able to help him. He had been sent to take Galen from the enemy. With Galen dead, he ought to go directly back to the Aventine Empire. Portia, the Master of Masters among Readers, would then reveal to the Emperor the plan known only to herself, Master Clement, and Torio, the brilliant young Reader who had been Lenardo's student and to whom he had chosen to confide the plan of Readers, by Readers, to stop Galen.

As the Aventine government did not know of their plan, though, it had gone ahead with its own, removing the Academy from the dangerous border town of Adigia to the safety of the capital at Tiberium. Master Clement had had to go but had left Torio in Adigia to wait for Lenardo to contact him. The news of Galen's death had been sad to report, but at the time he had told Torio to expect him back soon. Two days later, Lenardo had had to make a new report: Aradia had made him a lord.

With the shock of the event still ringing in his mind, he had closed the door of his room at Castle Nerius, hoping that Torio had not yet left Adigia. His Reading abilities were limited by distance; only by leaving his body could he contact the boy from so far away.

He smoothed the bedclothes, lay down, and relaxed his body. Easily, his consciousness drifted upward as he concentrated on Adigia. Instantly he was "there," in the room at the inn where he had found Torio two nights before.

But the room was empty. "Looking" around, he was relieved to see Torio's clothes still hung on pegs, his books scattered across the chest by the bed. The boy should have been at his studies until suppertime, but as the only Reader in Adigia, he could have been called to help someone.

The town was familiar; Lenardo had grown up there, had no fear of losing his conscious self among the streets and byways. But he hadn't far to search. Torio's disciplined mind stood out like a beacon from those of nonReaders. Blind from birth, Torio rarely stopped Reading, for if he did, the world disappeared.

Right now, however, he was engaged in a most unReaderlike activity: playing at dice with the stableboy and the smith's apprentice and proving beyond doubt that he had neither precognitive powers nor the ability to influence objects in motion.

//Torio!// Lenardo could not control his indignation.

The boy jumped and blushed hotly, but there was anger beneath his embarrassment until he realized who was contacting him. //Master Lenardo! I didn't think you would contact me again. Are you coming home?// Aloud, he said, "You've won enough for one day. Perhaps tomorrow my luck will be better."

Despite the protests of the other boys, Torio left them and headed across the innyard and up to his room.

//What are you doing gambling with servants instead of studying? Master Clement thought you could be left to work by yourself.//

//That's what I thought, too,// Torio told Lenardo in frustration. //Then this morning, he told me my testing has been postponed because of the time I've lost here. And I can't be a tutor, after all. He didn't test me, Master Lenardo, he just decided I hadn't kept up with my work—//

//And so you decided you might as well prove him right?//

//It was just today. I'd already decided to get back to

work tomorrow morning. I'll show Master Clement! I'll be ready for examination as soon as I get to Tiberium.//

//You won't be eighteen until autumn, no matter what you do. But I'm not worried about you, Torio—you'll pass.//

By this time Torio had reached his room, where he sprawled on the bed in the time-honored manner of schoolboys. //Of course I'll pass. But Master Lenardo, what's wrong? Why have you contacted me?//

//I won't be home as soon as I thought.//

//You said it might be weeks. Portia was angry, Master Clement said. She wants you back at once, to report to the Emperor that the leader of the savages is dead. Then while they're disorganized, we'll attack. You'll be a great hero.//

//Torio, I want to *prevent* war, not start it. Haven't we lost enough?''

//What can you do?//

Lenardo suddenly realized that if Portia intended to urge the Emperor to regain ·former empire territory, the news that Lenardo now claimed that territory as a savage Lord of the Land would make him a target rather than a hero. //I . . . cannot tell you, Torio. I must ask you to trust me.//

He felt the boy's throat tighten. //I do trust you. I thought you trusted me, Master.//

//Were you a Master Reader, I would tell you all, but until you reach your full powers, there will always be those who can Read what you know, whether you wish it or not.//

//But Masters Clement and Portia—//

//—Are not the only Readers in Tiberium,// Lenardo told him, although he wondered whether even Master Clement would approve of his plan. //I cannot reach Tiberium from where I am now, and I shall be no nearer for months. But Torio, under Oath of Truth, tell Clement and Portia that when I return, I hope to bring an end to the conflict and stop the savage encroachment upon our borders.//

//But I'm to leave here next week, Master Lenardo. You can't contact my replacement—he won't *know*. Oh, please, please come home now.//

//Torio, you are almost fully grown. You must complete

your studies and take your examinations, for I shall have work for Readers.//

//I don't understand. Why do you want to stay there with the savages? You haven't really turned traitor?//

//Do you think I could?//

//No, but Portia fears it.//

//Did Master Clement tell you that?//

//He didn't mean to. I felt it beneath what he told me. *He* trusts you, but Portia—//

//And he fears you may not pass your examinations? Torio, I've never known a Reader of your age who could Read what a Master Reader didn't want him to. No, I am no traitor, but I must have time to make preparations. A year, at the most—//

//A year!// Torio was horrified. //They'll never trust you after that long. Master Lenardo, you must come home now.//

//And start another war? I *cannot* do that, Torio. But don't you worry. When I do come to Tiberium, the Emperor will have to listen to me.//

Thinking back over that conversation with Torio, Lenardo realized again that Aradia was right. He was now trapped into seeking peace the way she wanted, from a position of power. And it was not Aradia who had trapped him—it was his own people. No, he could not hand over his lands to the Emperor. That would result in an immediate attack, using those lands as a base, on Aradia, Lilith, and Wulfston. His lands would be a wedge separating the three allies, which meant that Aradia trusted him not to make them such.

Thus hope and apprehension battled in Lenardo's mind as he rode toward Zendi at the head of an army—some soldiers but mostly civilians who had chosen to go with him into his new land. *My land.* It would never sound right. Nonetheless, he must live up to his duties to land and people until the day he could safely make the treaty he sought.

Lenardo noticed the well-developed crops beginning to wither in the fields. "No rain since the battle," he commented to Helmuth. "If we can find some clouds, we'll put Josa right to work. We can't afford to lose what food there is, or we'll be in for a hard winter." Josa was Helmuth's niece, one of the many people with minor Adept talents the old man had gathered for Lenardo's entourage.

"I'll help," said Arkus, who was riding on Lenardo's other side. "I can move anything light."

The young captain, promoted to commander of all that was left of Zendi's troops, was eager to dispel any doubts Lenardo had left about him. Arkus's future rested on Lenardo's. Human nature, as Aradia said. As long as it was in his own self-interest, Arkus would work faithfully for Lenardo.

Northgate stood open when they approached Zendi. At least no one opposed their entry. In the warmth of the day, the stench was unbelievable. Within the walls, all Lenardo could do was rein in and stare, too stunned even to Read.

The main market way through the city was strewn with corpses, human and animal. Debris littered the streets. What buildings were not burnt-out shells were looted, doors and shutters hanging, broken furniture tossed on the doorsteps.

People hid in the shadows, staring out in fear and hate—crowds of people in rags supplemented with bits of stolen finery. There was no coherent thought to be Read; they were like trapped animals: hungry, terrified, and desperate.

The gods help me, he thought. *Is this my capital city? Are these the people I'm supposed to teach to trust me?*

Paralyzed even beyond nausea, he sat hopelessly staring at . . . *my land.*

Chapter Two

Before Lenardo could even think of a command, Arkus turned his horse and began firing orders to his troops to clear people out of the looted buildings.

Helmuth shouted, "Greg, Vona! Up here and make us a clean path."

As two people rode forward, the corpses began to go up one by one in the roaring blaze of funeral pyres. The other debris burned with the bodies, and the paving stones were purified in the wake of the flames.

The obvious done, people began turning to Lenardo for orders. Dragging himself out of lethargy, he said, "We need a place to stay and a clean place to set up a kitchen and a hospital."

"Where, my lord?"

He Read the shambles all around them, despairing of clearing an area large enough to let his people—*my people*—sleep without the stench of death in their nostrils and rats crawling over their feet.

But there was one building. . . . He laughed as he realized it: "The one place Drakonius never used—the baths!"

The huge Aventine bathhouse, built to serve an entire city, was almost untouched. It stood on the edge of the forum, empty, unharmed by the looting because there was nothing in it to loot. The baths were dry, but the spring that served them had been diverted to form the city's water supply. Clean, fresh water tumbled from a pipe at the side of the bathhouse into the beginning of the ditch that had replaced the overloaded sewer system.

Lenardo led his train through the streets to the forum

and then pointed. "Sweep it out, scrub it down. Where's Sandor? Set up an infirmary and start processing the sick and injured. Call me if you can't see what's wrong."

"But my lord—"

"Give a mental shout—I'll be Reading." He turned to the cook and her staff, who were looking considerably sickened by the mess. "Those people the soldiers are rounding up are hungry. There's no food in the city, and we have our own to feed as well. No fireplaces in the baths—can you clear a place on the front steps and cook over an open fire?"

"Aye, my lord," said the woman who had volunteered to head his cooking staff, and set her people to hauling buckets of water to scrub down a section of the forum.

Once started, Lenardo found it easy enough to give orders. There was so much to be done. It was well after sunset when Cook descended on him with soup, bread, and cheese. He realized that he hadn't eaten all day.

As he sniffed the soup appreciatively, Cook said, "It's vegetable."

"I know," he replied, and she blushed.

"Sorry, me lord. I forget. But I didn't forget you don't eat meat."

"You didn't make special soup just for me?"

"Of course."

"With everything else you had to do today? Now, you mustn't do that again until we're settled and you're cooking just for me and my . . . household."

"Yes, me lord." But she was distressed.

"Thank you this time, Cook. The soup is delicious. If there's any left, I'll have it tomorrow, but no fussing over me. From now on, just bring me anything you have except meat."

Arkus found him still sitting on the steps outside the bathhouse, finishing the bread and cheese. "What shall we do with the prisoners, my lord?"

"What prisoners?"

"Why, all these people. We've rounded up over a thousand. Where are we going to put them for the night?"

"Let them sleep wherever they've been sleeping until we can create some kind of order."

"But they'll hide again."

"They'll come out for breakfast."

"Not," replied Arkus, "when they know the flogging starts tomorrow."

"Flogging?" Lenardo exclaimed. "What are you talking about?"

"They're thieves, my lord. They've stolen and destroyed your property. You must punish them, and since you're not an Adept, you can't do what Drakonius did."

"No, I'm not Drakonius," Lenardo murmured, recalling with a shudder the time he had observed, powerless, the Adept torturing Galen.

"Well, even Drakonius couldn't handle all the punishments himself. We always flog most of them."

"Not any more, you don't. Arkus, have you looked into the infirmary? There are over a hundred sick and injured people in there. Sandor's exhausted, and now you would deliberately injure a thousand more?"

"Sandor wouldn't have to heal them, and they must be punished," Arkus insisted stubbornly. "Do you want your people to think they can steal from you any time they feel like it?"

"No, but look around. There is an incredible amount of work to be done. Make them do it."

"I don't understand."

"Greg and Vona must burn the rest of the bodies to keep disease from spreading. Let the prisoners scrub down the streets. Then they can rebuild the houses they destroyed."

He could Read Arkus' grim disappointment as the young officer said, "What's the matter with you? You can't rule if you act like a country grandmother over a little bloodshed."

"I've shed my share of blood, Arkus. You've seen me fight when I had to. But consider this: how eager would you be to flog someone if you felt every stroke on your own back?"

Arkus's disappointment turned to dismay. "It must be a

whole different world for a Reader. Are you not tired, my lord?''

Tired of explaining that Reading did not use up physical energy the way Adept powers did, he simply said, "No, are you?"

"No, I've hardly used my talent today."

"Just to save my life," Lenardo reminded him. "Have you the strength to move some clouds before you sleep?"

"Of course. Let me set the guard first. You know, people still aren't going to come out tomorrow, because they'll be *afraid* of flogging."

"Arkus, will you stop worrying? I can *find* them."

"Yes, my lord!"

"And Arkus—"

"Yes, my lord?"

"There are far more than a thousand people in the city. I think the others will show themselves when they find out they'll be fed and not flogged."

That night Lenardo slept deeply and dreamlessly on a pallet on the marble floor. He had left Josa and Arkus to draw the cloud bank he had found toward Zendi. By morning it was raining, but not on the city. Moist breezes refreshed the workers, but the city streets remained dry.

Encountering Arkus and Josa hand in hand, Lenardo told them, "You're showing off."

"No one works well in the rain, my lord," Arkus replied. "Look how well your plan is working."

It did seem to be. Lenardo didn't like the fearful looks when he passed, but he hoped that would change when they got used to him. None of Aradia's people looked at her that way.

More people crept out of hiding as the news spread that there was food for all and no one had yet been flogged. On the fourth day, the test came.

They were attempting to provide only two meals a day, morning and evening. Lenardo, hot and thirsty, returned to the spring by the bathhouse to run cool water over his head and then take a long drink. The washing-up after the morning meal was completed, and already Cook had some of her staff preparing for evening. When she saw Lenardo, she hurried to his side.

"Are you hungry, me lord? Thirsty? One of the farmers brought in fresh berries."

"Thank him and tell him I'll have them for dinner," said Lenardo. "Do you have enough help, Cook? You're doing a fine job under difficult conditions."

She blushed under his praise. "Right now, people are grateful just for food. That won't last, me lord. Has Helmuth asked you—"

"About locating ale or beer? Yes. I told him to send men out to find as much as possible." He smiled at her. "I may have different dietary requirements than you're used to, but I wasn't raised totally apart from the real world. I know that after working so hard, people want something stronger than water or fruit juice. You know I like a cup of wine myself."

Although Lenardo hadn't meant it that way, Cook called, "Ho! Dorn! Wine for me lord!"

The boy ran into the bathhouse, where the casks of wine were kept cool, and returned with a goblet for Lenardo.

He was no longer thirsty, but he Read that Cook would like some wine, although she would neither ask for it nor help herself to the supply reserved for the Lord of the Land and his officers.

By savage custom, it was a sign of honor and friendship for two people to drink from the same goblet, and so Lenardo offered the wine to the cook, saying, "Will you try some?"

She blushed but dared not refuse. Although she rarely had wine for her own pleasure, she knew the varieties, which to choose to complement various dishes. This was an ordinary white wine, of which they had brought several kegs, but a good one. She held it for a moment to savor the bouquet before tasting.

Amused and happy that he could please this hardworking woman with such a simple gesture, Lenardo Read her reactions, careful not to invade the privacy of her thoughts.

As she sniffed the wine, her delight turned to puzzlement. She frowned and took another whiff. "Could the heat have spoiled it?'' she asked, and started to tilt the cup to taste.

Lenardo Read the wine curiously and then in panic grabbed the cup out of the woman's hand, sloshing wine over both of them. "It's poisoned!''

Cook gasped, "No! Oh, no, me lord, I never—"

"I know *you* didn't do it, but someone did—someone with access to the wine casks.''

Facing a life-threatening situation, Lenardo Read openly. Cook was trying to think of a suspect, still convinced that he would find her the most likely. She followed him into the bathhouse, where he Read the kegs. Only one was poisoned: the half-empty one he and his retainers had been served from.

"The wine was good yesterday,'' he said. "It was done last night or this morning.''

"But I've had thirty people in and out all morning,'' said Cook. "I *knew* we shouldn't have pressed those townspeople into service so near me lord's food, but where was I to get help?''

"Cook, I'm not blaming you,'' Lenardo insisted. "Your keen sense of smell just saved both our lives.''

"But you Read—''

"Only after you noticed something wrong. I'm not in the habit of Reading for poison in everything I eat or drink.''

Satisfied at last that he would not blame her, Cook asked, "Will you Read the workers, me lord? Find out who did this?''

"If he—or she—saw what just happened out there, the culprit is the person running away,'' Lenardo said.

But no one had run off. Most of the kitchen staff were resting; only the cooking staff—all of whom had come from Aradia's land—were beginning work on the evening meal. Lenardo sent for Arkus and then walked among them, Reading, finding neither hate, fear, nor resentment.

Arkus arrived as Lenardo confronted the puzzled, fearful townspeople pressed into scullery service. The terror of being called before the Lord of the Land so obscured individual thought that Lenardo wondered whether he would have to interview each one alone to find his would-be murderer. Although there was plenty of resentment, he could find no hatred strong enough to account for an attempt on his life.

He had not told them why he had gathered them; the thought in most minds was that they were to be pressed into some other work. But why would the lord himself bother with that? The Lord of the Land dealt with ordinary people only to punish, although this one had been heard to offer praise. . . .

That gave Lenardo an idea. "Arkus, these people are doing a fine job of keeping everyone well fed."

Puzzled, Arkus replied, "Yes, my lord."

"I wish to thank them. Instruct Cook to have wine brought from the open cask so that everyone may have a cup."

Thoroughly bewildered now, Arkus kept his composure only by reminding himself that he had sworn loyalty and obedience. *Why is he making me an errand boy for this riffraff?*

But blazing beyond Arkus' justified concern came a flare of fear and guilt and hatred, standing out clearly from the others' relieved pleasure. A man began edging his way toward the door.

"Arkus!" Lenardo's voice stopped the young commander in his tracks. "This man—" he pointed "—poisoned the cask of wine that you and I and our staff have been drinking from."

"No! It's a lie! I never—"

The man backed to the wall as Arkus advanced on him, sword drawn. But he was not suicidal: he stood pinned, sword at his throat, sweating, eyes popping, cursing himself for having moved.

To the other startled, frightened men and women, Lenardo said, "I'm sorry to trick you, but I had to find the culprit. And you shall have your wine—from a fresh cask—as soon as I determine what to do with this would-be murderer."

By the time they were left alone, the man was radiating

stormy defiance and contempt. Lenardo Read that he thought the new lord weak and stupid.

"What is your name?" he asked the man, who was dressed in tatters of what had recently been elegant clothes.

"I won't tell you."

"Your name is Bril. Why did you try to murder me?"

"You're not going to make *me* work like a scullery maid."

Lenardo knew the words a Lord Adept would say at that point: "You are my property." He did not say them. Instead, he said, "You are my responsibility, along with this city and all the surrounding countryside. I expect you to work for your food, clothing, and shelter like everyone else."

Arkus said, "Bril's a moneylender, my lord. He doesn't know what work is."

"It is not a motive for murder. What did you think to accomplish, Bril? Had you killed me, the Lady Aradia would have given Zendi to someone else or taken it herself. The new lord would be my friend and would avenge my death."

"Yes, a Lord Adept who would *do* something," Bril spat. "If anyone had tried to kill Drakonius, he wouldn't have wasted time talking. He'd have the person tortured to death in the forum as an example."

"You are quite right, Bril," said Lenardo, sick at heart. "Your punishment must be an example. Arkus, you may proceed with the flogging you've been wanting."

"At once, my lord," Arkus said with grim satisfaction. "I'll tell the whipman to make sure he takes a long time to die."

"No, I will not rule by torture. Bril will be flogged, but not to death."

"But my lord—"

"I want him alive so that people will remember that he *did not succeed*. The men who ambushed you and Helmuth and me did not succeed, but they are dead, and people have already forgotten." He turned to Bril. "I'm not like the Lords Adept you are accustomed to. You cannot fool me, Bril. You accomplished nothing, and yet you must suffer. Whether you admit it aloud or not, you will deliver this message to my people: Attacks on Lenardo are *not worth trying*."

Trembling inside but outwardly composed, Lenardo assessed Bril's physical condition. "Ten lashes," he ordered.

"For trying to kill you?" Arkus gasped.

"Look at him. He's never felt the lash before, and he's not young or strong. It will be the worst thing he's ever suffered, but he will recover and be able to work."

"You may be right," said Arkus, "but others, more hardened—"

"The idea," Lenardo said, "is for there to *be* no others!"

Arkus suddenly understood. "You really won't be able to . . . shut it out?"

"To a degree," Lenardo admitted, "if I stay at a distance." But he would have to witness his order being carried out.

Steeling himself, he stood on the bathhouse steps. There were plenty of witnesses: Arkus brought in all his soldiers and work crews, and other people mobbed the forum as the word spread that the Lord of the Land dealt punishment when it was deserved.

Bril was fastened to the old well-worn whipping post in the center of the forum. Arkus joined several soldiers there, gave one of them the lash, and, Lenardo Read, said softly, "My lord says no torture. Lay it on swift and certain."

Lenardo braced himself for the empathic reaction. He had to watch, nor could he shut out the sound of the lash or Bril's screams turning from fear to pain.

Yet something distracted his attention. He became aware at the seventh blow that for every crack of the lash, a wail from within the bathhouse rose in concert with Bril's scream.

Collecting his wits, he listened clearly to another two, and then on the last he heard the voice change to the mournful sobbing of a child in pain. He turned, following the sound and then Reading. Instantly his back was aflame, but he could tell himself that it was not his own pain and let it subside. The child could not.

He burst into the frigidarium, which was being scrubbed down before being put into operation. If the new lord had the functioning of the bathhouse high on his list of priorities, who dared question his idiosyncrasies?

A number of women had been working there while their children played about the building, but now one of those children was clinging to its mother, sobbing and then screaming when she touched its back. Everyone had stopped working to stare, and the room was awash in bewildered pity.

Knowing immediately what had happened, Lenardo set out to break the child's focus on Bril. //Child!// he projected at the most intense level.

Despite the pain, the response came clearly, the thrill of first contact with a compatible mind. The child turned huge brown eyes to him, and he smiled reassuringly. //Focus on me, and the pain will go away.//

Tears turned to laughter. The child dropped its clutch on its mother and ran to Lenardo, crying, "Mama, he talks to me! In my head, he talks to me!"

The mother screamed. Hate and terror filled the room as the other women cried, "Reader!" and converged on Lenardo and the child, one of them pulling a knife as she said, "I'll take care of it, me lord."

Astonished, Lenardo snatched the child out of their reach. "What's the matter with you?" he demanded. "Haven't you been told that Readers are not to be harmed anymore?"

Pounding feet, and Arkus skidded into the room, sword in hand. "What's going on?"

"This child—a Reader—they want to kill it!" And then, "Arkus, why don't these women know I'm a Reader rather than an Adept?"

The wave of renewed terror made Lenardo wince, and he recalled Helmuth stopping him from revealing himself to the peasants.

Arkus said, "I think you can Read why, my lord. Nobody lied to them. We just didn't spread the word. Now that you've established your authority, it'll be all right."

"By the gods," said Lenardo, "I want that decree

carried at once to every reach of the land. Any child who gives sign of Reading ability is to be brought to me *unharmed*.'' He was trembling, clutching the child tightly, his fear communicating itself to . . . her.

As he realized that it was a little girl he held, he thought in dismay, *I should never have touched her!* Although the scheduled testing in the empire was done by female Readers for girls and male Readers for boys, it naturally happened that unexpected discoveries were made by Readers of the opposite sex from the children discovered. At home, Lenardo would have avoided seeing the child, certainly never touched her, and sent her to the nearest Academy for girls.

But he was not at home.

Wait. I am *at home. This is my home, my land . . . and I make the laws for it.* He turned to the girl's mother. ''No one's going to hurt your child. She has a precious gift. I'll help you teach her to use it.''

''I don't want her, me lord,'' the woman answered, gasping. ''You take her!''

''Take the child, my lord,'' said Arkus. ''She's yours, anyway. But I'd still advise you to give the mother something for her, before witnesses.''

Lenardo nodded. He had often had to buy little boys from their families for the empire's Academies. ''Where is the child's father?'' he asked.

''I don't know,'' the woman said blankly, and Lenardo Read that what she meant was that she did not know which of a number of men was the father—nor did she care. ''What'll you give me for the girl?''

''A quarter measure of silver, or I will give her back to you to raise, and you will be severely punished if you neglect her or do her harm.''

''Don't want her poking in my head. She's yours, me lord.''

''Very good. Arkus, give the woman her money and get her mark witnessed on a paper signing the child over to me.''

Arkus covered his surprise with a ''Yes, my lord,'' but

as soon as they had left the room, he asked, "A paper? What do you mean?"

"A legal document," Lenardo explained. "Can you write, Arkus?"

"No, my lord. Helmuth can."

"Helmuth is out of the city today. I'd better write it."

As Arkus went off to the well-guarded room where their personal belongings and the treasure Aradia had insisted "went with Zendi" were stored, Lenardo turned his attention to the child in his arms. She was clinging to him like a little monkey, basking in the empathic flow between them. She didn't question leaving her mother, who had never responded to her growing gift. Lenardo knelt down and tried to set her on her feet.

//It's all right,// he told her, prying her clutching hands loose from his tunic. //See? You don't have to touch. What's your name?//

At first he didn't think she would respond. Reading abilities often operated sporadically for months before a child gained permanent control. She seemed terribly young and indeed looked like a monkey with her spindly limbs and her huge solemn eyes studying him from a too-thin face. Her hair had been lopped off any which way, apparently to save her mother the trouble of combing it.

He was about to ask her name aloud, when she said, "Julia."

He smiled approval. //That's a pretty name. Now, without saying it, try to tell me how old you are.//

//Eight.//

//Very good.//

The girl grinned, revealing that a front tooth was missing. Lenardo was surprised she was that old. She was no bigger than a five-year-old, and he had been guessing six only because of her response.

//Do you know who I am?// he asked.

In the heat of the day, Lenardo was wearing a plain tunic and sandals. Julia put a grubby finger on the dragon's-head brand on his arm and said, //That is the sign of the Lord of the Land.// She cocked her head, puzzled. //I thought he was old and ugly.//

//I am the *new* lord,// Lenardo explained. //What we are doing now—talking in our minds—is called Reading. I'm going to teach you to use your abilities, but around other people we must talk out loud. It's not polite to shut them out.//

"All right," she said, and held out her arms to be picked up again.

"You can walk," Lenardo told her. "As your Reading improves, you'll find you don't want to touch people. You feel what they're feeling, like that man's pain."

The dark eyes clouded. "Will that always happen?"

"I'll teach you how to stop it."

"Good," she said, idly scratching her head, where Lenardo Read lice.

"*That* is even easier to stop," he said. "I don't know which you need worse, a meal or a bath."

"Food! Don't want a bath."

"You'll have one anyway," he told her, taking her out onto the steps and turning her over to Cook. Lenardo then joined Arkus again to make the deal with Julia's mother.

"You don't have a seal, my lord," said Arkus, "but the city seal was in the treasure chest."

"That will do for now," Lenardo said. Something else he had not given a thought to. Some sort of symbol. What would Wulfston choose, he wondered, since the wolf's-head sign he had been named for belonged to Aradia?

Julia's mother watched curiously as Lenardo wrote out the document. When he pressed the seal into the wax, the woman pointed to the brand on his arm. "Is that how ye mark your sworn men, me lord?"

Choking down the horror of the idea, he replied, "No, indeed," and lifted the seal, only to find himself facing the dragon's head again, this time surmounting a tower, and beneath it the letter of the savage alphabet for the sound of "z."

If I don't do something about it soon, he thought, *I'll end up with the dragon as my symbol by default.*

In the infirmary, he found Sandor just finishing with Bril, who was still painfully sore. "Can't you help him any more than that?" he asked.

"I could, but do you want to have to flog him again tomorrow? I healed the cuts so he can't get infected. Let his own body do the rest, while the pain reminds him of what will happen if he turns on you again."

Lenardo said no more. Harsh physical punishment was the norm in the empire as well as here, but before he was branded and thrust beyond the pale, the worst that had ever happened to him personally was a sound thrashing the day he was caught kissing the innkeeper's daughter, when he was twelve years old.

Rubbing the mark on his arm, he told Bril, "Report to Arkus, and don't forget that it's no longer possible to sneak away and hide. I can find you no matter where you go."

Bril tried to look defiant, but the beating had taken most of the rebelliousness out of him. "You got a Reader working for you, like Drakonius had?"

"I *am* a Reader." Lenardo allowed a moment for the shock to register and then added, "You were a wealthy man, Bril. If you're clever and you work hard, you may be wealthy again—but it will be a long time before you earn back the right to be trusted."

Emotionally exhausted, Lenardo walked the streets of his city the rest of that afternoon, with some new instinct prompting him to show himself as the word spread of what he was. To his relief, acceptance followed the first shock. It was not that he was nonAdept, like the legendary Wulfston the Red, but that his abilities were different from the ones they were used to . . . and equally powerful. He Read the fear that had been growing since his arrival beginning to give way. Their lord had his own powers with which to protect his people. They were not defenseless, as they had begun to think.

But there were new fears as well: fear that he knew their most secret thoughts, fear that his powers were inadequate to protect them against Adept attack, and just the vague anxiety generated by another shock to people whose lives had been shattered too many times.

I should have been Reading my people more carefully,

he realized. Had he not been protecting their privacy, operating under the Readers' Code, he might have discovered days ago that his not exhibiting special powers frightened them far more than if he had been a tyrant like Drakonius, arbitrarily setting examples to keep them in line.

At Northgate he climbed the tower, greeted the watchman, and then turned to stare out over the city. He could have Read it from the ground, but somehow he needed the physical exertion of the climb and the actual view.

It no longer stank. Close by the tower, he could see that the buildings were empty shells, but the basic structure of the city was intact. From here to the forum a main street ran straight and clean; the other streets radiating from the forum were all clear now to the east and south. The west-to-northwest sector, though, was rubble. There, most of the buildings had been of wood and had burned down completely.

For now, he was having that area cleared of flammable debris and left alone. One day, after he had forged the treaty with the Aventine Empire, a new Academy would rise there, a place where Readers and Adepts would study together, share their skills—

But if that were to happen, Lenardo must first learn to rule. The dragon's-head brand on his arm seemed to glow in the late-afternoon sun. His people expected him to live up to that symbol. The empire, having seen it on the banners of those who attacked their walls for many generations, had deemed it the sign of the savage and used it to mark their exiles.

And here, thought Lenardo, *I am failing because I am not savage enough.* He wondered how Wulfston was faring— the young black man whom he had met as Aradia's foster brother and apprentice and to whom she had given the lands west of Lenardo's, to the sea. Was he managing to rule without the cruelty these people seemed to demand?

Cruelty? Or firmness? *Firmness I can give them,* Lenardo determined. *I'm a Master Reader. I don't have to invade people's private thoughts to stop plots before they get as far as Bril's poisoning the wine.*

But Lenardo was only one Reader, and if his actions that day had made many of his people feel more secure, they had also made one implacable enemy and generated enough fear to provide him with henchmen.

It was Julia's screaming that woke Lenardo well after midnight, just as Bril was poised to plunge a knife into his heart. Lenardo twisted, and the blade gashed his left shoulder. He hardly felt it, surging to his knees to drive his right shoulder into Bril's midsection, knocking the man back against the wall with a howl at the pain in his injured back.

Bril's knife clattered to the floor, but by that time another man had grabbed Lenardo from behind, seeking to cut his throat while two more reached for his arms. They could hardly see in the faint light from the window, but Lenardo could Read. He allowed the man behind him to get a grip and set his feet, grasped his knife hand so that he could not cut, and then used him for leverage, swinging his legs up to kick out sharply at the other two attackers. One he caught squarely on the point of the breastbone, full force, and the man dropped unconscious. The other he kicked in the diaphragm, leaving him only staggered, while Lenardo's weight drove the man behind him down, with Lenardo on top of him.

Lenardo arched over, twisting the knife out of his attacker's hand, bringing his full weight down on one knee on the man's forearm to the satisfying crunch of broken bones.

There were footsteps coming, help on the way, but Lenardo still faced two armed men, for Bril had reclaimed his weapon, mad with hopeless fury. With the growl of an animal, he launched himself at Lenardo, knife raised high, exposing himself to Lenardo's thrust between his ribs just as soldiers with swords and torches poured through the doorway.

Bril was falling at Lenardo's feet, one man lay unconscious, one sat moaning with the pain of a broken arm, and the fourth turned, knife in hand, and was promptly dispatched by one of the soldiers. Lenardo, breathless, surveyed the scene of carnage, revealed in the torchlight to be spattered with blood: his own and Bril's. His shoulder began to hurt in earnest.

The two men Lenardo had injured were still alive, and so was Bril, although he was bleeding badly. Lenardo's blade had missed his heart. Arkus and Helmuth were both in the room now, and Julia scooted between people's legs to Lenardo's side, crying, "Oh, they hurt you! Don't die, my lord—please don't die!"

"I'm not going to die," he said to reassure her.

At once, she pointed to his fallen attackers. "Kill *them*, my lord. Torture them to death."

Lenardo looked over the child's head to Arkus, who nodded, but it was Helmuth who said, "You must, my lord. This time you have no choice."

The three surviving attackers were taken to the infirmary, where Sandor put them to sleep, doing no more for Bril than to stop his bleeding so that he would survive for his execution.

The gash across Lenardo's shoulder was not deep. Sandor laid his hand over it, and the familiar heat of Adept healing spread through his shoulder as he sat on the edge of the infirmary table, talking with Helmuth and Arkus and Julia, who refused to be shepherded off to bed until she was certain that Lenardo was healed.

"They killed two guards on the way in here," Arkus said. "Slit their throats. But my lord, I don't understand. How could they sneak up on you? You've always known before."

"I was asleep," he explained.

Arkus and Helmuth looked blank, and Julia said, "So was I—and I Read them!"

"And that, child," said Lenardo, "is what saved my life. I thank you."

"But why didn't *you* Read them, my lord?" Helmuth asked.

"One of the most difficult lessons a Reader must learn," Lenardo explained, "is not to Read in his sleep. It is not that he might discover something but that he might reveal something, for no one can control his own dreams."

"I still don't understand," Arkus said. "Who could Read your dreams?"

"Julia or any other Reader. Where I come from, Arkus, people with varying degrees of Reading ability are as common as people with varying degrees of Adept talent are here. In the empire, a Reader with a slight talent—as you have a slight Adept talent—would be trained in an Academy to make the most he could of his ability. Can you imagine the chaos in an Academy full of children if each time one had a nightmare, it was broadcast to all the others? And what of the traumas of growing up? Consider how you might have felt had your adolescent fantasies been broadcast to all your fellow soldiers in training."

Arkus blushed scarlet. "I see," he murmured.

"But protection from embarrassment is not the main reason a Reader must guard his sleep. Theoretically, a stronger Reader might guide the dreams of a lesser one, specifically to elicit information. That is now a forbidden technique, for Readers are not gods. Because that technique, developed for teaching and for treating some of the problems Readers have, was in the past vilely misused, now every Reader is taught self-protection from earliest childhood. I shall have to teach Julia—a difficult task, as it means staying awake for many nights, monitoring her sleep. I fear it will have to wait until our situation here is much more stable."

"My lord," said Helmuth, "you are going to have to tell us how to protect you."

"Yes," added Arkus. "This incident tonight should have been prevented. Twice you have proved that you could Read danger and prepare for it, even recognize poisoned wine so that no one could be harmed. It crossed my mind last evening that after you revealed yourself as a Reader, I should increase the guard here, but then I thought, no, you will warn us far in advance of any attack. How much more effective to let your people see that you have no more need of an armed guard than the strongest Lord Adept."

"I haven't, except when I'm asleep," said Lenardo.

"But you must *tell* us when you are vulnerable," Helmuth

insisted. "A Lord Adept must have protection when he has used up his strength in applying his powers. Now that we know you must be guarded while you sleep, we will protect you."

"I'm still not used to thinking of myself as needing protection," Lenardo explained. "A clean battle is one thing, but assassins in the night—"

"You defeated them," Sandor put in. "No need to spread the word that you had even a small wound. Try your shoulder, my lord. Any soreness left?"

"No, Sandor. Thank you very much."

"Sandor is right," said Helmuth. "It won't hurt at all to let your people think you're invulnerable. Mutiny, poison, assassination—and there you are, unscathed, while your attackers are all dead or scheduled for execution. The word will spread tomorrow, my lord. With Bril dead, there is no one with a personal grudge. This should be the last attempt on your life until your people have a chance to see how you rule. And if you rule well, it may be the last attack ever."

Before the executions, Lenardo had the distasteful task of Reading the condemned men to discover whether they had acted alone or represented a larger group of malcontents. It was a skill he had learned years ago, interrogating savage prisoners for the Aventine Army. To his relief, he found that Bril had trusted no one but the three who had joined him, formerly wealthy businessmen with whom he had often traded financial favors.

When Lenardo stood once more on the steps, bracing himself to witness the executions, Julia joined him. "I told you to go to the watchtower, child."

"They tried to kill you. I want to see them die." Sensing that he would have her removed bodily, she tried a different tack. "Please, my lord. I must learn my duty."

Lenardo waved Sandor over. "Julia insists on witnessing the executions. I'll help her block the pain, but if it becomes too much for her, I want you to put her to sleep."

"It won't be too much," Julia insisted.

Lenardo was astonished at the girl's strength. He showed her how to block the worst pain of the men being flogged to death, but she had little control, and both of them were sick and shaking by the time the last of the attackers passed out. By Lenardo's order, they were not revived; the beatings continued until all three hearts had stopped.

Faint and nauseated, Lenardo stood his ground while the bodies were cut down. Greg and Vona stepped forward, and purifying fire consumed the bodies. Lenardo could not help but recall the burnt-out canyon in which Galen had died. A few bones were all they had ever found of the four Adepts and one Reader destroyed by powers Lenardo guided. Scavengers had made it impossible to know which of the scattered bones were whose.

Bril and his henchmen may not be accorded funeral rites, Lenardo thought, *but at least their bodies were not desecrated.*

The crowd broke up in silence, and Julia collapsed at Lenardo's feet. He picked her up, but Sandor quickly took the child.

"Come inside and lie down yourself, my lord."

Inside, Julia came to, threw up, and began to return to normal. "I should have had you carried to the tower," Lenardo told her.

"No," she insisted. "People mustn't think we're afraid to deal out punishment just because it hurts us."

He agreed with her in principle. The savage child seemed to understand instinctively what he was learning through trial and error, but he was faintly repelled at the way she sought to turn her abilities into power over others. *And yet that is what I must learn in order to achieve a treaty with the empire.*

As word spread that the new lord was a Reader, the population shifted. People fled across borders or into the hills, swelling the ranks of the hill bandits. In the city, as people came out of shock, Arkus' troops had their hands full as fights broke out between those willing to give their strange new lord a chance and those who feared his nonAdept status.

Even those on Lenardo's side resented his attempts to stop the regrowth of certain occupations; they were used to thievery, gambling, and prostitution as normal daily activities.

Helmuth advised Lenardo to punish theft and accept the other activities. "Sex doesn't harm ordinary people, my lord, and if some are foolish enough to pay for it, let them."

Lenardo sighed. In the Aventine Empire, prostitution was taxed along with everything else. Gambling would never stop—the problem was to prevent cheating. "Where is all the money coming from?" he asked. "We confiscated what the looters stole."

"You've been paying your army regularly."

"Helmuth, how can I allow—"

"My lord, you are worrying over which way the wind blows. Unless you plan to start a fire, it doesn't matter."

In the old man, Lenardo Read the wisdom of experience. "We've enough to do without starting fires, but all reports of anyone robbed or cheated come directly to me. It's easy enough for a Reader to discover who's lying."

Lenardo was constantly grateful for Helmuth's advice. When the old man had volunteered to join him, claiming that Lenardo's land was closer to Lilith's, where he had a daughter and grandchildren, Lenardo had hesitated. But there had been few in Aradia's land willing to throw in their lot with him, and Helmuth had quickly proved invaluable. It had been his idea to give Arkus and his troops a new chance, his connections who had scouted out Sandor, Greg, and Vona, all distantly related to him and all with the Adept powers Lenardo lacked. Josa was Helmuth's niece, entrusted to her uncle in hopes that in a new land she might find a suitable husband.

Once they were established in Zendi, Helmuth demonstrated new talents, for agriculture and for organizing people without antagonizing them. Lenardo couldn't have ruled without him.

As the summer passed, the crops were harvested, and the new lord's reputation for fairness spread. People began to return to Lenardo's land. There was plenty of work, as

Zendi had been the central trade city and all its warehouses had been destroyed in the burning and looting. Before winter, there must be not only food but shelter and clothing for everyone. The miserable huts that had served Drakonius' peasants were quickly replaced with more substantial homes. The materials were available, and willing hands could put up such a dwelling in a day or two, but Drakonius had never allowed them such comforts.

Everyone with Adept talent had fled before Lenardo arrived. Now many straggled back, offering their services. Healers were desperately needed, as Lenardo found chronic disease everywhere. Some would suffer all their lives from malnutrition in childhood. It would be many years before he could hope to have the robust population he had seen in Aradia's land.

Meanwhile, though, very few people were worse off than they had been under Drakonius. The vast majority, for the first time in their lives, were adequately fed and housed, and they worked with a will in return. Lenardo saw Helmuth's wisdom in not denying their leisuretime pleasures.

He could have used a hundred Readers, and frequently longed to be rid of the one he had. It wasn't that he didn't like Julia; no one could help loving the child, and that was her undoing. Lenardo had little time to spend with her, and so he assigned Helmuth to teach her to read and write and Josa to teach her "whatever girls are supposed to know." As it turned out, the old man melted at Julia's smiles, while Josa, a plain girl of an age when her society warned her to prepare for a life of lonely spinsterhood (*Twenty-five this winter!* Lenardo once caught her plaintive thought), took out her frustrated motherhood on the little girl, who, cleaned up and fed, her hair a halo of dark curls about her face, was turning into a pretty creature indeed.

Since Julia accepted Lenardo's authority and worked eagerly on her lessons in Reading, he did not at first realize that she was not performing equally well for her other teachers. Nor did any of them know the games she played when she was not under adult supervision.

A ruined city was a dangerous playground. The completely burnt-out sections were off limits, but Julia did not consider that the order applied to her. Unfortunately, she had little trouble persuading other children to join her in exploring and treasure hunting. They stole a rope and some digging tools and went into the abandoned northwest sector, where Julia Read a cache of coins at the bottom of an old well. They lowered Julia and two strong boys into the well to bring up the treasure, but inevitably their efforts caused the walls to start to collapse. When the three children above tried to haul up the rope, the terrified ones in the well all scrambled to be pulled up at once. Their thrashing dislodged more dirt to fall in on them, along with one of the girls hauling from above.

The other two children ran screaming for help, but long before they could reach the forum, Lenardo's mind was torn with, //Master Lenardo! My lord! Help!// and then a mental screech of panic, //Father! Father,// and a terrifying sense of suffocation.

"The gods help us," he cried, setting off at a run across the forum, Reading the whole picture before he had gone twenty paces.

Arkus loomed before him. "My lord—"

"Get men, ropes—follow me! Hurry!"

Arkus relayed the order and quickly caught up with Lenardo. When they encountered the two breathless children, Lenardo stopped only long enough to tell them: "We know. Help is on the way."

All the while, he was projecting to Julia, //I'm coming. Don't move,// for the struggles of the children threatened to bring more dirt down on them.

At the site, Lenardo Read all four children alive. The girl who had fallen in had a broken arm, but the other three were only scratched and bruised. They were half buried, though, and more wall threatened to cave in. "Where are those ropes?"

"They're coming, my lord," Arkus replied, peering cautiously into the depths of the well. "Who's down there?"

"Julia. Three other children. They *know* better!"

"Father?" a frightened voice called up to them.

"Hush! We're here. Keep still, all of you."

Men arrived with ropes, followed by Josa, Helmuth, and Sandor.

"Lower me into the well—" Lenardo began.

"No, my lord," said Arkus and Helmuth with one breath.

"The walls are collapsing. Someone must go down for them."

"We'll hold the walls," said Arkus. "Josa—"

The young woman hurried to his side, taking his hands and saying fearfully, "But heavy earth—"

"We don't have to move it," Arkus replied, "just make it stay in place. My lord, tell us where to concentrate. Someone small should go down there."

"I'll go, sir," said one of Arkus' soldiers, a compactly built young man with muscular shoulders.

In moments, although it seemed to take forever, the men laid a beam across the top of the well so that the soldier could be lowered without hitting the walls.

Arkus and Josa, facing each other with hands joined, concentrated on keeping more dirt from falling on the children.

The injured girl was brought up, and Sandor had her asleep and healing before the soldier reached the bottom of the well again. He had to dig the others out. One by one, he slung the rope about the boys and sent them up while he freed Julia.

She had calmed down, her confidence in Lenardo overpowering. *But I'm not doing anything,* he thought. *If only I had Adept powers.* Dust drifted down from the side of the well, and he said, "The side opposite. This side's already fallen. Hold that side!"

Arkus and Josa paled, but the wall held. With agonizing slowness the soldier freed Julia, started to put the sling on her—

"No," Lenardo called. "Both of you—the walls could go at any moment."

The hauling on the rope began again, backs bent with a will, but tired now, Arkus and Josa on the brink of collapse, the well wall threatening—

Lenardo grabbed the rope, adding his weight, instantly raising blisters in the uncalloused area of his hands between thumb and forefinger but not caring, needing to help.

The rope moved too slowly. The wall started to cave in. As guilt and fear ate at Lenardo, he Read Julia's panicked litany: //I love you, Father. I'll be good. Help me, oh, help me, Father! Don't leave me again! Father!//

Chapter Three

The rope came up bit by bit. Then eager hands pulled Julia
and the soldier over the brink as a cheer went up. Divested
of ropes, Julia leaped into Lenardo's arms as Arkus and
Josa let go, staggering and leaning heavily on each other.
The wall fell with a crash, and dust flew up from the
mouth to settle over everyone.

In the next few hours, operating purely by rote, Lenardo
Read the children and the rescuers, made sure that everyone with injury or strain was healed, distributed rewards
to all who had helped in the rescue, and finally bathed
the grime off himself in the cold water of the bathhouse.
His order that everyone bathe at least twice a week
had caused grumbling, but in the heat of summer it was
being obeyed. They'd have to get the warm and hot baths
functioning by winter. His people might think his insistence on bathing some personal quirk, but they did not
understand how cleanliness could disrupt the spread of
disease.

By the time Lenardo walked home, Cook had made
Julia presentable, and he was beginning to think that he
could face her. Home was now a large and beautiful town
house that had been looted but not burned—the only choice,
Helmuth had insisted, for the Lord of the Land. The place
was still empty. Lenardo refused to set carpenters to building him furniture when they were needed to repair other
buildings before winter.

His footsteps rang on the mosaic floor in the huge
entrance hall. Eventually this might become an all-purpose
audience room like Aradia's great hall. *By the gods, I'm
starting to think like a lord.* The title still seemed implau-

sible, and as her teacher, he had instructed Julia to call him Master Lenardo.

She was waiting in his room, which was furnished with a bed, two chairs, and a table, none of which matched. Julia sat on the window ledge, looking out into the courtyard. She did not turn at Lenardo's entrance, but he could feel her terrible tension as she tried to Read his mood.

"Julia," he said, "we must talk."

//Can't we—//

"No. We will discuss this like nonReaders, because you have caused several nonReaders to be badly hurt."

"Nobody was hurt bad," Julia protested, turning to face him and pulling her knees up to her chin, balancing on the sill. "Candida just got her arm broke. It'll be all right in a couple of days. When I got *my* arm broke, it took *weeks* to heal. Old Drakonius, he never healed nobody. You're lots nicer."

Ignoring her attempt to placate him, Lenardo said, "Candida's injury is the point, not that Sandor could heal her. He could not have healed her if she had died. Furthermore, Arkus and Josa were also hurt."

"Huh?"

"They expended far more energy than they could afford. Both have collapsed in exhaustion. If I had not Read when Josa's heart went into spasms, Sandor might not have noticed soon enough. She could have died."

"Everybody dies," Julia said coldly, but Lenardo Read that her words were a defense against a world in which ordinary people were considered dispensable.

"People should not die because those in power are careless," Lenardo began.

"Arkus'd be awful sad if Josa died," Julia interrupted. "They're funny, you know? She loves him and he loves her, and neither don't know it. Isn't that funny?"

"No, it is not funny. Neither is it your business. How can I stop you from Reading people's private thoughts?"

"They're *always* thinking about each other. How can I help knowing?"

"The same way I did not know until you told me—an even worse breach of Reader's Honor. Sometimes one finds out a nonReader's secret by accident. But to *reveal* it—" He let her feel the revulsion a Reader knew at such conduct and felt her cringe. Then he added, "Tell me why you went into the well."

"There's gold down there," she said eagerly. "More than twenty gold coins. I would've given it to you."

"You are lying. You wanted it for youself. Why? What do you lack?"

"Money for when I grow up. Mama always said she couldn't keep man nor money. She said if she'd kept all the money men gave her, she wouldn't need no one to take care of her."

"And why did you involve other children?" Lenardo pursued, ignoring the empty feeling her words produced in him.

"I couldn't get it alone. They'd each have got a gold piece. Then they'd have owed me more favors."

"You risked their lives and yours."

"I didn't know the well would fall in."

"No, you won't have the skill to Read such stresses for years. Why can't you learn to obey? I wish you could be sent to an Academy. They'd teach you some discipline."

Julia climbed down from the window and stood, shielding her thoughts as best she could. "I need to learn to rule, not obey. If you don't want me, Lord Wulfston will take me."

"What?" Then he remembered a recent letter from Wulfston: "So you have found an apprentice. Congratulations. If you should find any more Readers, I can certainly use someone with even a portion of your skills."

"You've been Reading my letters!"

"Well, you wanted me to practice." Defiant pride.

He stared at her helplessly. "What am I to do with you? Spank you? Helmuth, Josa, Cook—they've all punished you. What good has it done?"

Defiance melted as her eyes grew liquid. "You never punish me. You're the only one that's got the right, Father. Don't you care about me?"

He suddenly remembered that she had called him "Father" in her panic that afternoon. "I'm not your father," he said bluntly, not knowing how to approach the real problem.

"But you must be," Julia insisted. "There's nobody else like us, nobody that can talk in their minds. I *feel* it. You're the only one like me. You bought me from Mama. I thought you loved me because I was like you, but then you gave me to everybody else—and—and—" Angrily, she struck away the tears that rolled down her cheeks. "My mother was right. Men don't care nothing about their children, except great lords for the pride of it or the fear. I've got your powers. You had to claim me, but you don't want me. You don't love me. You just want me to stop using my powers so I won't use them against *you*!"

Lenardo was astonished. How could he handle this savage child? His only weapon was truth.

Kneeling before Julia, he took her hands. "Julia, you and I are not the only Readers in the world. I'm not your father, but if I were, I would certainly never have abandoned you. You're too young to understand that you're insecure because you never had anyone to rely on, not even your mother. Child, I will give you things you can trust in: your own abilities, the Readers' Honor, other Readers. But what you need right now is one *person* you can trust, and under the circumstances, that has to be me."

The wide brown eyes searched his.

"I'm going to open my mind to you, Julia. Read me."

Hesitantly, her thoughts met his. //You're not my father?//

//No. I never left the Aventine Empire before last spring.//

Because his memories were totally open to her, she caught a trace of the pain of his branding. //They hurt you,// she said, sliding her hand up his arm to rest over the dragon's head. //I hate them!//

//No, child, you mustn't hate people you don't know. I have many friends in the empire, Readers like us. You can trust any Reader, Julia, if you yourself are trustworthy.//

//I don't want other people, just you.//

//You have me. I promise, I'll take care of you. Trust me, Julia.// Stubbornness intruded, born of many disappointments. //Have I ever lied to you or broken a promise?//

//No, but you took me when you didn't want me.//

//I do want you. Can't you Read that?//

//Yes.// But she also felt walled off from him.

//Julia, I cannot give you every minute of my day. I have too much work. I'm the only Reader—// It suddenly occurred to him, //Child, would you like to help me?// In the empire, children were given Reading responsibilities within the Academies from the day they entered. There was no Academy for Julia, but the whole city could become her Academy.

//You'll let me work with you? All the time?//

//Not *all* the time but certainly a great deal *more* time, if you will work seriously. No tricks, and no spying on people's secret thoughts.//

Tears spilled again, but they were tears of joy. She flung her arms around his neck. //I promise! I'll be good. Oh, Master Lenardo, I want to be with you. I love you!//

He let her hold on to him for a moment and then gently removed her arms.

"Don't push me away," she pleaded.

"You don't have to touch, Julia." //Between Readers it's the same whether we're touching or not.//

//If it's the same, then I'd rather touch.//

He smiled, brushing her tears away and recalling that Torio had never formed a Reader's aversion to touching. *We assumed he needed that reassurance because of his blindness, and we didn't force him as we did the other boys.* Taking Julia's hand, he said, "Very well . . . for now. I'm far behind in today's work. Come along and see if you can learn to Read where the drainpipes have broken."

"Master Lenardo?" Julia's thoughts were guarded, and he did not seek to break her shield. "You *could* be my father. You could adopt me."

"I will take the matter under consideration."

"What does that mean?"

"I'll think about it."

"Oh." She was silent for a moment and then said, "I'll prove worthy. You'll see."

His first impulse was to discourage such ideas. Then he recalled who he was and where he was. If Julia could be taught honesty and responsibility, one day she would make a far better leader than he was. *I may need an heir, and where else am I going to find one?*

By the time autumn approached, Lenardo's lands were in good shape, the storage barns were full, and a large section of Zendi was in livable condition. They had, however, very little to trade for goods they did not produce.

Lenardo's land had little forest. His first inclination had been to allow people to hunt freely, but Helmuth warned him, "They'll kill off your game in one season, my lord. It would take years to replenish. You must appoint huntsmen to kill a proper limit and distribute the meat."

Wulfston, on the other hand, had large forests and little farmland. Along the coast, his people fished, and Lenardo sought for something to trade this year, when he could not afford to give up grain. "Trade your abilities," Wulfston wrote to him. "Come Read the iron deposits in the Western Hills and mark them for mining. Then negotiate with Aradia and me for a trade route across your land between my mines and her iron works." It was all so obvious to Wulfston and Aradia, raised to rule.

Lenardo's wider concerns were interrupted one day by Arkus. "My lord, I was your enemy, and you gave me the chance to become your friend."

"You have proved a good friend, Arkus. What is disturbing you?"

"My lord, it's Helmuth."

"Helmuth? But it was Helmuth who first suggested that I put you in charge of the troops from Zendi."

"I know, my lord. He's been most fair with me, but he is your chief adviser, while I am still commander of a fifty-man troop."

Lenardo was sorely tempted to Read exactly what was going on in Arkus' head. "Has Helmuth refused you a promotion? No one's been thinking in military terms since—"

"No, it isn't that. It's Josa." He blushed. "Where she comes from, what she's used to. I'd want to, anyway. I mean—"

"You want to get married," Lenardo finally interpreted.

"Yes, my lord."

"Then what is the problem? Does Josa want to marry you?"

"I think so, but I must ask Helmuth's permission. Josa's father entrusted her to him, to arrange a good marriage for her."

"Would you make her a good husband?"

Arkus sighed. "I'm a soldier, my lord. I don't know how to be anything else, and in peacetime there's no advancement."

Lenardo chuckled. "Arkus, you have spent the past three months rebuilding a city, and there is more to be done—years of work. Go find Helmuth and ask his permission. I'm sure he would be happy to have his niece marry the chief architect of Zendi."

Helmuth, coming to collect Julia for a lesson, was indeed pleased with Lenardo's appointment, but it was Julia who with childish bluntness told him, "What a good idea. Make it a big public ceremony, Master Lenardo. That way he can't ever forget what he owes you."

Lenardo agreed. "It *is* time for a party, isn't it? Everyone has worked hard all summer. We should hold a festival."

"Oh, yes," the girl said in normal childish excitement at the prospect of a party. But immediately his little savage began to scheme. "We must invite your Adept allies, Aradia and Wulfston and Lilith. That way everyone will see that you have powerful friends, and the Adepts will all be beholden to you."

Helmuth smothered a grin. "The child is right, my lord. I was about to suggest the same thing, although I would not have stated the motive so openly."

Lenardo said, "It was in my mind, too, although I was conscious only of wanting to invite my friends. I will write the invitations today."

The next day, Arkus formally asked Helmuth for Josa's hand, and the wedding became part of the festival plans. Julia quickly found out, for the news spread at once, and she spent hours each day Reading for the workmen still repairing the city. She had, quite effectively, cut Lenardo's work load in half. It seemed wrong to place such a burden on an eight-year-old child, but for Julia Reading was not work but play, satisfying her avid curiosity. She was developing a sensitivity Lenardo had seen only once before in so young a child, in Torio.

Moreover, she was determined to win Lenardo's favor, disciplining herself to be on time, clean, obedient, and—most difficult for her—honest. That afternoon, she bounced into Lenardo's room for her Reading lesson, curls flying, to plop down on his bed and tell him of her excitement about the wedding.

"I never knew nobody—anybody—who really got married. Only rich people, to other rich people, with dowries and things. Will you find me a rich husband, Master Lenardo?"

"No, Julia. Not if you live up to your potential. Readers do not marry."

He held his breath, but she didn't ask why. Instead, in mock dismay, she said, "Oh. I thought you didn't want to adopt me because you wanted me to grow up and marry you."

He let the teasing pass, gratefully, and hoped that he could persuade Aradia to explain to Julia the necessity for both Adepts and Readers to be virgin-sworn. The girl should know before she was old enough to feel the stirrings of womanhood. With her streetwise ways, he feared that Julia would recognize and act on such feelings only too easily.

Lenardo knew well that Readers were not immune to fleshly temptations. In the Aventine Empire, young Readers were strictly watched during adolescence. He himself had nearly yielded to nature's promptings. No, he *had* yielded, not understanding the power the pretty innkeeper's daughter held over male desire.

She had not understood, either, he now knew. She had been just a girl in her first bloom, enjoying the newly wakened stirrings of sexuality. Lenardo, then age twelve, had wanted her without truly understanding what he wanted. If Master Clement had not caught them in the first stage of passionate kisses and clumsy fumbling—

Lenardo's own willpower had had nothing to do with saving him that day. It was the horror he had Read in Master Clement's mind, much more than his punishment, that had made him understand what danger lurked within a Reader's normal human sensuality. Ever after he had avoided temptation, and eventually his adolescent fantasies had died away. He had helped to guide boys at the Adigia Academy through their own volatile years, but how was he to guide and protect a girl?

He would have to have Aradia's help, he decided as he went to the bathhouse. It was now in working order, ready for the influx of guests, but Lenardo admitted that if he had not had good reason for repairing the bathhouse, he would have invented one. The relaxing luxury of a proper bath was one sensory pleasure he had always savored.

As he sweated in the steam of the hot bath, his body relaxed and his mind wandered . . . back to a time at Castle Nerius just after Aradia had healed his branded arm. Pain and infection were gone, but Lenardo was still very weak. Aradia had insisted on bathing him, her hands soft on his body—

He pulled himself out of his reverie; such suggestive memories would not do! He missed Aradia and looked forward to seeing her again, but only as a friend, he instructed himself sharply.

Proceeding to the warm bath, Lenardo briskly scrubbed himself down. A group of young boys were spreading soapy water on the marble and running and sliding down one side of the shallow pool. He smiled at their antics but could not overcome his teacher's training.

"Don't you boys leave without rinsing all that soap away," he warned them. "You wouldn't want anyone to slip and fall."

Their momentary resentment turned to embarrassment when they recognized who had called them down. The intrusion of the adult world spoiled their fun, and with a "Yes, my lord," they cleaned up the soap and left. Lenardo could hear their voices echoing down the hall and the shouts and splashes as they jumped into the frigidarium pool.

NonReaders, nonAdepts—how young and free they were. They could do anything they wanted with their lives—

And so can I, Lenardo reminded himself, rinsing off in the warm water. *They will choose responsibilities, limit their lives as everyone must.*

He immersed himself up to his chin, and a fragmented vision rose before his eyes, fleeting and incomplete. He and Aradia, bathing together, laughing like children, flushed with desire.

It was gone as quickly as it had come, leaving Lenardo with the sensation of arousal. He fought it down, glad that he was alone. Fragmentary as it was, the vision had all the impact of one of his precognitive flashes, but it could not be true. He could not allow himself to desire Aradia. Even if he did, there could never be fulfillment of desire. She would never risk her powers. No, it was a fantasy, not a vision, and he put it firmly out of his mind.

The festival was Helmuth's responsibility. People from all over the land planned to come to the capital, for most had not yet seen their new lord. Lenardo's watchers worked harder than ever before to spread the news. The watchers were the savage means of sending messages in code, through lights flashed from one hilltop to another. Within a day, everyone in the land knew of the planned festivities.

The three Adepts sent whole trains of grain, fruit, wine, and cider; wagonloads of meat and fish; and herds of sheep and swine. The all-important feast would lack for nothing.

But while Zendi might house its people for the winter in minimum discomfort, there were no proper accommodations for a Lord and two Ladies Adept. Lenardo could provide a house for each but no furnishings. Even in his own house, he had the only bed. Julia's room had a couch that she would outgrow in a year or two, and everyone else still slept on pallets on the floor.

Helmuth had an answer. "Pavilions," he said. "Lord Wulfston thought of it, my lord. He sent a wagon full of blue, white, and black silk. The women wanted to make dresses of it, but I recognized Aradia's and Lilith's colors, and I assume Lord Wulfston has rather appropriately adopted black.''

"Where would Wulfston get all that silk?"

"He has a seaport, my lord. Merchants call there all the time. 'Tis a good thing you're allies. You can negotiate free passage between Zendi and the sea.''

Lenardo sighed. "Always more plotting. Pavilions?"

"When a Lord Adept makes a progress through his own land—not a march to battle but for some other purpose— he often sets up a silk pavilion as his quarters. Your guests will be appropriately housed. We can put the pavilions in the forum, and the Lords Adept can use their own travel goods inside them. Arkus and Josa will be busy, but we have others now who will see that rain does not spoil anyone's comfort.''

"Very well, Helmuth. I leave it in your hands.''

"As you should, my lord. Now, what about your own color, for banners? And your symbol?"

"You, too? The seamstress was in here this morning, pestering me about formal attire. I am a Master Reader, and so I shall wear scarlet robes. There was enough material in the supplies we brought with us. Perhaps scarlet banners—''

"No," said Helmuth, "white banners with the scarlet *dragon*.''

"Not the dragon," Lenardo insisted. "That was Drakonius's symbol.''

"The *black* dragon, on gold banners—and you've not seen a single one left in your land, have you? All burnt, the moment people knew Drakonius was dead.''

"Precisely why I should choose another symbol.''

"But you carry the red dragon on your arm, my lord— always. People take it as a sign.''

"Helmuth, everyone knows it's nothing but the brand of an Aventine Exile.''

"No, my lord. People say you were born with the mark, born to defeat Drakonius, to change the black dragon of terror to the red dragon of good fortune.''

"What utter nonsense.''

"No, it is not nonsense. Your people believe that their

destiny and yours are bound up together. You should encourage such beliefs, for who is to say they are wrong? There is an old saying: In the day of the white wolf and the red dragon, there shall be peace throughout the world. Aradia is the white wolf. You are the red dragon, the thing that cannot be, a Reader Lord in a land of Adepts. You are marked with the sign, my lord. Do not deny it.''

Wulfston was the first of Lenardo's guests to arrive. He came in style, at the head of his army, dressed in rich brown velvet embroidered in gold, riding a fine bay stallion. His banners bore the wolf's head, but in black on a white field. Lenardo was waiting for him in the forum, with Julia at his side. The girl still had some trouble visualizing what she Read: When Wulfston first came in sight, she gave a start.

//I've never seen a man all black like that before. Aren't you frightened, Master Lenardo?//

//Of course not. Lord Wulfston is our friend.//

//But I can't Read him!//

//Lords Adept cannot be Read, Julia. Considering your propensity for mischief, that is probably a very good thing.//

He stepped forward as Wulfston dismounted, and they exchanged formal greetings for the benefit of the gathered crowd. Julia managed a rather shaky curtsy, watching Wulfston warily. The fact that this was the first person she'd met whom she could not Read bothered her far more than his appearance.

Wulfston walked with Lenardo and Julia back to their house, maintaining formality for the staring crowds. Once they were inside, though, Lenardo found himself caught up in a bear hug.

"My, but I'm glad to see you," Wulfston exclaimed. "I missed you almost as much as Aradia." He held Lenardo at arm's length, looking him up and down. "But you look wonderful. Ruling agrees with you, eh? And your people. I don't have to Read to tell how they love you already."

"They'd respond favorably to anyone after Drakonius."

Wulfston laughed. "I won't frighten you with all the mistakes you *could* have made, but you've had good luck, too. Especially in finding an apprentice Reader.'' When he turned to Julia, she stepped back hesitantly, and Wulfston said, ''What's this? Surely you're not afraid of me? From what Lenardo told me, I didn't think you'd fear the ghost-king himself!''

He had instinctively taken the right tack. Julia bridled. ''I'm not afraid of anyone.''

''Then come and greet me properly, child.'' When he held out his arms to her, she launched herself into his embrace and was picked up easily, coming to rest astride his hip, her head on his shoulder, blissfully at home.

Wulfston hugged her and continued to carry her effortlessly as they walked through the house to Lenardo's room. ''What a joy this child must be to you, Lenardo. I can remember Nerius carrying me just this way. I always felt completely safe.''

''Master Lenardo doesn't like to hold me,'' Julia informed him.

Wulfston cast a puzzled glance at Lenardo, who said, ''Julia is a Reader. I've explained to you—''

''But she's just a *child*,'' said Wulfston, sitting down and establishing Julia on his lap. ''Surely at her age—'' Then he said apologetically; ''Lenardo, if I'm interfering in your discipline, I'm sorry. I didn't think.''

''It's all right,'' said Lenardo, sitting down opposite them. ''Julia will outgrow her compulsion to touch as her Reading ability develops. What upset her at first was that she can't Read you.'' Yet he felt a remote twinge of jealousy as he watched Julia settle happily.

''I can Read you now, my lord,'' she said, ''at least what you're feeling. You're awfully nice.''

''You caught me in a good mood,'' Wulfstone teased, no more taken in by her flattery than Lenardo. Yet it seemed that Wulfston automatically knew more of what Julia needed just now than Lenardo did. *No, not what she needs. What she wants.*

Julia lifted Wulfston's pendant. ''Look, Master Lenardo, just like yours!'' Then she held it against her cheek, saying, ''No, it tells a different story.''

''Hmm?'' Wulfston looked to Lenardo for clarification.

But Lenardo was just as puzzled. "What do you mean, Julia?"

"When I hold yours, it tells me about you . . . and an old man, a great Lord Adept . . . and a soldier, lots of battles—and then another soldier. I never went back any further because he died."

Lenardo felt the tingle of discovery. "Wulfston, do you mind if Julia Reads your wolf-stone? She could have gotten the history of mine from me, but I don't know how, as I've had no occasion to think about it."

"How can anyone Read a stone?" Wulfston asked.

"Let her try."

"You've been building a castle," said Julia. "Before that, another castle . . . the same old man—battle—he dies—terrible sorrow. He was your father. Before that, years of sadness . . . back further, great happiness. You and a little girl—such fun! I wish I could play with those children! People call them . . . Nerius' black and white wolf cubs. Further back you're a little boy, way younger than me. You draw the stone to you—terrible fear! Loss!"

"Stop, child," said Wulfston. With trembling hands, he extricated the stone from her clasp and then looked at Lenardo. "Can you do that?"

"No. It is a rare talent. I didn't know Julia had it until right now. That part about the wolf cubs—I never heard that before. And Julia cannot Read you."

"You can't Read things?" Julia asked Lenardo in astonishment.

"Not that way, Julia, not to tell their history. When I left the empire, of all Readers there were only three with that talent."

"Can nonReaders have it?" Wulfston asked.

"Yes, very rarely.

Wulfston nodded. "Like the many people with a single Adept talent."

"In a way, except that Reading is really a single talent, and one's skills are a matter of degree. Only two skills—this ability to Read the history of an inanimate object and the power of prophecy—never appear without the basic ability to Read thoughts. It's fortunate for me, though, that the varying Adept talents exist. Having none myself would put me at a great disadvantage were it not for all the people willing to use theirs to aid me.''

"A lord who knows everything about everybody is as powerful as a lord who can do anything to anybody," said Wulfston.

"People don't seem to mind that much," Lenardo replied. "When they first find out, they panic. But soon they learn that I don't care about their fantasies, their memories—"

"But they know you'd care about a plot to sieze power or to hurt or cheat people. You're better off than an Adept, Lenardo. You can stop such things when they begin. I can only punish after the fact.''

"Master Lenardo hardly never—ever—punishes nobody," said Julia.

"Yet there is order in his lands, Julia. You grow up to be just like him, and someday you will be a great ruler, too.''

Lenardo was finding the role of "great ruler" as awkward as an ill-fitting garment. Alone with Wulfston, and later Lilith, as cool and placid as ever in her blue traveling gown, he felt comfortable, at home among equals. But on display before his people, formally greeting his guests, he felt like a child playing a game and doing it badly.

Aradia was the last to arrive, in the greatest splendor, all in white—by some Adept power kept free of the dust of the road—and wearing her crown of twisted gold.

//Oh, isn't she *beautiful*!// was Julia's reaction. //She looks like the queen of all the world.//

But Aradia, too, shed her formality the moment they were away from the crowd, hugging Lilith and Lenardo and then throwing herself into Wulfston's arms. "How I've missed you, little brother. Oh, how fine you look—a true prince." She turned but remained standing with one arm about Wulfston's waist. "Lenardo, you've done wonders. And what audacity, to hold the first celebration when you had the worst conditions to overcome.''

"We've made a good start," he replied. "I hope you're willing to put up with some lack of elegance if not discomfort. In all this city, there were not four complete chairs, but by cobbling together some pieces, I've managed so that we can all sit down together.''

Lilith said, ''The pavilions are a charming idea. Quite proper, if not the usual accommodations one receives in a city.''

''You can thank Wulfston and Helmuth for them.''

As they sat down, Julia hovered near Lenardo, staring in awe at Aradia. She had been presented to give her curtsy in the forum, but now Aradia said, ''Your apprentice, Lenardo—what a beautiful child . . . and a Reader.''

''She was almost killed for revealing her ability, even after I was ruling here.''

''Yes,'' said Aradia. ''When you wrote me about it, I realized that people still had their old prejudices. I sent out a decree that no child who showed Reading talent was to be harmed, upon pain of death. If we find any, will you train them, Lenardo?''

''I'll have to,'' he said. ''Until we make peace with the empire, there's no one else to do it.''

''Of course I sent out the same decree,'' said Wulfston.

''And I,'' said Lilith, ''but we have found none.''

''In all the population of Zendi,'' said Lenardo, ''Julia is the only Reader I've discovered, and there were empire citizens trapped here when Drakonius took the city twenty-five years ago. In the empire, about one person in ten has some degree of Reading ability. Perhaps one in ten has some Adept talent, but only a few, like yourselves, have the full array of powers. I think over many generations, people carrying Adept powers in the empire have been killed off, while out here those who bear the Reading strain were killed. Both are clearly hereditary. I don't think you will find many Readers, because the strain has almost been killed off.''

''What would happen,'' asked Julia, ''if a Reader and an Adept had a baby? Maybe the child would have both powers.'' She paused thoughtfully. ''Lord Wulfston, will you marry me?''

''How old did you say you are, Julia?''

''Eight.''

''Ask me again in ten years.''

But when the laughter had faded, Aradia said, "How nice it would be if we were all Readers. Letters are not the same as being together. I think Reading would be much better, almost the same as really meeting."

"It *is* the same," said Lenardo. "Better than—" He cut off, wishing that he could recall the words, for it was clear from the faces of the three Adepts that they understood: *Better than really being with people who cannot Read.*

"Then Julia is an even greater blessing to you than I realized," Aradia said tightly. "Have you been terribly lonely among us, Lenardo?"

"No, I haven't," he replied honestly. "I expected to be. Lack of contact with other Readers should be the worst part of exile, but I have found I can make friends with nonReaders, very close and dear friends. Aradia, the fact is that ever since I met you—and Wulfston—I may have been angry, frustrated, fearful . . . but the one thing I haven't been is lonely. I have missed you, though. I keep feeling our separation is temporary, when I know that from now on we will meet only infrequently."

"Perhaps not," Aradia said thoughtfully.

"What are you plotting, Aradia?" Wulfston asked.

"Suppose the four of us were more than allies? Between us, we hold the largest area under one rule outside the Aventine Empire."

"But we are *not* under one rule," Lilith pointed out.

"We could be," Aradia replied. "We could form a central government, pool our resources, and be safe from any upstart, even one with the power of a Drakonius or a Nerius."

"But under whose rule would that central government exist?" Wulfston asked. "A beast with two heads tears itself apart. A beast with *four* heads—"

"I don't mean something like the Aventine Empire," Aradia protested. "Not a hereditary ruler. Certainly no such foolishness as a senate elected by the common people. No, I'm talking about a natural government by those with power, a government of Lords Adept . . . and Readers."

"You have not answered Wulfston's objection," Lilith

observed. "The four of us get on as friends and allies, but if we pooled our lands and attempted to govern as a body, we would soon quarrel over laws, projects, whose people were getting the most favors. Wulfston is right. It would tear us apart, Aradia."

"Obviously," said Aradia, "someone would have to be superior to the others, to decide when all could not agree. The strongest Adept—"

"Excellent, sister," said Wulfston. "I shall work diligently for the next few years, for by the time you form this government, I may well be the strongest Adept."

Sensing anger building and fearing any disagreement that might hinder his plan to attempt a treaty with the empire, Lenardo broke in, carefully keeping his voice at that pitch of total rationality that indicates the proposal of something completely absurd. "No, you are both wrong. Obviously, a Reader ought to head this new government. Only a Reader can truly know what the people want and need."

The three Adepts stared, taking him seriously for a moment. Then Julia chimed in, "The best Reader, and that's me! I have Reading powers Master Lenardo doesn't."

The tension broke. There was laughter, albeit slightly uneasy, and Aradia dropped the subject. However, Lenardo perceived something brewing beneath her calm surface even as she joined enthusiastically in the festival.

Zendi was a huge fair for the next two days. There were music, games, wrestling contests, footraces—and prizes of ribbons and banners carrying the scarlet dragon.

The activity was spread throughout the city, but the center was the forum. In the afternoon light, acrobats and dancers performed for Lenardo and his guests, but after the feast in the evening, a man with a lute came forward, offering to sing.

Lenardo had left the entertainment up to Helmuth, and so he never knew quite what to expect. What he did *not* expect was the story of how he had come to rule, made into a song that incorporated the basic facts but somehow made Lenardo the hero, relegating the Adepts to minor roles. It continued with how he had cleverly eluded each attack on his life—an invulnerable lord.

Embarrassed, he tried to form an apology, but Wulfston said, "That's how the story *should* go in your land, Lenardo. When you visit me, you'll find that I defeated Drakonius single-handed, to hear my bards tell of it."

"It's only right," Aradia added, "that your people see you as a hero. It will ensure their love and loyalty. Now reward your man before he makes up something scandalous about you, to an unforgettable tune!"

The formal activities were over for the night, although people continued to sing and dance. When Wulfston took Lilith to join a group of dancers, Aradia asked, "Have you learned to dance yet, Lenardo?"

"Somehow I haven't found time for dancing lessons."

"Then let us sit and watch," she said. "Perhaps when Lilith tires, Wulfston will dance with me. None of your men dare ask me."

"Ah, I can provide you with a partner. Ho! Arkus!" The young man was heading the small contingent guarding Lenardo and his guests. "Put off your sword and dance with the Lady Aradia. Surely partnering a great Lady Adept on the eve of your wedding will bring you good fortune."

Arkus blushed but stripped off his sword, saying, "You do me great honor, my lady."

When they had gone, Lenardo sat watching the dancers in the flickering firelight. Lilith was attired in green tonight, Aradia in violet, soft summer garments with tight bodices and pleated skirts that swirled as they moved. Wulfston was clearly enjoying himself. Perhaps Lenardo should learn to dance.

He Read Julia, dancing in a circle of little girls beyond the ring of adults. She greeted his intrusion with a merry laugh and continued concentrating on the steps she had just learned. //I'm not tired, Master Lenardo. Don't send me to bed.//

//No, no—go on dancing. I want to learn the steps.// He soon understood the basic pattern and then backed off to watch the differences in male and female movements in the adult dancers.

When he felt secure, he walked around the circle to collect Julia from among the children. She was delighted but protested, "I've never danced with a man."

"Read. The other dancers will tell you what to do."

They entered the dance at a point that allowed them to go through the pattern together before changing partners; by that time, Lenardo was feeling the flow of the steps in his own well-disciplined body. When the pattern brought him to Aradia, she said, "You certainly learn quickly."

"It helps to be able to Read the best dancers. Unfortunately, I cannot Read the best of all, my lady."

She laughed. "You're learning to turn a neat compliment, too. I knew power would be good for you, Lenardo. You're growing like a young tree that has reached the sunshine at last."

The dance called for her to pirouette and then raise her arms to clap her hands over her head while Lenardo watched, merely keeping rhythm. He had watched several other women perform the move, but Aradia did it with a twist of her hips that set her skirt to swirling, revealing her small feet in their neat slippers, ribbons tied about her delicate ankles. She turned faster, and her garment frothed just below her knees, revealing a swell of calf and enticing Lenardo to imagine what he would not Read.

The women came to an abrupt halt, and Aradia's skirts wrapped tightly about her body for one long instant, molding each feminine curve. Then it was over, her dress falling into its usual modest skimming of her figure as Lenardo nearly missed a step, wondering whether he could have imagined the seductive properties of the move that had seemed totally innocent when performed by other women.

Now it was his turn to clap and stamp, the men's version of this movement calling for more complicated footwork. He concentrated on that but slowly became aware of Aradia's eyes on him and of the picture he presented.

He was dressed appropriately for a savage lord, in a silk

shirt and hose in muted gold, topped with a richly embroidered tabard that under normal conditions rode modestly down over his hips. The dance movements, though, pulled it up to reveal the full length of his legs, even the bottom curve of his buttocks.

Again he realized that he had been through this figure half a dozen times without embarrassment. It was only under Aradia's scrutiny that he became aware of being on display. She was watching him avidly. He felt himself blush, but he determinedly kept to the pace of the dance as the final move called for him to take Aradia in his arms. Her violet eyes laughed up at him, but she said nothing. They were both breathing heavily, but it was a strenuous dance. Nevertheless, Lenardo was acutely conscious of his hand on Aradia's waist, her other hand in his, the peculiar intensity of performing the steps in unison.

The dance separated them then, and Lenardo's pulse returned to a rate that could be accounted for by the exercise. He went through the steps with two more women and was not aware of anything seductive in the moves. He performed his own steps without embarrassment, and by the time the music ended, he was quite certain that he had imagined the peculiar ambience of his dance with Aradia. Still, he was glad that she had finished the dance some distance away from him.

Julia, breathless and weary, was happier than Lenardo had seen her since the day he had showed her the joy of touching another Reader's mind.

"You really should go to bed, child," he told her.

"I'm too excited to sleep. Can't I stay up and watch?"

"Lie down on the cushions where Arkus left his sword, and watch until you fall asleep. I'll carry you to bed."

"If you're going to hold me, wake me up for it."

He sighed. "Julia, when are you going to stop thinking you get something more from touching flesh than from touching minds?"

"When it isn't true," she said. "But it is true," she added. "You'd know that if you didn't—" *lie to yourself* was in her mind, but she dared not speak the words.

He smiled at her. "You have years of growing up, child. All I can tell you now is, wait and see."

The next day was crowded with formal events. Lenardo had nothing to present his guests that remotely approached the value of the gifts they had sent him, but he could grant them free travel across his lands. After that, he began the announcements of formal offices, from the minor village heads up to official appointments for Arkus and Helmuth, in each case handing out a reward along with the title.

The last scheduled event was the wedding. Lenardo, however, had decided to add an event not on the schedule. Julia was sitting with the three Adepts, amusing herself through the long ceremony by Reading far and near, still trying to acquire the clear visual perception that was a young Reader's first major hurdle. She was dressed all in yellow today, a beautiful child sitting carefully in her first grown-up dress with its tight bodice and skirt of narrow pleats. Lenardo had instructed the seamstress to pattern Julia's outfit after the ones Aradia and Lilith wore, but his own was pure empire garb.

All summer, Lenardo had worn the all-purpose empire hot-weather outfit: a knee-length tunic. Soon the cool, comfortable, easy-to-make garment had become standard male garb throughout Zendi. Hair and beards were trimmed in imitation of Lenardo's shorter style, and the women put up their hair and modeled their dresses on those of the women who had come with Lenardo from Aradia's lands.

His people were proud of Lenardo. He had surprised them today, for they had never seen the formal attire of a Master Reader before. He wore a white ankle-length tunic, banded and belted in black, and over it a floor-length robe of scarlet, the sleeves bias-cut and so wide that they almost touched the ground. When he lifted his hands, the wide sleeves fell from his wrists like wings. It was the first time he had ever worn the robes.

Never in his life had he made so many decisions. The matter of clothing was trivial; his other decision for this occasion was not, and he had really made up his mind only last night, when he had carried Julia to bed. She had cuddled against him when he picked her up, and at home, when he laid her on her couch, she gave a small cry of pain. Wondering if she had made herself sick with excitement and rich food, he Read her and found her in the midst of a nightmare.

She found her mother, but it was as if the woman could not see or hear her. Then Lenardo appeared. She saw him through the crowd, lost him, found him at the end of a long, narrow passage and tried to run to him. He walked on, out of sight. Again she found him, ran to him, tried to throw her arms around him, but he thrust her away, saying, "No, child. I am not your father."

"But I love you," she sobbed.

"Don't touch me," said Lenardo.

Julia's dream brought back a memory. For many months after he had come to the Academy, Torio had had nightmares in which he lost the power to Read and was plunged back into darkness. Both Lenardo and Master Clement had often had to hold the boy in the night until his fear subsided.

Now Lenardo sat down on Julia's couch and took her in his arms, telling her, //It's all right. I'm here.//

She didn't wake, but her dream turned to bliss. Safe at last, she clung to him as he reassured her. //Sleep now. If you need me, call. I'll be here for you.//

Since he had made the commitment personally, he might as well make it publicly. A search through the treasure chests yielded the token he needed.

Now, before his people gathered in the forum, he called, "Julia. Come here, child."

//???// But she came quickly, excitement stirring her blood.

Lenardo turned her to face the crowd, his hands on her shoulders. "As most of you know, this is Julia, a Reader like myself. She is progressing well in the use of her gift and is learning the Readers' Honor."

Julia glowed with happiness as the crowd cheered. Making public speeches, Lenardo was learning, was not very different from lecturing in a classroom and certainly got a more enthusiastic response.

"So on this day of celebration and recognition, I want to make formal something that has been growing in my heart ever since this child came into my life. Here, before my people, before my allies and dearest friends, I ask you all to bear witness as I declare this child, Julia, to be my adopted daughter—"

In the wild applause drowning out his words, Lenardo fastened the gold fillet he had found in the treasure chest across Julia's brow. She reached up to touch it in disbelief, all thought suspended as the cheering died down and Lenardo finished triumphantly, "—hereafter to be known as Julia, daughter of Lenardo."

Turning Julia to face him, he knelt, feeling her restrain her longing to throw her arms about him, merely letting him kiss her formally on either cheek. Her warmth came instead in a joyous rush into his mind. //You *do* want me! You *do* love me!//

//Yes, child, and now I *am* your father.//

After that, the wedding was almost an anticlimax, although not, of course, for the principals. Josa was so happy, she looked positively beautiful, but Lenardo Read that Arkus, proudly paying the bride-price to Josa's father, who had come in Aradia's train for the occasion, had long since looked beyond Josa's exterior to the spirit beneath. If he could not Read them, he might have thought the quiet, steadfast young woman and the boisterous soldier an unlikely match.

The couple pledged to live, work, and rear children together, with their families as witness to the pledge. As Arkus had no family, Lenardo witnessed for him. Then, his official duties over, he joined his guests.

Tomorrow morning Lilith would leave, as would most of the people who had piled into the city for the festival. Wulfston and Aradia planned to stay a few extra days, and after that Wulfston wanted Lenardo to come with him, "just for a couple of weeks, so I can start mining before bad weather sets in."

"I understand," said Lenardo, "but there's still so much to do here. Julia is a tremendous help, but—"

"You said Julia can locate metal, didn't you?" Aradia asked.

"Yes, she's good at that—one of the first skills she learned."

"Well, that's all Wulfston needs. Why don't you lend him your daughter?"

"Aradia—" Wulfston protested, but she went right on.

"You do *trust* Wulfston with Julia, don't you?"

"Of course I do. The worst he could do is spoil her to death. Actually, she could locate your iron ore as well as I could, Wulfston, but she's had so little training—"

"I understand," said Wulfston. "You don't want to go away from Julia, or send her away, either one—and I can't blame you."

"However," said Aradia, "you have made Wulfston a promise, Lenardo. If Julia can do the job and cannot do your work here in Zendi—"

"I'll talk to her," said Lenardo. "You must remember that she's only eight years old."

Julia immediately hated the idea, but she did not say so. He could feel her trying to Read what he wanted her to say, and he kept his own thoughts neutral.

"It would be only for two weeks," he said, "and you like Lord Wulfston. I must tell you, Julia, that with only two Readers, the time will quickly come when we must divide our skills."

"We already do," she replied, "but I know you're here in the city. I can't Read even from here to Northgate. If I go into another land—"

"*I* can Read that far, Julia. We'll set a time, every day, when I will contact you. You can't miss your lessons for two weeks, you know, whether you go or I do."

"You mean you'll go if I don't? Then what difference does it make?" She remained silent for a moment and then added, "One day I shall rule a land of my own. I must think of what is best for our people. I shall go and repay your debt to Lord Wulfston." The grand lady disappeared, and the little girl was back. "Besides, he holds me on his lap, and he told me if I ever visit his land, he'll take me to the sea. Have you ever seen the sea, Father?"

"Yes, I have. I know you'll have a good time, Julia, and I know you will Read accurately for Lord Wulfston. I'm proud of you." He let the warmth of his feelings flow to her, and she responded in kind from across the room.

Still, it was hard for Lenardo to watch Julia ride away with Wulfston a few days later.

Aradia had not yet set her departure date and made no mention of one now. The white pavilion stood alone in the forum.

"Poor Julia," Lenardo said to her as they walked back to his house. "When I adopted her, I didn't realize she would immediately inherit my debts."

"You did find yourself an heir rather quickly."

"*My* heir, perhaps," he said as they entered his room, "but I did not name her heir to my lands because I cannot know how good a Reader she will become—and I'm not altogether certain a Reader ought to try to hold power this way."

"But you are doing beautifully," Aradia protested. "Look at all you have done for your people in a single summer."

"In a totally artificial situation. Suppose you had given me land with different Lords Adept as neighbors? How long before they discovered that I am no Adept and that the most fearsome thing any of my people can do is start a few fires? How long do you think I would hold such lands?"

"If your Adept opponent has no Reader, he becomes a bear on a tether. You tell your minor Adepts where he is, and he goes up in flames, or his heart is stopped—and his lands are yours for the taking. Besides, you have powerful allies. No one would dare attack the alliance that defeated Drakonius. In fact, I have already received tentative overtures from two other lords to join our alliance."

"That's wonderful, Aradia. You may yet achieve peace through all the lands of the Adepts."

"It's not that simple. Remember Hron. He was my ally only until he thought Drakonius could defeat me."

"Unfortunately, nature does not always bestow the gifts of great power on those with great strength of will."

"You are thinking of Galen as well as Hron," said Aradia. "Such people must be guided. Lenardo, my father always said that the greatest strength lay with those who were right. Conversely, right lies with the strongest, and even the strength of a Drakonius is powerless against it. I have a plan that will bring peace and prevent defections such as Hron's."

"The empire of Adepts you mentioned earlier?"

"Yes. Wulfston is right that a government must have one head, but he is wrong that the solution is many governments. Moreover, our alliance is not binding on our heirs. Wulfston and I do not even *have* heirs, while you and Lilith are each training a child whose potential is yet unknown."

"I didn't know Lilith had an apprentice."

"Her son. He is eleven and probably the reason Lilith's power is not equal to mine. She chose to have a child young, while her powers were still growing. There is a theory that a woman may thus regain most of her ability once her child is born. It seems to have worked for her, but of course no one will ever know what strength she might have had."

"And is her son an Adept?"

"Of course. He will be a Lord Adept, but it will be ten years yet before we can begin to predict his mature powers." Aradia rose abruptly and went to the window, looking out into the courtyard. With her back to Lenardo, she said, "I must think about an heir myself . . . and soon. Despite the danger to a woman, I want my own child, Lenardo."

Even her emotions were beyond Reading. Every defense was up. Before Lenardo could say anything, she continued.

"My parents wanted their own child as heir. They risked their powers for me. My father recovered . . . but my mother—"

Lenardo knew the story. Aradia's mother had blamed the child for her diminished powers. "It doesn't have to be that way," he said quickly.

"But it might be! I hardly remember my mother, but because of her I would not dare emulate Lilith. If I ever decide to have a child, I want the father of that child with me to raise and protect and train it if I cannot. As my father was there for me.''

''Surely any man worth considering would want—''

She turned, her eyes flashing. ''You think it is that easy? A fully empowered lord who would not simply take the child for himself and cast me aside if my powers were permanently damaged?''

''There is Wulfston—''

''Wulfston is my *brother*.''

''What I started to say is that Wulfston would protect you in such a situation. But he is *not* your brother by blood, Aradia.''

''He is in every other way,'' she replied. ''If my father had taken Wulfston ward instead of son, raised us not to think of each other as brother and sister, we might have been drawn to each other, or we might not. Father wanted us to have a tie as strong as blood, not dependent on attraction after we reached adulthood, and not to be severed if and when we each chose other partners. An unbreakable alliance, Lenardo. Surely you can see that there is no changing our sense of family now. Wulfston and I could not possibly be lovers. We could never have a child.''

He had known that, and yet it was somehow reassuring to have it formally stated that Wulfston's protectiveness of Aradia, particularly when they had first met, had no other basis than brotherly devotion. But why should he care? He had no designs on Aradia; he even had a potential heir and thus no reason ever to risk his own powers. Yet if he were to risk them for anyone—

He cut off the absurd train of thought. Aradia would seek an Adept to father her child one day, not a Reader. She was trusting to his friendship in revealing her concerns this way. He had no right to the urge he felt to take her in his arms and promise her his care and protection.

She was watching him warily. Deliberately, he forced his tense muscles to relax and sat back in his chair. ''If we make the peace we seek, no Adept will have to have such fears of losing power, even temporarily. Already our alliance protects us.''

Aradia's violet eyes grew dark with . . . what? Surprise? Then she shook off the moment's vulnerability and accepted his change of mood. Coming to sit opposite him again, she said, ''We must have more than an alliance. Would Julia retain alliance with me if you were gone? Would Lilith's son honor his mother's commitments? Who protects Julia's rights if you die while she is too young to rule? If any one of us should die tomorrow, war could erupt over the disposition of our property.''

''I see,'' said Lenardo, grimly noting Aradia's tenacity. ''That must happen often.''

''There is only one way to stop it: with a central government that takes precedence over the local lords and has the strength to maintain order. In that one thing, the Aventine Empire is right. They have no internal wars over who owns what.''

''No wars,'' he agreed. ''Fights and occasionally murders; the empire is by no means crime-free. But no internal wars or cities destroyed as Zendi was. Disputes are settled in the courts.''

''Then you agree with me?''

''That a central government would benefit our people? Certainly. However, the *kind* of government—''

''A government of the strongest,'' she said. ''A natural government with the strongest of all Adepts at its head. Wulfston and Lilith fear that their lands would be taken, but that is not my intention. They would rule their own way, as would you, Lenardo. All the Lords Adept would be part of my council.''

''*Your* council?''

''Only the most powerful of Adepts can make this plan work. You would all be bound to me, your armies and your powers at my disposal, but in return you would be protected, and your chosen heirs after you. For example, I have promised Lilith that if anything happened to her, I would take her son as my apprentice. But suppose she died suddenly? Before I got there, her neighbors could overrun her land and kill her son. But if I were Empress, no one would dare. I could hold the land of an heir until he was grown, and then, provided only that he proved a true Lord Adept—or Reader—he would receive it. All would answer to me. If a Lord Adept died without an heir, instead of his neighbors warring through his land, I would choose who was to rule it, peacefully."

"Why *you*, Aradia?" Lenardo asked.

"Because I can do it. No, because you and I can do it together. We can set up a government that will long outlive us. We are fated to do it." She took his right hand and traced the dragon's head on his forearm with one finger. "You have taken the red dragon as your symbol."

"That just happened. Aradia, surely you don't believe in that old saying—"

"Then you've heard it. You know we are meant to seize the chance, now, while I am the only Adept with a Reader to guide me."

"You could start a war. Is that how you plan to achieve peace?"

Aradia shook her head. "You've changed so much, but you still have much to learn. It is necessary to demonstrate power in order to rule peacefully. Even you have had to have people executed."

"Three in all, and all in the first few days I was here."

"You see? Demonstrate power on a few, and the rest come into line."

"I won't help you, Aradia."

"Not today," she said, holding his hand in both of hers. "I will be thirty years old next spring. The last and slowest growth of my powers will come in the next five years, and in that time I and my allies have our own lands to rebuild. Then, Lenardo, you will help me convince others, or perhaps Julia will."

It was a patent threat. As she stood there, gently holding his hand, she could as easily kill him. She could stop his heart. If she didn't want a body to dispose of, she could burn him to ashes. Then she could take Julia and bend the child to her will. Was Wulfston a part of the plot? Had he taken Julia out of the way in case Aradia decided to kill Lenardo?

"Five years," he said.

"Oh, perhaps not so long. You will learn, Lenardo. Every day you are more like one of us. Look how happy you have made your people, and think how much better, safer, their lives could be."

When Aradia left him, Lenardo sat down on the window ledge, numb. *I thought I knew her! I thought she truly expected me to make a treaty with the empire. What is she? Benevolent dictator, true, but is that not what I have become? Now she wants to rule the world, and who is to stop her? I can pretend to cooperate . . . until she tests me.*

What was he to do? His first instinct was to ride after Wulfston and bring Julia home. Yet he had sensed sincerity in Wulfston's indignation when Aradia first brought up her plan. Julia might be safer with Wulfston than in Zendi just now.

He must convince Aradia that she was wrong. She believed that might made right. He had been in the savage lands long enough to know that there was no use trying to bridge that basic philosophical gap.

Aradia had thought out reasons for her plan that were sound enough. If she could rule peacefully as she described, people *would* be better off. She would hardly take seriously the argument that power corrupts and would deny that anything she had said was a threat against Lenardo or Julia.

How can I convince her she's wrong? I can't.

He felt as frustrated as he had months ago, when he had found himself a helpless prisoner in Aradia's castle. He had won her respect then . . . through his powers. Power was one thing Aradia respected. She considered herself to be the most powerful practicing Adept. What would convince her that she did not have enough power to become Empress?

A thought licked at the back of his mind, from a realm so absurd he could not even let it take form. Yet having considered and discarded all reasonable approaches to the problem, Lenardo finally allowed the absurd thought to surface: *The only thing that permanently weakens an A-dept's power is sexual activity.*

And what am I to do, try to rape her? He could think of more pleasant ways to commit suicide.

The thought was a long time coming, but it finally thrust its way into his consciousness: *I must seduce her.*

It was surely the most ridiculous thought he had ever entertained. What did he know about women? And what would happen if he succeeded? His own powers would be impaired—but how badly? Only failed Readers ever engaged in sex, to produce new generations of Readers. No Master Reader had ever. . . .

If those Readers who did not reach the top two ranks still retained some Reading ability, a Master Reader ought to retain a great deal. Certainly he would lose range, accuracy—exactly the things that made him most valuable to Aradia in battle. That was all to the good. And if he lost it all—if he found himself blind even to thoughts—was it not a necessary sacrifice to stop Aradia?

The thought terrified him. *No one ever loses it all,* he told himself firmly. He would certainly be able to continue to rule Zendi, to teach Julia until he could make peace with the empire and get her proper tutors. And then, with Readers spreading into other lands, Aradia would not be able to put her plan into action, no matter how much of her own power she might retain or recover.

Very well, he had a plan.

But by every god who had ever amused himself by dallying with human women, how was he ever going to implement it?

Chapter Four

It was afternoon, the time for men to use the bathhouse. Lenardo found several off-duty soldiers playing ball in the gymnasium and joined them, working up a sweat as he tried to banish his tension. When he finally slammed the ball with such force that the receiver was knocked over, one of the men called out, "You're sure you've no Adept power, me lord?"

He managed an almost natural laugh and said, panting, "Perhaps it's contagious, eh?"

As he helped the fallen soldier to his feet, the young man said, "Then stick around me, my lord, and see if Reading rubs off. Would that I could Read what's happening in sweet Nerissa's mind!"

As the other men proceeded to tell him what they thought was on Nerissa's mind, Lenardo excused himself and went to bathe. Even when he plunged into the pool of cold water, the last step in his daily routine, he was still unsettled.

I can't do it, he told himself as he toweled off and put on a clean tunic. *It's not something I'm capable of, nor something Aradia would succumb to.* At once he felt better, until he remembered that that left him without a plan at all. Perhaps if he talked with her again. . . .

Emerging from the bathhouse, he walked across the forum to the white pavilion. Pepyi, one of Aradia's retainers, was standing guard at the entrance. "Is the Lady Aradia within?" Lenardo asked.

"Yes, my lord. One moment, please."

Almost at once, Peply came back, along with Aradia's maid. "My lady will see you, Lord Lenardo. Please enter."

He threaded his way through the hanging that provided

79

privacy to the large central area where Aradia's furnishings were set out. Grass mats covered the paving stones of the forum; on them were set a small folding table and two chairs, a chest, and several tall candelabra, unlit now, as daylight filtered through the white silk. A bedroll covered with silken sheets and heaped with cushions occupied one end of the inner room formed by the hangings.

Aradia was sitting at the table, wearing an amethyst silk dress; the surcoat she had worn earlier was folded neatly on top of the chest.

"Come sit down, Lenardo," she said, gesturing to the other chair. "Will you have some wine?"

"Thank you."

With her back to him, Aradia poured the wine and produced two goblets, not one. So she acknowledged that they were not in accord. "Why have you come here?" she asked.

He had no answer; he didn't know what he hoped to accomplish.

Aradia reached out to touch his damp hair. "You're wet."

"I just came from the baths."

"Yes, you smell nice and clean. I've been using your baths every morning—such luxury! Did you know that your people are so mystified about your putting the baths in order before anything else that they've decided a Reader must immerse in water every day to keep his powers?"

He laughed. "How did I miss Reading *that* bit of nonsense? No, Aradia. When I first came here, the entire population was infested with fleas and lice. I had to do something to prevent the spread of disease, and the bathhouse was there."

Aradia shuddered. "I'm glad you got rid of the fleas and lice before we got here!"

"But an Adept can just—"

"I'd rather not have them at all, thank you. Can we change the subject?"

"Of course."

But she fell silent, sipping her wine, and Lenardo followed suit. The wine was not the light beverage he had become used to. It was strong and spicy and seemed to go straight to his head. Aradia studied him over the rim of her goblet and then put it down and reached for his hand. Again, her fingers traced the brand on his forearm.

"Tell me what you want for your people, Lenardo."

"Hmm?" He forced himself to concentrate.

"After you rebuild Zendi, then what?" Aradia asked, pouring him more wine.

He ignored the wine and said flatly, "You know my plans. They have not changed."

"A treaty with the Aventine Empire?"

"You once thought it a good idea."

"I still do. I need skilled Readers, not untrained children, to carry out my plans. Go on—what else do you plan?"

"I would like to see all my people comfortably clothed and housed and free to earn a living as they choose. There is terrible ignorance here; few people survive from the time before Drakonius took this land, none of them scholars, artists, or even skilled artisans. The younger men don't even know how to hunt, as Drakonius allowed only his own huntsmen into the forests to get meat for his tables, and be damned if the peasants were starving."

"Lenardo, that is a way of keeping Adepts from flourishing. Keep meat a rarity among most of your populace, and you won't find a Lord Adept suddenly grown up among the peasants to challenge you."

Lenardo felt a sickness at the pit of his stomach. "Deliberately stunt the growth of their powers? Aradia . . . in your lands—"

"You have seen how I feed my people. I want everyone with Adept power to use it to the fullest—for me. Diet cannot create powers a person was not born with, but inadequate diet can blunt Adept powers just as it can make a child physically and mentally weak. Your Julia, now—"

"Ironically, Drakonius' restrictions worked in her favor. Apparently she got enough—barely enough—to eat, though. She's certainly bright, and she's growing like a weed now that someone's taking care of her."

"What happened to her mother?" Aradia asked.

"She disappeared as soon as I lifted travel restrictions. I don't know why."

"I do. If Drakonius had adopted a child, he would certainly have killed her parents to be sure she had no other ties."

Lenardo sighed. "It will be a long time before my people get over Drakonius. Still, I don't think Julia misses her mother very much. She couldn't communicate with her the way she does with me. I can't really explain to a nonReader. What seems odd is that I feel the same closeness with Adepts—and look at Julia and Wulfston."

"People with extraordinary powers," said Aradia. "We have a great deal in common."

She continued to hold his hand with one of hers. Lenardo waited, somehow unable to initiate further conversation when he was so aware of her touch. He had never seen her like this, apparently open and vulnerable. In a sense, she was on vacation. She had no responsibilities here; she was his guest. Everything was up to Lenardo.

Not really believing that he was going to try his plot, Lenardo remained waiting, suspended. Maybe they could just talk, come to a better understanding if Aradia were relaxed. . . .

Aradia uncurled the fingers of Lenardo's hand, staring at the palm. "You have such nice hands. Why don't you ever touch people?"

"I touch people—"

"To heal. To lift Julia up onto Wulfston's horse. But you never really *touch*."

"Readers don't."

"I'm not a Reader," she said, placing her palm over his, her fingers tickling the sensitive skin on the inside of his wrist. "Julia thinks you don't care about her because you don't hug or kiss her."

"Julia can Read directly how I feel about her . . . but you can't," he said, his heart pounding in terror at his boldness.

He hadn't expected the opportunity, and surely it would never come again. *Take one step and see what happens,* he told himself firmly. He closed his hand around hers, and when she didn't pull away, he leaned forward and kissed her.

His position was awkward. He could not remain kissing her long, just a touching of lips that brought no answering response from her except a pang of startlement. Before his muscles went into spasm, he sank back into his chair, waiting for Aradia's reaction.

She blushed but gripped his hand more tightly. She had once told him that she could make good use of energy created by frustrated desire. Probably she thought that she could kiss him safely enough, let herself become aroused, and then stop short. If she did, he had lost nothing except his composure. But if he could Read her feelings well enough to tip the balance—

He got up, drawing Aradia to her feet. She made no resistance when he took her into his arms but held him, her head against his shoulder. Her quickened breathing and faint trembling told him that she was excited, and he Read her heart beating as rapidly as his own. Only once before in his life had Lenardo held a woman thus, and for the first time he blessed that innkeeper's daughter, only wishing that they had not been caught quite so soon.

Despite the close contact, he felt no unpleasant over-burdening of emotion. It was more pleasant than holding Julia, something highly charged with expectancy communicating from Aradia's body to his. A faint, clean smell rose from her, the sweet aroma of her hair. During the days of ceremonial appearances, she had worn it in intricate arrangements of braids and curls. Now she had pulled it into a simple coil at the nape of her neck; it looked as if all that held it were three gold combs set with amethysts. Experimentally, he pulled out the combs, and her pale blond hair tumbled free.

At that, she lifted her face up, and it seemed the most natural thing in the world to kiss her again. This time it was more successful—they seemed to fit together. As he pressed his lips to hers, her mouth yielded, softening invitingly, and a charge of pure desire struck through him. Pleasure blurred the edges of his fear. It became harder to think, easier to act.

He felt a strange yearning to get closer to her. He could Read her hesitant desire but could not reach her mind. As if physical closeness could compensate, he held her tighter, his hands seeking over her body but encountering only the fabric of her gown where he sought to feel flesh on flesh.

Finally he found the tiny hooks fastening her gown, fumbling as he fought a wish to tear the fabric. That violent notion brought him back to reality long enough to complete the task while he made a decision. *It's up to Aradia now. I want her, and I'll take her if she'll let me.* He didn't pause to question when his duty to stop Aradia from trying to rule the world had become his personal desire. His touch-starved body merely acted, feeling Aradia pliant, willing, shy—

He couldn't remember getting out of his own clothing, but he was naked and was trying to find Aradia beneath layers of filmy undergarments, until he finally stripped away the last one and she stood pale and shimmering before him, veiled now only with the soft aura of her hair.

He couldn't even pause to look at her but lifted her and knelt to lay her in the bed. In his hasty and inexperienced passion, when he kissed her aggressively, their teeth met in a painful jolt. But her soft outcry only inflamed him. She was his now, helpless beneath him. He was annoyed momentarily when her hair got in his mouth, shifting his weight when her sense of suffocation reached him, but at the core he took her on a rush of power such as he had never known before.

Emotion peaked. With a cry of triumph at the burst of total pleasure, Lenardo dropped panting, sweating, onto Aradia's breast, burnt out and unbelievably satisfied. The last thing he felt was her hands pushing at him until he slid off her, feeling somehow that he ought to investigate why her feelings seemed so distant from his, but he was too content, too tired.

Blackness claimed him.

Lenardo woke to the thob of a headache. It was dark, almost midnight. Instead of the pale square of his window,

there was milky grayness all around him, the night color of
Aradia's white pavilion. Memory flooded back. His first
instinct was to run, but it hurt incredibly when he moved
his head, and there was Aradia—

Despite the pain, he Read her. She was curled up with
her back to him, now wearing a long-sleeved, high-necked
loose robe and clutching the covers about herself protec-
tively, as if she feared attack. From the state of her body,
he could Read that she had wept long and hard before
falling into exhausted sleep.

Lenardo was filled with utter self-loathing. He deserved
however much his head ached and was surprised that he
could Read at all. Now he knew why Master Clement had
beaten him so that time. Was the beast loosed this afternoon locked within every man, or had his teachers recognized a particular danger in him and tried to restrain it with
special strictness? If he had never left the Academy, he
might never have known—

Now I can never go back.

What was he to do? First things first: take himself out of
Aradia's way. She wouldn't want to face him when she
woke. *Why am I still alive?* he wondered. *Can I have
damaged her powers that much?* He would certainly have
wanted to kill anyone who had so brutally used him.

The headache was interfering with his thinking. He got
to his knees, swaying, and sought his clothes. He Read
them, finally, neatly hung on one of the chairs, his sandals
under it. Aradia's attempts to restore order made his heart
ache.

As he struggled to his feet, the world tilted and the pain
in his head redoubled. Fighting to suppress a moan, he
winced in agony when the candles burst into flame.

"Lenardo."

Helplessly, he turned to face Aradia. "Don't leave,"
she whispered.

"How can you—" he began, but the effort of talking
set the room spinning, and he staggered, putting both
hands to his head as the jar of regaining his balance sent
another lance through his skull.

"You're in pain," Aradia gasped, and was at his side,

one cool hand on his forehead. The pain dissolved; the world oriented itself, and he stared in astonishment into her anxious eyes.

"How can you stand to touch me?" he asked.

She looked away, suddenly shy. "I wanted it, too," she said. "I didn't know it would be like that."

She seemed so forlorn that he wanted to comfort her, started to reach for her, and pulled back—but she turned into his arms, clinging to him.

"I'm sorry," he murmured helplessly. "I didn't mean to hurt you." *Not that way.* "I'll never do it again."

At the disgust in his tone, she backed off. "Am I repellent to you now?"

He closed his eyes, trying to Read some sense in her attitude, but all he got was a haze of shame, anxiety, and self-recrimination.

"Aradia—" If he could only touch her mind, assure her that his loathing was toward himself. But he could not. So he held out his hands, not reaching for her, just available. "Whatever you want."

What she wanted was to sleep in his arms, it seemed. He didn't understand, but he was grateful. As he lay awake long after Aradia, he realized that he didn't want to leave her. Perhaps not ever.

The next morning, having faced down the guards when he left Aradia's pavilion, Lenardo prepared to keep his appointment with Julia and discovered that his powers had indeed deteriorated. He could not leave his body; it was as if the lead weight of his animal nature held his spirit prisoner.

Fast and meditation, he told himself. *You cannot have regressed permanently.* Those Readers who were judged capable of trying for the two highest ranks when they took their tests at eighteen were given instruction in leaving the body. Anyone who could not do it by the time he was twenty was judged a failure.

And had I failed this miserably at that time, they would have married me off, and what I did last night I would

*have done to some poor female Reader—but worse, be-
cause I'd have assaulted her mind as well as her body.*

He cringed from that line of thought. Julia was waiting.
He had to calm himself and try to reach her. He had Read
farther than to Wulfston's castle without leaving his body
before. But that was indeed before.

He knew where Wulfston was building his castle—actually
expanding one of Drakonius' old fortifications into a
dwelling—but he had never been there or Read it before.
By the time he found it, his relief was so intense that Julia
caught it.

//You're late, Father. What's wrong? Are you ill?//

//Yes—no—not exactly. It's nothing for you to worry
about, Julia.//

//I'm coming home!//

//No!// He forced himself to be calm, feeling as if he
were the eight-year-old.

Julia was already up and running out of her room and
down the hall to pound on Wulfston's door and then burst
in to declare, "Lord Wulfston, I've got to go home! It's
Father!"

"What?"

"He's sick."

//No. No, Julia.//

Wulfston was saying, "Hasn't he contacted you?"

"Yes. He's . . . here. In my head, I mean."

Wulfston squatted down so that he could look directly
into Julia's eyes. "Lenardo, can you have Julia tell me
what's wrong? We can ride today if you need us."

//Tell Lord Wulfston you got scared, Julia. There's
nothing wrong at all.//

When Julia remained silent, Wulfston demanded, "What
does he say?"

"He says there's nothing wrong. I don't believe it."

Wulfston studied the girl's face. "Julia, if you don't
like it here and want to go home, just tell me. Don't make
up stories about your father being ill."

//Tell him I am ill . . . in a way. It's nothing serious.//

"Father says he is ill, but it's nothing serious," Julia
relayed. "He says his Reading powers are—im-paired?—but

they'll come back. You remember how his powers were impaired''—this time she was certain she had the word— ''when he was so sick at Castle Nerius. It's not nearly that bad, he'll be fine, and he . . . he wants me to stay here.'' Then she added her own interpretation. ''I think he's scared about me.''

''Well, you know, Julia,'' said Wulfston, ''some illnesses are much more serious for children than for adults. It's probably something he doesn't want you to catch. Now, don't you worry. Aradia's there to heal Lenardo.''

//That's right,// Lenardo told her. //Tell Wulfston that Aradia has already helped me.//

When Julia relayed the message, Wulfston said, ''There, you see? The healing has used up Lenardo's strength. It's nothing to worry about.''

Between them, Lenardo and Wulfston calmed Julia, and she settled down to her lesson. However, Lenardo found it difficult to maintain contact over that distance and warned Julia that when Wulfston took her on the promised excursion to the sea, she was not to worry if he could not reach her there. *But surely,* he told himself, *my abilities will improve soon.*

If only he could take two or three days to fast and meditate. But there was work to be done, and he still had a guest. When he emerged from his lesson with Julia, he fully expected a polite message saying that Aradia was leaving. But there was none, and as he crossed the forum on his way to the day's work site, there was no sign of activity about the white pavilion.

He passed people busily rebuilding, who smiled and waved to him as they might on any other day. If the news had spread that the Lord of Zendi had spent the night in Aradia's pavilion, he could not Read that anyone suspected what had happened there. He caught some curiosity about what a Lord Reader and a Lady Adept might be plotting together and slowly realized that those endowed with the full range of powers were not thought to have the same temptations of the flesh as ordinary people. *How disillusioned they would be if they knew!*

Lenardo had started his rebuilding program from the

forum outward. As the city now held approximately the number of people it was designed for, Lenardo hoped to put everything back in order and then expand the facilities as the population increased. Trade would grow again, he knew. People with talent and business skill would sort themselves out from the rest. The excellent Aventine road would keep Zendi flourishing, and Lenardo foresaw a time when it would outshine its heyday as a prime Aventine trade city.

The sewer system under the forum had been cleared and repaired during Lenardo's first month in Zendi, the ditch closed and paved over all along the main market way to Northgate. Water no longer flowed from the bathhouse pipe but bubbled merrily from the forum fountain and two others some distance away. Lenardo had been amused to discover that bringing the long-dry fountains to life was regarded as an act worthy of the most powerful Adept.

Today, work continued along another main street branching out from the forum. Yesterday, Lenardo had Read a section of broken pipe, and when he joined the workmen this morning, he found them just laying the cobbles back over the completed repair. He Read the new pipe neatly joined to the old and said, "Good job. We'll have this whole section finished before winter sets in."

The workmen picked up their tools and followed Lenardo as he Read the water and sewer pipes beneath the street. "The water pipes are sound now all the way to the fountain, but the sewer pipe is clogged solid. Vona?"

They had tried various Adept abilities on the pipes and had found that fire was best at clearing them. As there was little air in the pipes, though, fire was difficult to sustain, and their two best fire talents alternated days and still could not work for long. There were patches where it was best to have the workmen dig up the pipes.

"Show me, my lord," said Vona, coming to stand beside Lenardo.

She was in her midforties, hair graying from auburn, calm and steady and easy to work with. She was also, Lenardo realized for the first time, a soft, warm woman. His reaction startled him, but it vanished instantly once he recognized it. *Thank the gods, I can control the beast when I try!*

To enable Vona to visualize the blockage, Lenardo chalked the dimensions of the clogged pipe on the paving stones and then held a stick upright over the center, marking it as he said, "This deep to the top of the pipe, this deep to the bottom."

Vona studied the markings and then sat down cross-legged in the roadway and began to concentrate. Heat smoldered through the debris in the pipe. Parts of it charred, but not enough to unblock the pipe. Lenardo told Vona what was happening, encouraging her. But as her heart pounded and her breathing grew ragged, he had to stop her.

"Sorry, men, you'll have to dig this one up," he told them, and chalked the joinings of the pipe on the roadway.

When Vona had rested, she and Lenardo moved down the street, where they removed two other clogs in the pipe and located another that would not respond. Soon lunch arrived. Lenardo, who had not been able to face breakfast, found his appetite returned. The workmen and Vona ate at least three times what Lenardo did, including the usual large slices of meat, but the novelty of Lenardo's vegetarian diet had worn off, and talk was of other things.

When he was sure that Vona would not faint along the way, Lenardo sent her home and directed the workmen to the second section of pipe to be dug up. The second pipe was harder to get at, for it had at some time leaked around the joining, and the earth surrounding it had become as solid as stone. Clay pipe was scarce. They had enough to replace without breaking any that could be salvaged.

As they approached the pipe, Lenardo took a pick and began to work around the most delicate area himself, enjoying putting his back into the hard labor. The afternoon was warm, and all of them stripped to the least clothing possible. Lenardo took off his tunic and refastened it around his waist as a sort of loincloth.

He was concentrating on the difficulty of landing heavy blows to break through the mortarlike earth without striking the clay pipe, when he was interrupted by a feminine voice.

"What in the *world* are you doing?"

Lenardo turned to find Aradia watching him in surprise and amusement.

"My lord's doing work we can't, milady," the head of the work crew immediately said defensively, "nor our Adept talents can't handle it."

"We're clearing a blocked pipe," Lenardo explained.

"By hand? When you have a Lady Adept available?"

"Lady Aradia, you are my guest," said Lenardo. "I did not invite you to clean the sewers."

She burst into rich laughter and said, "Come out of there, all of you. Why should you put such hard labor into something I can do in a moment?"

The workers were quick enough to scramble out of the hole, with a grateful "Yes, my lady." Lenardo climbed out more slowly and explained the situation, trying very hard not to be embarrassed.

As Aradia did it, the job was easy. The pipe did not have to be dug up and its contents scraped out; rather, when fire did not work, she concentrated, and the impacted mass crumbled into dust that would wash away as soon as water was turned into the pipe.

"Now," she said, "is there anything more like that? As long as I'm here, Lenardo, let me help you. I will certainly never hesitate to call on *your* services."

It occurred to him that she might be testing her powers, and so he said, "If you really don't mind, you can save us several days of work," and led her into the next street on his agenda, telling the workmen to quit for the day once they had filled in their last dig.

Aradia made no reference to yesterday's debacle; nor did she seem the least bit embarrassed. *She wants to forget it,* Lenardo thought. *So do I, if I only could.* But he was surprised at her ease with him.

They worked their way up the street toward the forum, with Lenardo Reading and Aradia clearing the pipes. Where there were broken spots, Lenardo chalked instructions for the workmen to follow tomorrow, but with Aradia's help he completed as much in an hour as he could do with the workmen in two days.

Perhaps it was the incredible mundaneness of the task that made it so natural for them to work together. Healing a sorcerer of a brain tumor, fighting in a battle won by Adept power—those were rare occurrences that by now seemed almost dreams, or stories the bards sang. Their repair of pipes was *real*, the sort of unromantic but extremely important work that Readers and Adepts would one day routinely do together.

"Why are you so intent on the pipes?" Aradia asked.

"It's easy to repair them now," Lenardo explained. "Once there's heavy traffic in these streets, such repairs become a nuisance. This quadrant of the city will house everyone for the winter. These are old Aventine buildings. The houses have hot-water heating systems that I hope to restore. But maybe *I* won't have to restore them."

"What do you mean?"

"Drakonius rewarded his officers with property like this, letting them take whatever rent they could force from the tenants. I also plan to give out some of these buildings as rewards, but I hope the new owners will put them in repair and rent out the apartments reasonably."

"Apartments," said Aradia. "Rents." She shook her head. "I chose the right person to give a city. I've never lived in one, so I had no idea how a city is run. It doesn't have to be ugly and dirty, overcrowded, and infested with rats, does it?"

"I take it you were in Zendi when it was under Drakonius' rule?"

"Only when I had to be. I don't think it would have occurred to me to begin improvements with the underground pipes. In fact, I wouldn't have known they were there."

"But you would never have allowed garbage in the streets," said Lenardo. "Before we cleared the first sewer line, our biggest problem was persuading people not to throw everything into the streets but to take it to the waste stations to be burned. Now we're trying to teach people what cannot go into the drains. I didn't realize they didn't know, and our newly cleared sewer line was clogged the very day it was opened.''

Aradia laughed. ''The glamorous occupation of ruling a land. No, I'm not laughing at you. I'm remembering two years ago, when in the worst heat of the summer, Wulfston and I had to go out among the swine to stop an epidemic of running sores. It was bad enough going into the mud wallows, enduring the stink, but there were also clouds of stinging flies. I could keep them off me until I would focus on healing an animal. Then, while I was concentrating, the flies would settle all over me.'' She shook herself as if shaking off the insects. ''I prefer a nice comfortable job like cleaning out sewers.''

They reached another clog in the pipe. Lenardo Read it carefully and said, ''There's a pocket of explosive gas here.''

''Explosive gas?''

''Yes, the matter in the pipes creates it. Occasionally, we find a spot like this, so airtight that the gas has not leaked away over the years. There's a huge pocket of it under Southgate, where the culvert out of the city collapsed years ago. It's very deep underground.''

''Isn't that dangerous?''

''Not so long as no spark of fire can get at it. One day, when we begin work in that area, we'll have to put a shaft down and release the gas. But doing that before we're ready to work there would create a dangerous constant gas leak. It's better left alone.''

''How do we get rid of the pocket of gas here?''

''I've been marking such places to be dug up with caution, for one spark—''

''I understand. But I can make a crack in the earth to release the gas. Show me where.''

Under Aradia's concentration, the paving stones separated, forming an uneven line not wide enough to insert a finger.

''Now the pipe,'' said Lenardo. ''A small crack won't harm its function.''

A *snap* rose from the fissure, followed by a soft *whoosh*

of released gas. Aradia, who had been holding her breath, sniffed cautiously. "I don't smell anything."

"Marsh gas," said Lenardo. "It forms in mines sometimes, too. The fact that it's odorless makes it very dangerous. It takes a Reader to detect it."

His heart gave a heave of guilt as he suddenly realized how careless he had been today. It had not occurred to him to test whether he still had the sensitivity to distinguish gases—and if he had not, he could have blown up himself, his work crew, Aradia—

He swallowed hard and made a mental note to test himself before taking on any more "routine" tasks. Aradia, meanwhile, cleared the pipe and let the earth settle back over it. They continued on, talking as they worked, as much in harmony as if yesterday had never happened.

Lenardo was so busy Reading the pipes under the street that he was not Reading Aradia, nor was he paying attention to the time. The afternoon dwindled into shadow as the sun dropped behind the buildings, although there was still sunlight in the open forum they approached. An entire street done in one afternoon; if, that is, they cleared one more blockage.

"This is the last one," Lenardo said as he chalked the marks to guide Aradia.

For the first time, instead of Reading on ahead, he watched her. She was wearing a pale wheat-colored silk dress, the same color as her hair, no robe over it, as she had come out in the warmth of the afternoon. Now Lenardo saw her shiver slightly. Yet he was not cold, even bare-legged and bare-chested. Aradia's body was exhausted.

It had not occurred to him to keep watch on Aradia the way he did on Vona. This work should have been nothing to her strength. Her powers were diminished just as his were. Why hadn't she said something?

"Aradia, that's enough," he said. "You're worn out."

"Oh, no," she replied. "Why, this much I can—" She staggered, half fainting.

Lenardo caught her, held her against him to support her, panic rising and then subsiding as her heart recovered its strong, steady beat. She clung to him for a moment and then stood on her own. He saw that the grime on his body from the dusty, sweaty work he'd been doing had transferred itself to her cheek, her hands, and all down the front of her dress.

When she realized what had happened, Aradia laughed.

"I'm sorry," Lenardo began.

"It's nothing," she replied. "I can clean the dress, but tomorrow, I think. For myself, I'll make use again of your luxurious bathhouse."

"It's just closed," he said. "I'll have water brought—"

"Lenardo," said Aradia, "that is *your* bathhouse. You can use it any time you want, and I doubt that ever in your life have you needed it more."

He was far dirtier than she was, although it was certainly not the first time. Ordinarily, he stopped early enough to use the last half hour of the men's time in the baths.

"These are no attendants now, but you're right, of course. There's no reason I can't go in and scrub off this grime."

"Good," she said. "I'll get a clean dress and meet you there." She set off toward her pavilion.

Lenardo went for clean clothes and then got the key to the bathhouse from the attendant, who took one look at him and made no query as to why he wanted it. The only reason the bathhouse was locked at night was Lenardo's fear that children might sneak in and drown. Unlike the small bathhouse at the Academy, this one had a frigidarium pool big enough to swim in.

There were a number of changing rooms, but Aradia followed Lenardo into one near the hot bath. Having done plenty of sweating in his work today, he planned simply to scrub off the grime and then take a brief swim.

When Aradia hung her clean clothes on the peg beside his, he said, "Uh . . . do you want to bathe first, Aradia? I'll go and—"

"There are no attendants, Lenardo. We'll have to attend each other."

"Aradia, surely—"

"Lenardo, when you can Read right through clothing, how can nudity mean anything to you? How can you be so modest?"

"After yesterday, how can you ask such a thing?" he asked bitterly, immediately regretting having brought up the subject.

He had turned away from her. Aradia circled him until they were face to face. "You know I wanted you, or I could have stopped you. It shouldn't have happened that way, Lenardo, but I wanted it to happen. And you promised you wouldn't hurt me again. I believe you."

I'll never touch *you again!* he thought, but she was the one touching him, her hand on his arm, on the dragon's-head brand. It seemed to leap into flame.

Aradia was looking up at him expectantly. "Come on," she said. "I've scrubbed your back before. Now it's your turn to scrub mine."

How could she be so casual? Perhaps because she was too tired to feel desire, she thought that he was. He couldn't seem to convince anyone that Reading took no energy, and today he had done only half the physical labor he was capable of.

Although the furnace had been banked for the night, the water in the caldarium was still quite warm. Totally un-selfconscious, Aradia plunged into the water, emerged, and began lathering her body with the soap that was so plentiful in the savage lands. Lenardo remained soaking, stretching his muscles, until Aradia said, "You promised to scrub my back."

He hadn't, but he couldn't decide whether it would be more embarrassing to argue with her or do as she asked. Then he realized that she was making a gesture of trust. Perhaps she knew that he needed to prove to himself that he could touch her without erupting into mindless lust.

He climbed out of the pool and lathered her back and shoulders, being very careful to remain as detached as when, as a young teacher, he had sometimes had to scrub the smallest boys at the Academy, for budding Readers showed the same affinity for mud as any other little boys.

When he did not go beyond the slender contours of her back, Aradia relaxed against his hands. "Rub harder. Oh, that feels good."

He kneaded her shoulders, Reading the tenseness of the

muscles give way. She seemed to be bouncing back from her exhaustion; perhaps a meal and a night's sleep—

She turned in his arms and said, "My turn," starting to lather soap onto Lenardo's chest.

"That's not my back."

"Oh, but you are dirty all over," she replied, reaching up to work the soap through his hair and beard. "I know how to do it. I've bathed you before—remember?"

"At the time, I couldn't stop you."

"Do you want to stop me now?" Her wide eyes invited candor.

"No," he replied, "and that is why I must."

"Lenardo—" there was a terrible uncertainty in her voice, "—do you really not want me?"

Her utter vulnerability struck through him like a sword of ice. "Of course I want you," he said harshly, "but look what I've done to you already."

The hurt in the depths of her eyes abated slightly. "I think," she whispered, and he Read how immensely difficult it was for her to say it, "if we tried, we could make it worth . . . anything."

What had he done to her? What was she doing to him that her foolish words seemed to make perfect sense, that he suddenly didn't care if he woke up tomorrow a nonReader if he could have Aradia? What did it matter what they did together, as long as it *was* together? Hadn't he just spent one of the happiest days of his life cleaning out sewers?

"Aradia," he said, bemused at the beauty of her name. He knew the words but had never dreamed they might apply to him. "I love you."

Her violet eyes lit with joy, and then her arms went around his neck as he felt dread sorrow give way to happiness. He kissed her then, gently, tenderly, tensed against the beast that had been roused yesterday. But no animal lust stirred in him, although desire sang sweetly in his blood as their soap-slick bodies slid easily against each other. His beard was full of soap, and in a moment they both had a mouthful of lather and drew apart, giggling like children.

Plunging into the warm pool, they rinsed each other,

hands exploring bodies, Lenardo marveling at his own exuberance, untouched by any hint of violence. When they emerged and toweled off, he kissed Aradia again, easily quelling his impatience when he Read that she was glowing in response to his touch but nowhere near ready for completion of the act.

He knew that sex ought to be as pleasant and satisfying for a woman as for a man. What he didn't know was how to make it that way. Reading, though, even if he could not reach Aradia's thoughts, made it possible to discover what pleased her. He sensed fear beneath her desire and knew that he would have to gain her trust. He dared not pause to question by what miracle the desire remained.

They needed a comfortable couch; the marble floor was cold and uninviting. His practical nature suggested that they dress and return to Aradia's pavilion, but some new instinct told him that it would be devastating to break their mood that way.

There were massage tables in a nearby room, too high and narrow for lovemaking but covered with soft mats. He carried Aradia in there and set her down on one of the tables.

She laughed. "We'll fall off!"

"Just stay there, safe from the dragons, my lady, while I prepare a bower."

"I don't want to be safe from *all* the dragons," she said as Lenardo stripped the clean coverings off the other tables laid ready for morning, put the mats on the floor, and covered them with the clean cloth. As he did so, he became aware that Aradia was watching his body as he moved, the play of his muscles as he bent and stretched. His faint embarrassment was overshadowed by his delight that she found pleasure in the sight of him.

When he had finished, he turned and looked at Aradia, letting himself for the first time in his life be completely immersed in the sight of a beautiful woman. Her skin was ivory, marbled with faintest shadows of blue veins where her blood flowed near the surface. Her breasts were small and round, lifted pertly, inviting his caress. Only because her waist was tiny did her hips curve in womanly fashion;

she was slender as a boy, her legs molded into smooth contours from walking, running, and riding. Her hands and feet were small, her wrists and ankles so slender, it seemed they might snap like twigs. Everything about her fragile appearance belied the enormous power she could command.

As Lenardo moved toward her, his gaze focused on her face, flushed with expectancy. Her lips, already swollen with his kisses, were slightly parted; her violet eyes were dark with passion. She had fastened her luxurious hair on top of her head for bathing, but soft tendrils had come loose, creating a halo about her face.

His heart pounding, Lenardo kissed her once more, gently exploring, feeling her respond eagerly when he did not demand. Some guiding force led him to trail gentle kisses down the soft column of her neck, to tickle the hollow of her throat with his tongue. Her hand stroked his hair, wordlessly encouraging. When he kissed her breasts, she gasped softly, and her heart began to pound in expectation.

When he finally lifted her from the table, she cried softly, "Yes. Take me to the dragon's lair. Devour me!"

He found her eager for him, moving with him in a natural rhythm. Lenardo was wide open to anything he might Read in Aradia but otherwise no longer controlling, rising on waves of shared passion until with a small cry Aradia melted into bliss, triggering Lenardo helplessly to follow, soaring and then floating, this time to a fully conscious sense of satisfaction for both of them.

Aradia did not have to push his weight off her. He turned onto his back, gathering her against him, touching her and Reading her at once to be sure she was real. She snuggled against him, drifting in contentment, one hand caressing his chest, fingers twining in the hair growing there.

"I love you," he repeated, and when she turned her face up, he kissed her again.

"I knew we were meant for each other," said Aradia. "Mmm. I could stay here forever."

"No one's going to chase us away."

Aradia pulled herself up to kiss Lenardo's forehead, his eyes, even the tip of his nose. "Can a Reader live on love?" she asked.

"I feel as if I could."

"I fear I'm not so romantic," she said in mock sadness. "I'm hungry."

Lenardo laughed. "Shall I have supper served here?"

"No. I don't want to share this with anyone else." She rose to her knees. "I don't want to share *you* with anyone else, but I'll manage."

Lenardo sat up, and they kissed again. He never wanted to stop touching her.

"Let's swim first," said Aradia, "then go and eat. And then—"

"And then we'll see what happens," agreed Lenardo as they climbed to their feet. "Oh, my—I'll have to put this room back in order first."

He carried the rumpled sheets out to the linen hamper. When he returned with clean coverings, he found that Aradia had already replaced the mats on the tables. She stood back and watched as he flung the sheets open and each one settled, unwrinkled and perfectly aligned.

Then they swam, dressed, and returned to Lenardo's house for a huge meal. He found himself eating more than usual, even a piece of fish, although he had had eggs for lunch. He had become used to having meat on the table, as he frequently had guests. Tonight, though, the roast actually smelled good, and he didn't avoid looking at Aradia as she consumed great quantities of it. *Love does the strangest things!*

Although the day that had so changed Lenardo's life seemed long, it was far from over. They had not even been late to supper. Lenardo Read no suspicion of what had happened, although he was sure that his happiness was plain on his face.

For he was happy, strangely, ecstatically happy and unwilling to break the mood by giving thought to the future. Aradia had her own land to rule; soon she would return to Castle Nerius, and it might be months before he saw her again. But tonight, with Aradia falling asleep in his arms under the pale, milky glow of the white pavilion, all he could feel was that at last he knew contentment.

The next morning, not wanting to upset himself and thus Julia, Lenardo did not attempt to leave his body but simply Read Wulfston's castle. As he had located it yesterday, the contact was much easier today. The lesson went well, and when it was over, Julia said, //You're better today. I can tell.//

//Yes, Julia, much better.//

//I'm glad. I'm sorry I got so frightened.//

//I understand,// Lenardo told her. //I worry about you, too.// Sensing her desire to retain contact, he asked, //Has Lord Wulfston put you to work yet?//

Julia was only too delighted to give him a detailed account of her activities, which included Reading the foundations of Wulfston's castle so that the architect could take advantage of what was already there. She had made fast friends with the stableboy by warning him of a pebble caught in the hoof of Wulfston's gray mare. That would have earned the boy a beating from the head groom had the horse gone lame while the Lord of the Land was riding it. Relieved of her worry over Lenardo, Julia was clearly enjoying herself. He left her to convey his greetings to Wulfston and went about the day's business with a light heart.

It seemed to be one of Lenardo's flashes of premonition: he *knew* that Aradia was not going to leave him. No matter how often he told himself that it was wishful thinking, the conviction remained, and he moved in a cloud of good cheer.

Late in the morning, Aradia joined Lenardo at the repair of a burned-out warehouse. Scaffolding had been built across from the buildings on either side, and with great effort men were hoisting heavy roof beams up. Arkus and Josa stood ready to attempt to keep the beams from swinging out of control when the workmen tried to put them in place.

The newly married couple glowed with happiness. *I know*

how you feel, thought Lenardo, but he was surprised a while later to discover Arkus studying him, putting his manner together with the rumor that he had spent the past two nights in Aradia's pavilion and dismissing the obvious conclusion as ridiculous.

Aradia told Arkus and Josa not to waste their strength and guided the beams into place herself. It didn't seem to tire her at all.

"I wasn't moving the beams," she explained. "The workmen were. I don't think there's ever been an Adept with the strength to move something that heavy straight up in the air. All I did was let the chance swinging of the beam allow it to go right into place."

"Now wait," said Lenardo. "If you were guiding the swinging of the beam, then chance was not operating."

"Yes it was," she insisted. "There were all kinds of chances as to what the beam would do. I simply encouraged the chance that it would swing right into place."

"I'll never learn to think like an Adept."

"You should," said Aradia. "Your Adept talents could be doing much more with far less effort if you knew how to train them. Either Arkus or Josa could have done that job alone today, but the way they do it, trying to will the beam to go where they want it instead of *letting* it go in the right direction, they exhaust themselves."

"I'm not sure I understand the distinction," said Lenardo, "but I hope you'll teach it to Arkus and Josa."

"It's simply understanding nature," Aradia explained. "You see if there is any way what you want done would happen naturally, and then you let it happen that way. For example, you are in a valley, and a rock dislodges above you. If it comes bouncing down the hillside, what do you do?"

"Me? I run out of its path, hoping it doesn't bounce in my direction."

"And if you were an Adept?"

"I suppose . . . I could guide the rock to bounce away from me. Oh, I see—I think. The chances that it would land right on me are not very high, anyway, so I shouldn't waste energy forcing it to the other end of the valley but just concentrate on having it *not* hit *me*."

"Very good," she said. "Now, instead of a valley, you're in a canyon. A rock dislodges from the top and is falling straight down on you. As an Adept, what do you do?"

He thought a moment. "My guess is that it would be almost impossible for an Adept to change the path of a heavy free-falling object. So I run out from under it."

Aradia waited a moment and then said, "Right, as far as you've gone. But a rock falling from such a height is going to bounce—"

"And I have to see that by chance it doesn't bounce right on me," Lenardo said with a laugh. "Would that I could, not that I have often been threatened by falling rocks." Recalling the earthquake that had almost brought the Adigia Academy down on him, he added, "Only once." Then he said seriously, "Will you stay here in Zendi long enough to teach some of this to Arkus and Josa and the others? I don't think they've had any formal training in using their talents."

"People with a single talent usually don't. Wulfston and I worked with a few around Castle Nerius. My father's idea of Academies for Adepts, though—"

"Why not?" asked Lenardo.

She took his hand. "Think a moment. Suppose you had a group of people with Adept talents, trained since childhood. Together, they might be as strong as a Lord Adept or even two or three. And if- they were guided by a Reader. . . ."

"That is the second time you have suggested it, Aradia."

"Yes, for if it is on my mind, it will be on others'. Here, in your land, is where the first Academy must be, protected by the lands of your allies. Because you are not an Adept, it will not appear to those who might be your enemies as a preparation to mount an offensive. As time passes and you do not use your trained Adept talents to conquer, you will earn more trust."

"Aradia," he said in amazement.

"No, Lenardo, I have not lost my head along with my

heart. You must be prepared to defend yourself at all times. Lilith, Wulfston, and I know you. We have fought side by side. Other allies will come.''

In the next few days, Aradia spent part of each day teaching Lenardo's people with Adept talents to use them more efficiently. She also helped in the construction work and the continuing job of repairing the water and sewer systems. Their bath together at the end of each day became a ritual, and by now everyone knew that it was no rumor that Lenardo spent his nights in Aradia's pavilion.

However, they did not make love again. It was enough to lie in one another's arms, warm and content. Reading what little he could of Aradia, Lenardo suspected that she was waiting to see how much of her Adept strength returned. As he hoped that his own skills would also approach normal again, he curbed the desire that the sight and touch of her body awoke in him and learned to appreciate their simple nearness. His range of Reading seemed to be returning to normal, as was the clarity of his perceptions. Something kept him from further attempts to leave his body; perhaps it was that he was so thoroughly enjoying being within it.

Soon Wulfston would bring Julia home, though, and before that she would get her promised excursion to the sea. Lenardo would have to try his powers then and face explaining his apparent hypocrisy to his daughter on her return. Julia would not be in Zendi for an hour before she would know of his time spent with Aradia, and her devious little mind would quickly draw the proper, or improper, conclusion.

But Lenardo would deal with those problems when they arose. For the moment, he had a growing relationship with Aradia, and a sweet contentment he had not known even in the Academy.

One cool, bright morning, Lenardo was listening to Helmuth's report on agricultural plans for next year, doing nothing more than agree, as he knew little about farming. As usual, he was neither trying to Read Helmuth nor completely blocking against Reading.

Suddenly a shock of pure terror struck through his gut, along with the sensation of being hurled upward, falling, and intense, unbearable pain. He screamed in agony before he could shut it out, and then he found Helmuth on his feet, his face white, staring at him. "My lord—"

"An explosion," Lenardo gasped. "Near Northgate. The man's still alive. Get Sandor!" As he ran out, he added, "Get Aradia. Hurry!"

He was breathless by the time he arrived at the site of the tragedy, both from running halfway across the city and from Reading the victim's pain. Aradia was already on the scene, trailed by Greg and Vona. She glanced up at Lenardo, saying, "I heard him scream," and returned her concentration to the injured man, putting him to sleep.

It was easy enough to see what had happened. One of the workers digging around the foundation of a warehouse, to repair a crack before it weakened the structure, had struck a yet-uncleared sewer line with a pocket of gas in it. His metal pick must have produced a spark, and the pipe had exploded, slamming the man against the wall of the building.

He had slight superficial burns, not serious, but the blow had broken his left arm and leg, which had hit the wall.

"Where is the internal bleeding?" Aradia was asking.

How did she know that? Then Lenardo actually looked at the man he had been Reading and saw that his lips were turning blue. "Two broken ribs have pierced his lung."

"Guide me," said Aradia, laying her hands over the man's side.

This, Lenardo understood, was working against nature, forcing the broken ribs to withdraw and return to place. An Aventine surgeon might have done it by cutting into the man's chest, but in the time it took, the patient might bleed to death. If he lived, he would develop an infection untreatable with the antiseptics they understood. But Aradia could work in the knowledge that if she saved the man immediately, she could drive out any infection with healing fire.

When the ribs were back in place, Lenardo Read the bleeding veins and arteries, while Aradia, in such rapport with him that a single word seemed to guide her to the right spot, joined them and then closed the punctures in the lung tissue.

The man was out of danger now. Worried that Aradia would use up her strength, Lenardo said, "Let Sandor take care of his burns and broken bones. He's good at that."

"They're not simple fractures," Aradia said. "He'll be lame if his leg is not set right."

Sandor, who had been hovering nearby for some time, said, "It's a blessing you are here, my lady. I don't think I could have saved him, even with Lord Lenardo's help. But now we should take him to my house so that after the bones are set, he won't have to be moved again."

Several boards were quickly lashed together, and the injured man was carefully lifted onto them and carried to the house near the bathhouse, where the infirmary was. It was an elegant home, with which Sandor's wife was greatly pleased, although Lenardo's main motivation in giving it to the healer was the central location and the size, which permitted a number of rooms to be used as a hospital and still leave plenty of room for the family.

Aradia did not seem inordinately fatigued. "When we healed Nerius," Lenardo said, "although it took a long time because the work was so delicate, it was certainly not so *much* work as you have done already today. Yet both you and Wulfston were so exhausted that you collapsed."

"Oh, no," she replied, "that was enormously harder work. We didn't just move my father's tumor, we destroyed it. There was no way to burn it or otherwise remove it in a natural way. It had to be disintegrated, made not to be. That was more against nature than any work I have ever done before or since."

Made not to be. A chill went through Lenardo as he realized the implications of what he had Read but not understood. *I didn't understand because I could not conceive of such a thing.* He still could not, but he let it pass. There was work to be done.

Lenardo, Aradia, and Sandor set to work on the injured man's arm and leg. It was tedious work, combining physical manipulation wherever they could with Adept influence to align the bones and set every chip and splinter back in place. Again, Lenardo found an astonishing rapport with Aradia. The work did not seem to tire her beyond what the same amount of physical labor would have done. Perhaps she had regained her full strength. Lenardo was glad. He no longer wanted to blunt her powers.

When they finally finished, it was late afternoon. Sandor, pale and drawn, was assured that his patient was healing now and was sent off to sleep himself.

"You should sleep, too, Aradia," said Lenardo.

"Oh, I will, but first I want a bath and some food."

"I can't believe you're not as tired as Sandor. You did far more of the work."

"But I am a Lady Adept, fully empowered. I am bone-weary, Lenardo, but I won't collapse. Give me a good meal and let me sleep through till I wake on my own, and tomorrow I won't know I did all that today."

They found the patient's wife waiting in the hall, three children clustered around her. She had already been told that her husband would recover fully, and her gratitude rang far beyond her inadequate words.

"Your husband's going to be just fine," Lenardo told her. "If you and your children need anything before he's better, come to me."

The woman managed a smile at Lenardo's naivete. "Brad ain't my husband, not like fine ladies got. But he's my man, and these is his children. I guess we're just stuck like glue."

"Some people are," Aradia murmured. "Now, don't you worry. You can go in and look at your man if you want to, but he'll be sound asleep for several days. Then you'll have to care for him until he gets his strength back."

"Oh, my lady, 'twas fate you was nearby! The other men said Brad was so scared he didn't even cry out."

As she and Lenardo left the building, Aradia said in a

puzzled tone, "I know I heard him scream. That's why I came running."

"You must have heard the explosion."

"No, I don't remember hearing that at all, just a scream of such fear and pain—" She shivered.

"Whatever brought you there, I'm thankful," said Lenardo. "I am partly responsible for what happened to Brad. I Read the crack in the foundation, and I Read the sewer line close to the buildings along there and warned them not to break it."

"Well, then, it was the man's own carelessness."

"No, it was mine. I didn't even think to Read for gas in those pipes. Then that work was interrupted for the festival, and the workmen had proabably forgotten all about my warning by the time they got back to it." He sighed. "There ought to be a Reader checking every work crew every day. A child could have prevented the accident today, not by Reading the gas but by Reading the pipe."

Aradia studied him, but it was obvious that she was too tired to concentrate. "Lenardo, we will talk tomorrow. Right now I need a bath, a good meal, and sleep."

Although she knew that she would be virtually unconscious from the moment she lay down, Aradia insisted that Lenardo come and sleep with her. He finished his interrupted work, inspected the city as he did each evening without leaving his room—but with more thoroughness than usual—and then crossed the forum to Aradia's pavilion. The guards and Aradia's maid said pleasantly, "Good night, my lord," as he passed. His presence on this night when Aradia was already deep in the Adepts' recuperative sleep confirmed their certainty that whatever the reason a Reader and a Lady Adept were spending their nights together, it wasn't sex.

Lenardo slept almost as deeply as Aradia but woke as the pale light of early dawn filtered into the pavilion. Beside him, Aradia lay curled up on her side, her hair spread across the pillow, the covers pulled up to her chin against the chill of early morning. *I think it's time,* he told himself, *that I stop having the rain diverted around Zendi and invite Aradia into my house.* But instead, she might leave. Yes, Lenardo admitted, he knew perfectly well why up to now he had avoided suggesting the obvious.

Aradia would probably not waken before noon, but he had time before he had to be up, and so he lay comfortably in the warm bed and Read outward. In the outer chamber, Aradia's maid was also sleeping. Outside the pavilion, her guards were moving back and forth to keep awake until their replacements came. Otherwise, the forum was empty, but Lenardo Read a few early risers wakening here and there. Soon, from his own house, Dorn came to fill buckets at the fountain, and he read Cook poking the kitchen maid to make her get up and start work.

It was a shivery cool morning with a promise of autumn. Lenardo began to Read visually to enjoy the beauty of the sunrise. It was something he did perhaps four or five times a year, but each time it brought back the morning he had taken seven-year-old Torio up to the Academy tower and let the little blind boy see the sunrise through his eyes. Master Clement had scolded Lenardo, who had just passed his own exams the year before, for awakening in the boy a yearning for something he would not be able to do for a year or more. But within six months Torio was Reading visually with ease, and Lenardo was quite certain that it was because he had learned to want to see such beauty.

This morning the sunrise was equally beautiful, breaking through the clouds in a palette of magnificent colors. *I wonder if Torio is watching the sunrise today.*

As effortlessly as forming the thought, Lenardo was in a room he had never seen before, where Torio, still in his nightshirt, was standing "looking" out the window. Before the boy's sightless eyes were the buildings of a city, blocking any view of the sun until it was far overhead. But Torio was indeed watching the sunrise, seeing it in unrestricted glory by Reading.

Confused, Lenardo wondered where the boy could be, so close by? And then he recognized the city: Tiberium.

Heart pounding, Lenardo sat up in shock, but even so he lost neither clarity nor contact. He was really Reading

Tiberium, and directly, all the way from Zendi, without leaving his body!

But that's impossible!

//What's im— Master Lenardo! Is that you?//

Beside Lenardo, Aradia woke with a start. "What's wrong?"

Not knowing what to tell Torio, Lenardo withdrew without confirming contact. Let the boy think it was his imagination.

"Nothing's wrong," he assured Aradia, although he did not at all understand what had happened. *Could it have been* my *imagination?*

"Did you have a bad dream?" Aradia asked. "I was having such a beautiful dream until you shouted and woke me up."

"I didn't shout," he said. "That must have been part of your dream."

She laughed. "Yes, you did. As clearly as anything, you said, 'That's impossible!' "

Could he have said it aloud? Never. Not after all his years of training. He was not delirious now. But how could Aradia know? Yesterday she had heard a scream that wasn't uttered. *But that is completely impossible.*

"Will you stop saying it's impossible and tell me what you're talking about?"

"Aradia," he whispered as chills crawled up his spine. "Tell me what you were dreaming."

"Mmm? It wasn't prophetic or anything. I was just watching the most beautiful sunrise." At his stricken look she broke off, eyes wide. "Lenardo, were you Reading me?" she asked in a small, frightened voice.

"No," he said, slowly shaking his head. "Aradia, *you* were Reading *me*."

"But that's—" her eyes searched his "impossible?"

He nodded. "Exactly what I was thinking."

"Coincidence?"

//I was Reading the sunrise,// he projected at the intense level used to test children.

"Well, at this time of day, anyone—" She froze. "You didn't *say* that, did you?"

//No.//

No. It can't be!

//Obviously it *can* be, for it *is*.//

Her eyes grew wide with terror, and she reached for Lenardo, overwhelming him with panic as she clung to him, pleading, "No. Stop it. Tell me how to make it stop!"

Chapter Five

Fighting his way out of Aradia's desperate fear, Lenardo tried to project soothing calm. //Aradia, Reading is nothing to be afraid of.// He had never seen such a reaction before. The awakening of Reading ability was a cause for rejoicing, not despair.

//But you can Read me, everything I'm thinking!// Flashes of incoherent scenes that meant guilt to Aradia but nothing to Lenardo.

//You'll learn to shield your thoughts. Besides, there's no one here but me to Read them, and I love you.//

He let the warmth of his caring flow to her, feeling her respond and open to it, giving back joy for joy. Her fear dissolved as she yielded her mind to him as completely as she had her body. For a long time, neither had a coherent thought, but such a height could not be sustained.

Lenardo's own thoughts began to intrude. How could this have happened? And what of his own experience just before Aradia wakened? He had to find out if it had been his imagination, half a dream—

Very gently, he removed himself from Aradia's embrace, remaining with his hands on her shoulders. She looked at him expectantly.

He said, "You'll be confused at first about whether people are talking or thinking. Try not to answer their thoughts. That is very disconcerting to nonReaders. It is also against the Readers' Code. Whatever you Read by accident, you are supposed to forget."

"Lenardo, I'm not a child. I can exercise discretion. What I must learn are techniques. Most important, how do I keep you, or especially Julia, from Reading me?"

"The simplest way is to stop Reading."

She frowned. "I can't. Right now I'm getting a sort of echo effect—what you're going to say just before you say it."

"Is it gone now?"

"Yes. What did you do?"

"Stopped Reading. You see? That keeps you from Reading me. There are ways to Read and at the same time keep other Readers from Reading you, but they are difficult to master. They won't work against any Reader more sensitive than you are, and you can slip up and reveal yourself to a less sensitive Reader. For the moment, what you need is to be able to guarantee your own privacy of thought. Refinements can come later."

"How do I stop?" she asked, screwing up her face in concentration.

"Not like that." He laughed. "All right, I'm open to you again."

"I can tell."

//Very well.// He fell into the exercise for teaching children. //Hear the tune playing in my head? Stop listening to it. Just blot it out.//

He sat concentrating on the music, but Aradia's feelings intruded: frustration, anger, fear.

"I can't," she burst out. "I can't shut it out."

"Aradia, relax. That's your own fear preventing you, a double fear. First that you'll never be able to keep the whole world out of your private thoughts, and second that if you once stop Reading, you'll never be able to start again."

"Damn you, Lenardo. How can you Read my thoughts better than I can myself?"

"I have taught hundreds of Readers. Over half of them had the same problem."

"But I'm not a *child*," she said in irritation. "I'm a full-grown, fully empowered Adept." The small cushion from one of the chairs went sailing toward Lenardo on the force of Aradia's frustration.

He caught it, laughing. "And *that* solves your problem."

"Hmm?"

"You're not Reading me anymore, and I can't Read you. I should have remembered that when you're functioning as an Adept, I can't Read a thing about you, not even your feelings."

"Oh, you're right. That's a relief, and it seems what's happened hasn't affected my Adept powers." Then, thoughtfully, "Lenardo, exactly what *has* happened?"

"You're a Reader, Aradia. I've never heard of the ability not appearing until adulthood, but your Adept talent showed first and was trained, and you shut out Reading while you exercised it. And of course you grew up in a society that feared and hated Readers, so you probably suppressed Reading, didn't even recognize it until you got to know and trust a Reader."

"On the other hand," she said, "maybe I caught it from you."

"It's not a disease."

"Perhaps Readers and Adepts don't have two separate talents at all," she suggested. "Maybe it's which one you look for and train and which one you fear. Lenardo, if I can do both, why can't you?"

When he didn't answer, "Try it," Aradia prodded him. "Something easy—light the candle."

"I really don't want to carry it out to find a fire."

"No, don't joke. Try to light the candle, Lenardo. Concentrate. It was made to burn. Fire is its natural state. Envision the flame."

Lenardo concentrated until his head began to ache, but no flame appeared. Finally he said, "It's not going to work, Aradia."

"But it has to. If I can Read—"

"You simply have both talents. Some people are painters, and some people are musicians. Rarely, there is someone who can do both. So you have two talents. You are both Adept and Reader."

"Possibly," she said. "But what do I do now?"

"I'll teach you everything I can," said Lenardo. "We'll see how much ability you can develop. Right now, though, you should get some more rest. You said you'd need to sleep till noon today."

"I'm too excited to feel tired. I want to try Reading everything. But what if it's only you I can Read?"

"It may seem that way at first, if you develop the way a child does. It takes a while to Read thoughts other than those a Reader is deliberately projecting. Aradia, you know meditation exercises. Rest this morning and then don't eat until after we try some tests this afternoon."

"Don't eat?"

"One morning's fast can't hurt you, but what kind of dietary compromise can we find for you?"

"Don't even bother to suggest that horse fodder you eat."

"A few days of purifying diet won't hurt you, any more than a few meat meals at your castle hurt me."

"Yes, Master," she said in mock obedience, but she lay down. Although her thoughts were completely unReadable once more, he could see that she went quickly to sleep.

Lenardo had to exercise careful control to stop trembling before he could dress and leave Aradia's pavilion. At home he ate the hot cereal Cook placed before him, not because he wanted it but to avoid another lecture about keeping up his strength. As soon as he dared, he escaped to his room and began to Read.

Zendi was all around him, the morning bustle well begun, the harvesters already in the fields outside the walls, a caravan a three-hour journey away packing up camp to head into the city, while in the hills—

He was Reading effortlessly in every direction, well beyond the city walls that had previously approximated the radius of his nondirected perception. Incredulously, he let the circle expand, Reading east and west slightly beyond his borders and not quite to them north and south, as his lands expanded farther in those directions.

He found the same exquisite clarity that he had previously known only within the small circle of awareness, and he could focus on one thing and see it as if it were there within his grasp, complete to the smallest detail.

What is happening to me? I committed the cardinal abuse, impaired my powers . . . and now this!

Reading outward in a single direction, he was aware not

only of Wulfston's castle but just as easily and at the same time the sea far beyond.

A sleepy Julia was allowing one of the women of Wulfston's household to comb her hair, while the lord of the castle was in his own room, dressing for travel. Then Wulfston went to Julia's room.

"Ready for breakfast?"

"But we can't leave yet," she protested. "Father hasn't contacted me, and he may not be able to reach me at the sea."

//I'll reach you.//

"Oh!" Joy bubbled up in Julia's mind. "Father's here now, Lord Wulfston."

"Hello, Lenardo. Feeling better?"

"Father says he's completely recovered," Julia relayed, "and there's no hurry about returning to Zendi. Lady Aradia is still there."

"Still? Lenardo, what are you two up to?"

Julia must have caught something of the consternation Lenardo tried to cover, for she giggled as she told Wulfston, "He says you wouldn't guess in a hundred lifetimes. And . . . he thinks Aradia should tell you herself."

"If that means Aradia will stay until we get there, I'm delighted," said Wulfston. Then, guiding the gaping servant woman out, he told Julia, "Meet me in the kitchen when you're through with your lesson, and don't forget to tell your father about helping Demetrius find his mares."

"Aww, that was easy," said Julia, but she nonetheless eagerly told Lenardo of helping one of Wulfston's men locate five horses lured into the hills by a wild stallion. He gathered that his foster daughter would soon have a swollen head if left to the adulation of nonReaders.

Only years of training and concentration allowed Lenardo to put this morning's events out of his mind and give Julia her lesson. She was improving rapidly, happy in her work, but she was now torn between her promised holiday and her consuming curiosity about what was happening in Zendi.

//Go and have a good time,// Lenardo told her, //but don't be a nuisance to Lord Wulfston.//

He managed to get through his morning's work and clear the afternoon for Aradia. Beginning with the simplest tests, he sought the limits of her current ability, similar to those of a child whose powers were newly wakened. When Lenardo verbalized his thoughts, she could Read them clearly. Other people were a blur of emotion except for an occasional clear thought, and she could not even sense inanimate objects, let alone visualize them.

"So I'm considerably less of a Reader than Julia," she said when Lenardo decided that it was time to stop.

"At the moment, yes. If you were Julia's age, I'd pat you on the head and encourage you to do better tomorrow. As it is, I don't want to discourage you, but I don't want to raise false hopes, either."

They were in Lenardo's room, seated on either side of his worktable. Now Aradia went to the window, staring out at the courtyard. "I don't know if I want to Read any better."

"Why not?"

"All my life I've judged people by their actions. I'm not sure I want to know their motivations."

"I don't understand."

"I know people act from selfish motives," Aradia explained, turning to face him. "My goal is to make working for me in my people's best interest, yet there are those who become caught up in patriotic fervor, and I might be tempted to trust such people more than those who were merely doing what was expedient."

"Since you recognize the danger, Aradia, I do not think you will fall prey to it."

Her violet eyes studied him. "So you agree."

He nodded slowly. "Galen always acted from enthusiasm. I was the object of his enthusiasm for a time, but then came a time when I disagreed with him. He became disillusioned with me and was easy prey for Drakonius."

"Who wasted no time making it expedient for Galen to work for him," said Aradia. She sat on the edge of the worktable, facing Lenardo. "You have learned quickly, now that you are over the blindness your empire instilled in you. You will be a great leader, Lenardo."

"No," he replied. "I was not meant to rule. With every day that passes, I wonder what mistakes I have made."

"You think I do not? Every conscientious ruler worries, but he acts. I did not know whether you could act, Lenardo. That's why I gave you Zendi. You have proved yourself here."

"Insulated. Untested."

"When the test comes, it will be against all of us, and we have passed the test against Drakonius. It will be a long time before anyone will dare attack us. But if we do nothing for long enough, that attack will come." Again her fingers traced the brand on his arm. "Lenardo, I don't want to leave you."

"I don't want you to leave."

"Then—"

"No. Don't say it. Come here." He drew her onto his lap, where she leaned against him, her head on his shoulder. "Aradia, I don't know protocol among Lords Adept, so I've been making up my own rules."

"You have the right to make the rules in your own land."

"Then in my land, the right and honorable thing for me to do, because I love you and I want you with me always, is to ask you to marry me. I realize that that will present difficulties. We each have a land to rule, and your people might well object to your forming a permanent alliance with a Reader, and one who has been on this side of the pale less than half a year. Still, I want you to know what I would do if it were possible."

She was glowing with serene happiness. "I'm glad you said it first," she murmured. "We'll combine our lands and rule jointly. We have the right to set precedents. Lenardo, I was willing to sacrifice some of my powers for you, as my parents did when they married. After that first time, my strength and accuracy were greatly diminished."

"So were mine," said Lenardo. "But later—"

"Yes," Aradia whispered fiercely, "later. There is something fated between you and me, foretold in ancient legend. When I woke today, after you had gone, I tested my powers. I removed one of the cobbles from the forum floor and lifted it. I split it, Lenardo, and then I crumbled part of it to powder, and I still felt so strong that I broke off a small piece and disintegrated it.''

He recalled what she had said about disintegrating her father's tumor. ''How is it you are not exhausted?''

''I don't know. I have never had such strength. And you?''

''I can Read farther and more easily than ever before. I was having difficulty reaching Julia at Wulfston's castle, and then this morning I discovered that without effort I could Read all the way to the sea. I haven't yet dared to try leaving my body. I felt as if I could Read the whole world.''

''Leaving your body? What do you mean?''

''The highest, most difficult form of Reading is to dissociate one's . . . self . . . from one's body. I did it the day I first Read Drakonius's stronghold for you. You thought I had fainted, remember?''

She studied his face, and he could feel her trying to Read him. ''No, I don't think you're lying,'' she said. ''I'm sure you believe that some sort of separate spirit leaves your body. But if that were possible, legends like that of the ghost-king would be fact, not fairy tale.''

Lenardo considered. ''Was this ghost-king one of your ancestors, Aradia?''

''I'm not joking.''

''Neither am I. Someone like you, both Adept and Reader—''

''No!'' She wrenched out of his embrace, shoving hard against his chest as she jumped to her feet. ''No. There cannot be any life separate from the body. The legend of the ghost-king is meant to warn of the folly of such nonsense.''

Reading how upset Aradia was, Lenardo recalled what he knew of savage beliefs. No dieties, no afterlife. ''Life is the greatest value,'' Aradia had once told him. She believed that there was nothing more than her physical life; he remembered that the subject was particularly painful to her because her mother had taken her own life, the worst thing a savage could do. He decided that it was best to change the subject.

"You will understand more as your abilities increase. There's nothing to fear, and we have joyful plans to make."

"Indeed we have. Lenardo, let's not tell anyone yet. I want Wulfston to know first."

"And Julia."

"Julia," Aradia said. "Oh, my. Do you think she'll accept your marriage?"

"You do see the point precisely. As long as she is assured that she will not be losing me but gaining you, I have no fear that she will object. However, there is the matter of explaining to a literal-minded child my seeming hypocrisy. I told her that Readers never marry."

"In the Aventine Empire," said Aradia. "And most Readers *are* married off, if I understand the system, to produce new Readers. What seems wrong, though, is that only second-rate Readers reproduce; where do Readers like you come from?"

"My parents were, as you put it, second-rate Readers. I don't remember them very well."

"Has there never been an instance of two Master Readers having a child?"

"Male and female Readers are rigorously segregated."

"But you Read each other."

"Yes."

She put her hand along the side of his face. //I fell in love with you before I could Read you, but now there is so much more. Lenardo, how can man and woman touch minds like this and not desire to join bodies?//

//They do. That is why the marriages arranged for those who do not reach the top ranks of Readers are generally successful. But for those who remain in the Academies, the mental union with other Readers far more than suffices for physical touch. Aradia, you need not touch me now.//

//I *want* to touch you!// Her fingers slid into his hair, and she bent to kiss his mouth possessively. Fire stirred in his veins, and she laughed. //You see? You excite me,

Lenardo, and now it will be even more exciting to touch, to make love—//

Passion threatened to overwhelm his control, but he forced common sense to prevail. "I love you, Aradia," he said aloud, "but I don't think we want to announce our intentions to the world by having Helmuth or Arkus walk in on us like this."

"Very well, then," she said wistfully. "Later."

But later, although she moved into Lenardo's room and into his bed, Aradia did not want to make love. Now that she was open to Reading, Lenardo knew that it was not teasing, that she wanted him but felt compelled to wait. He could not find the reason without invading her privacy, but he sensed that she was waiting for something she both feared and longed for.

But when he tried to ask her about it, she avoided the subject, again demanding that he try to exercise Adept power. "Fire talent is the most common and the easiest of all even for the Lord Adept," she told him. But although he tried to cooperate and then at her insistence tried to make the silken hangings move, all he achieved was a tension headache. He wondered idly if that was what she had intended.

Three days later, Julia arrived home with Wulfston. When Lenardo lifted his daughter down from her horse, he did not resist her embrace but squeezed her in return, enjoying her happy surprise at his leniency. He could feel her trying to Read him, knowing that something important had happened while she was away.

Wulfston, too, was brimming with curiosity. As soon as they were all together in Lenardo's room, he demanded, "Now, what scheme are you two plotting?"

"No scheme," Aradia replied. "Just happy plans."

Wulfston looked from one to the other and said, "I think I can guess."

"In the Aventine Empire," said Lenardo, "I would have to ask your permission, Wulfston, as Aradia's nearest male kin. Here, however, Aradia is her own mistress."

The black man nodded. "I've been expecting as much

ever since fate dropped a man of appropriate age and endowments into Aradia's path. In fact, I feared this very development at first. Aradia, are you certain?''

''I'm certain. Lenardo and I have agreed to marry, unite our lands, and rule jointly. We wanted you and Julia to be the first to know.''

Julia was wide-eyed. ''But Father, you said—''

''It is not always possible for us to follow the customs of the Aventine Empire,'' Lenardo said. ''We must seek the right way for Readers to live *here*, child.''

''Julia,'' said Aradia, ''won't you be my daughter, too?''

''Lenardo,'' Wulfston added, ''This makes us brothers. Julia, I'll be your uncle. Can you stand so much new family all at once?''

Lenardo hoped that Aradia did not Read that Julia was uncertain about her new mother but delighted to be suddenly related to Wulfston. Searching carefully for the right words, the girl said, ''I think it will be very nice. Are you going to have a real wedding, like Arkus and Josa?''

''Indeed,'' said Lenardo, ''and you shall witness for me.''

''When does the great event take place?'' Wulfston asked.

''As soon as possible,'' Lenardo said, but Aradia objected.

''We've just had a festival, and we must draw up all the agreements between us. Better to fight it out now than after other parties are involved.''

''But Aradia,'' Lenardo began.

Wulfston let out a burst of laughter. ''Oh, you are off to a fine start. You haven't even agreed on a date?''

''Midwinter,'' said Aradia. ''It will be a marvelous excuse for a party at the dreariest time of year.''

''Surely we can make it sooner,'' said Lenardo.

//We're discussing only the formal ceremony,// Aradia told him without thinking.

Julia gasped, and Aradia's shock of realization of what she'd done rang through all three Readers.

The only one unaffected, Wulfston, said, ''Julia, when

two people fall in love, it's normal for them to want to marry as soon as possible.''

''But she— But they—''

Wulfston realized then that Julia had Read something to upset her. ''What has happened? Lenardo? Aradia?''

Julia, remembering that nonReaders sometimes projected a thought at a Reader without saying it aloud, stared at Aradia. //Can you Read me?// she demanded.

There was a long moment's suspense before Aradia admitted it. //Yes, Julia, I can.//

Wulfston looked from the girl to the woman and back, then to Lenardo. ''Are they—''

Lenardo nodded. ''Aradia has learned to Read.''

''By the gods,'' Wulfston whispered, the Aventine oath of his childhood slipping out in his astonishment. Then he grinned. ''I was right. I never dared to believe it, but I've suspected all along. It *is* all the same power—the difference is in how you are trained. Aradia, how did you learn?''

She blushed. ''I don't really know how I learned,'' she replied finally. ''One morning I just woke up Reading.''

''I can't explain it, either,'' Lenardo added.

''What about you?'' Wulfston demanded. ''Have you mastered Adept powers now?''

''Not in the slightest,'' Lenardo replied. ''Wulfston, I think Aradia inherited both abilities from her father.''

''Of course she did. But I ought to have both powers, too, even if Nerius was my father only by adoption.''

''Wulfston,'' said Lenardo, ''none of us, not Aradia in all her studies, not I in my years at the Academy, ever heard of one person exhibiting both Reading and Adept powers . . . except Nerius.''

''Nerius?'' Wulfston frowned. ''Nerius was no Reader.''

''He never consciously used the power. But when you brought me to Castle Nerius while he lay in a coma, he Read me. You remember after we healed him, when he first saw me, he claimed to have seen me in his nightmares?''

Aradia mused, ''We thought he simply put Lenardo's face to his faceless fears, but apparently he had actually Read him. And feared him. He tried to kill him.''

"What?" asked Wulfston. "I don't recall."

"You were with me," said Lenardo. "It was the day you brought me back to Castle Nerius after I had escaped. Nerius had one of his convulsive attacks. Most of his blows went wild, but two were definitely aimed at me. One killed my horse. Then, inside the castle, he flung a spear at me."

"But it would have hit *me*," Wulfston protested, "if you hadn't knocked me out of the way. Nerius would never have harmed me, Lenardo. I was as much his son as Aradia was his daughter."

"I know that. He didn't know you were there, Wulfston. Adepts cannot be Read. Nerius was completely untrained as a Reader. Because I am a Reader, he could focus on me, but you and Aradia were unReadable, invisible to him."

Wulfston pondered that. "The first day you were well, then, Nerius also tried to hurt you. Do you remember? He flung a shield across the room at you."

Aradia said, her throat tight, "I think my father sacrificed his life to save mine. The night of the battle, he knocked me out of the way and took that last thunderbolt himself. How could he know, if he had not Read it? Lenardo, you could not relay as fast as the attacks were coming."

He nodded. "Nerius would have done anything to protect you, Aradia. Wulfston—"

"I'm going to learn to Read, Lenardo," the black man said firmly. "If you won't teach me, Julia will, and I will teach her Adept powers."

Both Lenardo and Aradia Read Julia's eager response. The desire for power was as strong in the child as ever.

Remembering that Julia could Read her, Aradia held her response in control and then went blank to Reading, poised to use her Adept powers.

In moments, the atmosphere in the room had changed from happy family camaraderie to armed truce. Julia moved from her seat next to Lenardo to Wulfston's side, saying, "I'm still learning, but I'll teach you everything I know, Lord Wulfston."

"And I will teach you all I can, child," he replied, becoming as unReadable as Aradia, poised for attack.

Lenardo felt hollow. The news that was supposed to have united them all instead had brother faced off against sister, daughter against father.

"Wulfston," said Lenardo, fully open to Reading so that Julia would know he spoke the truth, "of course I will teach you, or try to. What I said was not an excuse to refuse but an attempt to explain why I have been unable to learn Adept abilities. But you are free to teach Julia all she can learn. Aradia will teach her, too. We are sworn allies, not enemies."

Wulfston looked to Aradia. "Sister, does Lenardo speak for you?"

"In this matter, yes. But he speaks truly. He has not mastered even the simplest Adept functions, and he has sincerely tried."

"But we will try further," Lenardo said encouragingly. His soothing was not entirely successful; although his guests maintained courtesy, they continued on guard, and Julia felt betrayed.

He tried to make up to the child that day by allowing her to touch, admitting, "You were right, Julia. There's no harm in touching."

But as he tucked her into bed that night, Julia hugged him for a moment and then said, "You've prepared a room for Lord Wulfston."

"Yes. Josa's father brought her furniture as a wedding present, remember? Arkus and Josa have lent me enough to furnish a room for our guest."

"But no room for Aradia, and her pavilion's gone. Father, can't you see what she's doing? My mother used men that way—"

"Hush! This is not at all the same thing, Julia. You mustn't be jealous. Just because I love Aradia, that doesn't mean I love you any less. I'm your father now, and I always will be. Soon Aradia will be your mother. You must learn to love her, Julia."

"She doesn't want to be *my* mother," the girl said sullenly.

"Of course she does. Now you go to sleep, and tomorrow you and Aradia spend some time together, get to know each other."

There were tears in Julia's eyes. "She's chained your mind and stolen your powers. You don't believe me now, but you'll find out."

Julia was not Reading. Lenardo knew that she feared Aradia might be eavesdropping, and let it go. He could understand the child's jealousy and uncertainty. He would have to prove to her that she could still rely on him. But Aradia's task would be even more difficult.

Neither Julia nor Aradia had yet been trained not to Read in her sleep, and Lenardo slept restlessly, worried that there might be a clash of nightmares. If there was, he didn't know of it, and in the morning he had the bright idea of setting the two women in his life to teaching each other. That way they would be forced to get to know each other. If Julia spent time Reading with Aradia, she would have to see that there was no ill will in her.

Lenardo took Wulfston with him on his morning's work, trying to explain how to Read. But there were no words for *how* it was done, and Wulfston protested that he was doing no more than describing *what* he Read. Nor was Wulfston any more successful than Aradia in teaching Lenardo Adept talent. After an hour's frustration, they gave up and turned to using their individual talents in mutual cooperation.

Their friendship seemed to be back to normal by the time they returned to Lenardo's house at midday, only to find Julia and Aradia in separate rooms.

"She hates me," Julia informed Lenardo when he entered her room. She was sitting on the window ledge, poised as if to jump out into the courtyard.

"Of course Aradia does not hate you," Lenardo said firmly. "It's difficult for a grown woman to take lessons from a child. You must be grown-up enough to understand that."

She swung around and let her legs dangle inside the room. "She's an awful Reader. She can't hardly Read anybody but you or me, and she didn't want to start the lesson off with the Code of Honor. Why did you ever teach her to Read, Father?''

"I didn't teach her, any more than I taught you. She has developed the ability, and now we must teach her to *use* it."

"She doesn't trust me. I don't think she was really trying to teach me Adept tricks, neither."

"Julia," he said, taking her hands and pulling her off the window ledge, "I don't think she *can* teach you. Do you?"

"Yes. I think if she'd once learn to Read real good, she could show you and me both how she does it."

"Well, perhaps," he said, but he didn't believe it.

One reason Aradia's Reading powers were limited was that she had refused after two days of purifying diet to continue the Readers' dietary restrictions. The problem came up again at the midday meal as Aradia and Wulfston helped themselves to huge servings of meat.

"Aradia," said Lenardo, "can you not at least wait until the evening meal to clog your system?"

"No, I can't, not if I am going to maintain my strength. Wulfston, you should have seen me when I tried Lenardo's diet. By the end of the second day, I couldn't lift a pebble."

"You are exaggerating," said Lenardo.

Wulfston paused with a piece of meat halfway to his mouth. He put it back on his plate and said, "I had forgotten. Let me try your Readers' diet, Lenardo. And you should try ours. It did not harm your Reading powers when we fed you a strengthening diet at Castle Nerius."

"It didn't make me an Adept, either," he pointed out. "Wulfston, you are willing to compromise. I wish you would persuade Aradia. She *has* both powers but resists my attempts to find a nutritional balance that would allow her to use both efficiently."

"I wonder if that is possible," Wulfston mused, but he left his meat and ate only what Lenardo did.

Wulfston's willingness to cooperate had no effect on Aradia. "I need my strength," she insisted, and beneath her words Lenardo sensed some gleeful hope she was holding secret. Had she found some further extension of her powers?

In the afternoon, they changed partners, with Wulfston and Julia attempting to teach each other while Lenardo and Aradia had their regular lesson. But Aradia was closed to Reading.

"Can't Julia Read us?"

"If we are Reading, yes, except that she is busy doing something else. And she has passed the beginning exercises that you are doing, Aradia. They won't interest her."

"Can she Read us talking if we're not Reading?"

"No. That is, she could not without deep concentration. In a year or so, she'll find it easy enough. Aradia, you're not going to start worrying that Julia is spying, are you?"

"Last night, while I was sleeping, I think she tried."

"I don't think so," Lenardo assured her. "At most, you may have Read one of her dreams. Julia abides by the Readers' Code of Honor."

"You don't," Aradia pointed out. "Why should she? And how can I accept it? I cannot swear celibacy, not any longer."

"That is only for the two highest ranks. I ask you to accept only the basic oath which governs all Readers, even the married ones. Misuse of your powers leads to weakened abilities, Aradia."

"You, of all people, should know that that is mere superstition. You broke your Oath, and your powers have increased."

"I did not misuse my powers," he insisted. "I invaded no one's privacy; I did not use something I Read to harm another or for personal gain. I kept all precepts that govern every Reader of every rank, and that is all I am asking you to do, Aradia. Accept the Code and the diet—"

"I *can't*," she said in irritation. "I cannot swear to something that will limit my powers to govern, to protect my people, to form the empire that will put an end to the constant power struggles between Lords Adept."

He stared at her. "I thought you had given up that idea."

"I had, until I discovered I could Read. Lenardo, how

can you be so blind? I have *both powers*. I thought—''
She shook her head, frowning denial of whatever she had
begun to say. ''No, *I* must do it, with you by my side.''

Still she was not Reading, but she responded to Lenardo's
stricken look. ''Can't you understand? I must do this for
us, for our people, for our children, Lenardo. What kind
of world do you want them to grow up in?''

''Not a world,'' he replied, ''in which power is used
only to gain more power. Will you never stop, Aradia? If
you form your empire, will your first move be to take the
Aventine Empire, and be damned to attempts to make a
treaty with them? And what next? Drive north? Take all
the savage lands, one after another, war upon war just to
prove that you have power? I'll be no party to it, nor will
Julia. Your Reading powers will disappear if you use them
for personal gain. You'll still be a Lady Adept, but which
will you be? Someone like your father, building for the
future and making a better life for your people? Or will
you become another Drakonius, caring for nothing but
conquest—murdering, destroying, until in desperation other
Adepts form an alliance strong enough to destroy *you*?''

All color had drained from her face, and her eyes dilated
so that they appeared black. But Lenardo turned on his
heel and stalked out, heading for Wulfston's room at the
other end of the house. Behind him, the door slammed
shut.

As he approached, laughter came from Wulfston's room—
the Adept's and Julia's. He paused. Wulfston opposed
Aradia's plan, and there was little chance now that she
could get Julia's cooperation. She would have to come
around, and if she did, it would be best if her brother did
not know that she had temporarily fallen back into power
madness. It had to be temporary. Aradia was too intelli-
gent to cling to a plan that would set her brother and her
allies against her.

His fury fading, Lenardo was sorry for his angry tirade.
That was no way to handle Aradia. It would only make her
more stubborn. If he went back and apologized . . .

He paced the hallway, trying to determine what to do.

Finally he decided to Read Aradia, just a superficial Reading with no intrusion.

She was lying on his bed, tears streaking her face, a sodden kerchief in her hand. But she was not crying now, and she was completely blocked to Reading.

He knocked at the door and then entered when she neither replied nor Read him.

"Have you thought up more accusations?" she asked, but the words lacked sharpness.

"No," he said, sitting on the edge of the bed, "I've thought up an apology. I know you don't intend mindless conquest, or war. I should not have shouted at you. Will you forgive me?"

"Will you listen to me without jumping to conclusions?" she countered warily.

"Yes."

"Then I forgive you. And you must forgive me, Lenardo."

"For what? For being yourself? I don't suppose you'll ever lose the desire for power. But as long as you care about your people, you will not allow the desire for power to rule you. I should have remembered that, Aradia. With all your power, you would never deliberately hurt anyone."

"Oh, Lenardo!"

She sat up and threw her arms about him, open to Reading—and just as had happened the first time, a whole flood of regretted incidents tumbled into her consciousness. This time, though, there were things he understood, and foremost was the hope she had fostered the past few days that she was carrying his child.

She wanted it very much, he saw, even though she feared what pregnancy might do to her powers. He let his own delight flow to her even as he Read that her flux had begun today, spoiling her hopes.

Before he could attempt to reassure her that they would try again, his pleasure was destroyed by a further flood of guilty memories: she had set out to seduce him as much as he had her! When he had made Julia his daughter, Aradia had feared that the girl would become his heir. But she was certain that he would prefer a child of his own flesh over Julia: Aradia's child, raised and trained in her ways. And the child might inherit both their powers. Educated by Aradia, he would have the unquestionable right, by law of nature, to unite the world under his rule.

For one moment, Lenardo found incredibly funny—and therefore forgivable—the idea that each had set out to seduce the other for ulterior motives. He knew that he had not realized he loved Aradia until after that fateful afternoon, so how could he blame her for reacting the same way? As long as she loved him now, wanted his child out of love, for he could Read Aradia's sincere wish that she had conceived the second time they made love, and not in that first betrayal—

Betrayal? He pursued the idea.

Aradia had thought him impervious to seduction. So, intending to invite him to her pavilion, she had procured the spicy wine and a drug—

Lenardo thrust her away in horror. "You drugged me?"

"You can break a command implanted in your mind. It was the only way I could be certain—"

"By the gods! Ever since, I have hated myself for what I did that day. But it was not my lust at all, it was your manipulation. I trusted you. It never occurred to me to Read the wine."

Reading his revulsion, she bristled. "You were manipulating *me*, weren't you?"

"Not by destroying your will."

"Only my powers," she said grimly.

He saw himself through her eyes and cringed. "Yes, I meant to blunt your powers. Manipulation. Deceit. I've learned your savage ways, Aradia, but I will not live by them. I cannot stand what I have become, and I will not have my daughter grow up to be like you. I'm going home."

"Lenardo, this *is* your home. You may throw me out—"

"No, Aradia, this is *your* home. You and Wulfston and Lilith can fight out among yourselves how you divide the lands that were mine. I'm taking Julia to Tiberium."

"You can't. They'll kill you."

"Perhaps. But Julia will be placed in an Academy, where she will learn a Reader's disciplines. I don't know if her savage heritage can be controlled, but we must try."

He didn't know whether Aradia was trying to Read him; he had closed his mind to her. But she was clever enough to guess.

"You think Julia will get you through the gates, despite the brand on your arm. Delivering a young Reader from the savages is a fine heroic act."

"Aradia, I am expected to return. You know that. I told you I was sent to stop Galen. The brand is just a ruse."

"One that almost killed you," she said. "That's how much your empire cares about Master Readers. But go back. Tell them of your land left rulerless, theirs for the taking. Maybe it will buy you a few more weeks of life. But it will buy death for hundreds of your people when the empire attacks."

"No, Aradia, you will not use me again. I will neither endanger the people who have come to trust me nor send empire troops into the trap you and your allies would prepare for them. I am through with both deceit and power struggles. If you want to stop me, you will have to kill me . . . and even if you destroy my body, you will have a difficult time gaining the loyalty of my people if I mysteriously disappear."

Just then Julia burst in, tugging Wulfston by the hand. "Father, what's wrong?"

"We are leaving, Julia. Go and pack. Take anything truly precious to you, for we will not return."

"But—"

"Go! I will explain on the road."

Wulfston looked from Lenardo to Aradia, his dark skin graying as he recognized the finality of their confrontation. "What has happened here? Julia said you were fighting."

"It's over, Wulfston," said Lenardo. "I got a good look at myself as a savage lord. I cannot live this way."

"Then change it."

Because the young black Adept was completely sincere, Lenardo said, "Perhaps you will change it, Wulfston, or perhaps as you come into the full strength of your powers, you will succumb to the same temptations Aradia has—and I have. Undisciplined power is too dangerous. It may be too late for me, but I can try to see that Julia is not corrupted.''

''Where will you go?''

''Tiberium. I could be executed, though I doubt it. They'll find some harmless job for me, but Julia will be safe in an Academy. Wulfston, will you try to make the transition as painless as possible for the people of this land?''

Wulfston went to Aradia, who was now sitting on the edge of the bed, and sat down beside her, putting his arm around her. ''We will hold your land as your regents until you return.''

''I won't return.''

Aradia, who had sat silently since Wulfston's entrance, now leaned into the protection of her brother's arms and said, ''Father was right.'' Her voice was tense with controlled emotion. ''Wulfston, do you remember? 'You would steal my daughter's powers,' he said. He called Lenardo 'the foul beast who would ravish my daughter.' ''

''Ravish?'' Wulfston stiffened, all conciliation gone. ''He tried to—''

''He succeeded. But he could not steal my powers. I stole his.''

But Wulfston paid no heed to Aradia's satisfied tone. He rose, stalking Lenardo like the wolf that was his emblem. ''You deliberately—you dared to—''

Lenardo could not answer—he could not move: Wulfston held him under Adept control.

''I should kill you,'' Wulfston said. ''If ever I see you again, I will. But for Julia's sake, go.''

Aradia asked warily, ''Will you keep the child, Wulfston?''

''A Reader? How could I ever trust her? She is a child now, but she would grow up to be like her father. No, Lenardo. Take her back to your empire and let things return to their natural order. We are born enemies, and we must never again forget that fact.''

Wulfston took Aradia's arm and led her out past Lenardo, who still could not move. He wanted to explain, but

Wulfston would never believe in his sister's treachery. Even if Aradia had betrayed Lenardo, it was not without his full cooperation.

The spell lifted suddenly, and Lenardo collapsed to his knees. He wished he could just lie down and forget everything, but he couldn't. He must get Julia away before either Adept decided that she might be worth keeping after all. He changed quickly into traveling clothes and called for horses and food for a journey. His own packing was simple: the barest necessities. He was a Reader again; he needed no crown, no seal of office, no treasure. Even the robes of the Master Reader that he had worn at the festival he left in the chest. He had forfeited the right to wear them.

The wolf-stone pendant he left lying on top of the chest, for he no longer had any loyalty to Aradia. How neatly she had manipulated Wulfston today. Would she finally win her brother to her plan? And Lilith? It was no longer his problem. To the Aventine Empire, Aradia's plans could mean a chance to rebuild and recoup losses if she set the savages fighting among themselves. With his newfound powers, he could Read what was happening here, keep the Emperor informed—

If he was once granted the opportunity to display what he could now do, he need not fear execution.

He was just leaving the room, when Helmuth entered. "My lord, where are you going? Why was I not told of your travel plans? You must have a retinue—"

"No, Helmuth. Julia and I are leaving. No one else."

"But it is not seemly, my lord. And messengers must be sent ahead, accommodations prepared."

"No, Helmuth."

The old man studied him sadly. "Something is very wrong, my lord."

"Yes. And the only way I can correct it is to take this journey. When I am gone, you do whatever Lady Aradia or Lord Wulfston says. Tell Arkus."

"But when will you return?"

Lenardo looked into the anxious eyes and Read the sincere concern for him. If he told the truth, Helmuth and many others would quickly guess that Aradia and Wulfston had driven him away. He did not want any kind of revolt, Adept punishments of his people—

"I cannot say, Helmuth. Take care of my people for me and obey Aradia and Wulfston."

"Yes, my lord."

Lenardo and Julia were seen leaving the city, of course, by the Southgate, where Lenardo had entered on his search for Galen—was it only four months ago?

People waved, and Lenardo waved back. He must make it appear that nothing unusual was happening. Once they were on the main road south, few people came near enough to recognize them. A man and a child in traveling clothes might be anyone, their fine horses indicating no more than that they had found favor with the Lord of the Land.

Julia was astonishingly silent as Lenardo set a pace to cover ground as rapidly as possible without overtiring their horses. Finally she asked, "Father, where are we going?"

"Home," he replied.

"But we just *left* home."

"We are going to *my* home, Julia, back to the Aventine Empire where I came from. There you will meet other Readers and get a proper education."

"You're not going to leave me there?"

He Read her panic, the normal child's fear of losing a parent, compounded by the terrible uncertainties she had known in her short life. "No, Julia," he told her. "I'm going to stay in the empire, too."

He didn't tell her that once he placed her safely in Portia's hands, they would never see each other again. Once she touched the minds of her teachers and classmates in the Academy, she would forget him as quickly as he had forgotten his own parents. *I will be the one who will sorely miss Julia,* he realized sadly.

Lenardo intended to Read ahead, contact Master Clement, and have his message relayed to Adigia so that the gates would be opened for them on their arrival. He would not rest securely until they were within the walls of the empire.

Before the mysterious expansion of his powers, Lenardo

would have had to ride to the wall, find a secure place to hide, and leave his body in order to Read all the way to Tiberium. Now, though still several hours from the border, he could contact Master Clement without even stopping.

But just as he decided to do so, he Read pursuit. Arkus and a troop of ten men were galloping along the road several miles behind them. *Lord Lenardo*, Arkus projected. *Lord Wulfston wants you to return to Zendi.*

I'll just bet he does. "Julia, we are being pursued. We must hide."

She didn't question him but followed him off the road into a patch of woods. In a few minutes the soldiers galloped past, Arkus still broadcasting his order.

Julia looked wide-eyed at Lenardo. //Why don't you trust Lord Wulfston anymore?//

//We dare not trust any Adept, Julia. I fear it is you he wants, to bend to his will . . . or to Aradia's.//

//They couldn't. I'm a Reader. I'd know—//

//You have forgotten already how Drakonius treated people to make them obey him.//

//Lord Wulfston's not like that. And anyway, a Reader can always get away, like we're doing.// They were continuing through the woods, pausing each time they had to cross an open area to Read whether anyone might see them.

//Galen could not get away,// Lenardo told her. //I've mentioned Galen, my student, who went over to the enemy, Reading for Drakonius and his henchmen.//

//Yes. That's why you came here—to stop him.//

//That's right. But Julia, Galen was not an evil person, merely young and very foolish. He blamed other people for his problems instead of trying to solve them himself. And I suppose that is why he allied himself with Drakonius, thinking such a powerful Adept would give him wealth and power in exchange for his services. But do you know what Drakonius made him do, to test his loyalty?//

//No. What?//

//Help him attack Adigia, the town Galen had come from, where all his old friends were.//

Julia did not respond, trying to shield her thoughts as

she pondered that. Then she observed, //If anyone did that to me, I would think it was wicked. But if I was trying to test someone's loyalty, what better way?//

//Child, you are far too old for your years,// Lenardo told her wearily.

//But what happened? Did Galen pass the test?//

//He Read a fault in the rock beneath the Academy at Adigia. By jarring it just a little, the Adepts could cause an earthquake.//

//Oh, I remember. The ground trembled in Zendi. But it didn't work right. Almost our whole army got killed. The mountain fell on them.//

//Yes, and Drakonius blamed Galen.//

//Did Galen do it?//

//We will never know, child. By the time I found him, Galen's mind was so twisted from Drakonius' tortures that he himself did not know when he spoke truth.//

//What did Drakonius do to him?// Julia asked with child-ish curiosity.

//The soldiers are far ahead of us now,// said Lenardo. //We can return to the road, where we can move faster.//

//The watchers will tell everybody.//

Lenardo could Read that Wulfston's command to him to return was being relayed throughout the land, but the message would have to be sent by foot or on horseback into every settlement, for only the watchers knew the code of flashing lights. By the time it had disseminated widely, Lenardo and Julia would be in the no-man's-land near the border, where no one lived.

It was incredibly easy for two Readers in a mind-blind society to elude pursuit. Aradia could do nothing. Her powers were far less than Julia's.

//I was caught by watchers once, Julia. I won't be again, nor will you.//

The little girl might not have been able to do it alone. Lenardo estimated that her range was about what his had been limited to by illness and exhaustion the time Aradia's watchers had located him. But with Julia Reading near and Lenardo far, they were able to use the good road to travel quickly when there was no one about and leave it to skirt settlements and avoid other people on the road.

They passed harvesters in the fields, making no attempt to hide when they Read that these people had no idea that they were fugitives. There was a sharp contrast between the well-clothed, well-fed, well-housed people they passed and the hungry, hopeless people Lenardo had Read along this same road on his journey northward last spring. *So I have done some good,* he thought. *Aradia and Wulfston will keep it up. They would never let their people suffer the way Drakonius did.*

//What did Drakonius do to Galen?// Julia's tenacious curiosity demanded to be satisfied.

//I don't know all of it, child. When I found him, he was caged like an animal. One time I Read Drakonius break the bones in Galen's hand—as a warning, he said. He healed him afterward, but that did not lessen Galen's pain at the time.//

//Do you think Aradia or Lord Wulfston would do something like that?//

//Their methods are more subtle, Julia. Aradia once kept me locked in her castle by planting in my mind the idea that I could not open the door of my room. I don't know if you can understand that that is much more wicked than outright torture.//

She thought it over. //If they can make people think whatever they want, why don't they make us think we want to go back?//

//I don't think they could implant an idea in the mind of a healthy Reader. They did it to me when I was very ill, while they had me in healing sleep. I was not yet completely well when I found out what they had done, drove the command from my mind, and escaped. So they know they cannot hold a Reader that way. And Aradia tells me no one can be forced by that method to do something he believes to be wrong. It may be that Drakonius tried to chain Galen's mind, and Galen caused the avalanche to fall on Drakonius' army without knowing what he was doing. But now we'll never know.//

//Did you kill Galen, Father?//

//No, not personally. I was guiding Aradia, Wulfston, Lilith, and Nerius. They trapped Drakonius and Galen with the other Adepts and burned them to death.//

He withdrew into his own thoughts, remembering having no time to think or to grieve—not over Galen and not over Nerius—but having to go on into the combat between the armies, with Drakonius' troops still fighting fiercely, not knowing that their leader was dead.

At the mass funeral three days later, Lenardo had not been able to bring himself to speak for Galen. He could not believe that all the boy's bright potential had died so horribly, nor was his ability to accept Galen's death aided by the fact that those who had gone to collect the charred remains in the burnt-out canyon found nothing but a few scattered bones.

Suddenly, imposed on the memory of that charred canyon, rose the vision that had plagued him months before: Castle Nerius in ruins beneath the golden harvest moon, Aradia dead—

"Father! Father, they're coming back!"

Julia's cry jolted Lenardo back to the present. Four of Arkus' men were indeed coming back toward them. He and Julia rode quickly over a swell of ground, the only nearby shelter. On the other side, they reined in, got down from their horses, and pulled the animals' heads down as they crouched, waiting. The horses began to crop the stubble in the newly harvested field. Lenardo wished for a moment that a field of grain shielded them, until he realized that in an unharvested field they would have left a trampled trail to lead the soldiers right to them.

The men were moving slowly, peering out on either side of the road. They didn't expect to find their quarry in the fields, though. As they passed, one of the men ordered, "Erik, Tav, ride around that patch of woods ahead, then come through it toward us."

Lenardo Read the soldiers carefully. They were puzzled but doing their duty. Why the Lord of the Land would be hiding from his own troops was a total mystery. At least two of them were of the opinion that it was a war game to see whether nonReaders could figure out how to capture someone who could Read their every move, part of whatever plans Lord Lenardo and Lady Aradia had been working on together.

Julia, Reading with Lenardo, smothered a giggle. He touched her touseled curls and told her, //We won't have any trouble eluding *that* kind of pursuit, will we?//

When the soldiers were out of sight, Lenardo and Julia took to the road again. The sun was low in the sky as they reached the part of the road that had fallen into disrepair. Close to the wall, the road became a wide highway again, but for many miles it narrowed to a badly rutted wagon track, full of holes that could throw a horse if the rider was not careful.

Ironically, there was plenty of shelter here and no one to take shelter from. The fields had been abandoned in Lenardo's childhood, and the woods encroached on them, after all these years almost coming together to form a forest.

They were still more than two hours from Adigia, and Julia was getting tired and cranky. They stopped to eat and rest, while Lenardo Read on ahead to find Arkus setting a trap.

Every savage knew the danger of coming near the walls of the Aventine Empire because of the Readers therein. Near the gates of Adigia, a huge area was kept clear. Even in the blackest night, a Reader with bow and arrow could pick off anyone attempting to approach the gates.

Lenardo had stood watch atop that wall many a time. It was routine duty for boys from the Academy, from the ages of twelve to fifteen. What Arkus did not know was that with the Academy gone and only three Readers now in the town, there was no longer a Reader atop the tower at all times. There was none now, just two guards from the garrison.

Torio was gone, of course, and the three Readers who had replaced him did not know Lenardo's situation. Two of them did not even know Lenardo, a husband and wife he Read just sitting down to their evening meal with a chubby little boy of perhaps three. It was easy to Read them, not intruding, without their being aware of him.

The third Reader was Secundus, who had been the healer at the Academy. He was a few years older than Lenardo, a quiet, gentle man who had barely achieved the rank of magister and perhaps might have been denied it except that he was skilled at healing, and such people were always badly needed.

Secundus now had Torio's old room at the inn and was also unaware of Lenardo's scrutiny, being deep into a book of remedies in search of something to cure a catarrh that had so far eluded his skills.

But Arkus could not know that there was no Reader keeping watch from Adïgia's wall, and so as the sun set, he deployed his men in a semicircle just out of range of arrows shot from the gatetower. On either side, at a distance from the gate, men lurked near the wall. The rest were close enough to one another in their arc that Lenardo and Julia could not ride between any two undetected.

He considered abandoning the horses and attempting to sneak through on foot. By the time he contacted Master Clement and the message was relayed to Secundus to admit him, it would be well after midnight. Arkus' men would be bored and sleepy.

Arkus' men? No, not the way the young commander kept them trained. And Julia was still a child. If she was weary now, what would she be in a few more hours?

Adigia's troops could be called out, but Lenardo did not want a battle, the slaughter of Arkus and his few men. He realized that the young man trusted him not to call out an army against seven, or not to be able to.

Julia, her supper half eaten, nodded off to sleep. Lenardo let her sleep while he thought. The nearest gate other than the one at Adigia was beyond the Western Hills, in Wulfston's land. It would take several days of difficult travel to reach it, and with the watchers alerting everyone, he was sure that it would be well guarded before they could get there.

The next gate to the east was even farther away, in Aradia's land. The problem was the same. The wall between them, however, passed through dense woods, areas where no one went for years at a time. He could Read places where the trees had so encroached upon the wall that it might be possible to climb over. They would håve to abandon the horses, but with any luck they would be safely inside the Aventine Empire by morning.

But he must let Masters Clement and Portia know that he was coming. He Read carefully all around him to be sure no dangers could creep up on them while his attention was far away. No people between them and the gates of Adigia and none for miles in any other direction. No wild animals except some deer in the woods. The deer were skittish and nervous, but since Lenardo could Read nothing else to disturb them, he decided that he and Julia must be the cause. All around them birds were chirping, too, although it was fully dark.

With the incredible ease he had developed these past few days, Lenardo Read to Tiberium. Master Clement was in his study, deep in conversation with Portia, who was, of course, in her own room within the female Academy.

//But I found Drusina's performance well above average,// Clement was saying. //I recommend that you send her for her medical training and then test her for admission to the rank of magister. I'm certain she is capable, Portia.//

//Clement, Clement, you were out there on the border too long,// Portia replied. //This girl might barely qualify in a time when there was a dearth of fine Readers—//

//There is *always* a dearth of fine Readers. Just last month you refused Quintus admission to magister rank, even though he passed every test. Master Tervo wept when you denied his candidate—he needed Quintus for his Academy. I need an assistant until Lenardo returns. We are old, Portia. Three Readers of the Council of Masters have died just since I returned to Tiberium. We cannot afford to set an arbitrary standard if no one can meet it. We must admit our best young Readers to the upper ranks or there will be no one to train new Readers when we are gone.//

At Clement's mention of his name, Lenardo almost made his presence known, but as he was about to interrupt, he Read something from Portia—a denial she was hiding from Clement. She did not expect Lenardo to return—no surprise there. But what was surprising was her faint, pervasive guilt, beginning with his mention and continuing through Clement's plea. He felt her force it away as she said, //That is precisely why we must allow only the very best into our ranks—and Clement, you know that control is as important as strength to a Reader. These young people lack discipline. How can they discipline others?//

//Perhaps,// replied Clement, but Lenardo could sense his old master's deep concern about Portia's attitude.

It was that concern, along with the strange emotions he had Read from Portia, that kept Lenardo from making his presence known. Portia was Master of Masters; she headed the Council-of Masters, with full veto power. The Reader who held that post was the best of all Readers, yet Lenardo was able to eavesdrop on her without detection. That could be a fluke, as her attention was elsewhere, but he should not have been able to Read feelings she hid successfully from Clement.

Both Masters were old; Lenardo wondered whether the infirmities of age could be weakening their powers, just as any other infirmity might. He had no idea how old Portia was, but it seemed to be many years older than Clement. Was it senility? Or were her powers impaired because she had misused them? Why guilt?

Confused and ashamed at what he was thinking, Lenardo nonetheless withdrew without making contact. He would try later, when Clement was alone. His old master would know the proper way to approach Portia to use her influence for Lenardo's safe return.

When he brought his attention back to the nearby surroundings and to Julia, she was awake. //What's wrong, Father?//

How easily the child Read him. //Arkus is guarding the gate at Adigia. We will have to go home by a different way. It will be a difficult journey, but I've found a place where we can climb the wall.//

They cut cross-country at a diagonal, struggling through thick, overgrown forest as they approached the area Lenardo had Read. The trees overhead obscured the stars; the underbrush forced them to twist and turn to find a way through. Anyone but a Reader would be certain to lose himself in such wilderness.

It was well after midnight when they finally reached the wall, leading their tired horses. Julia stumbled with weariness. Lenardo wondered whether she would be able to make the climb and had her sit down on a fallen log to rest while he stripped the horses and began to lighten their packs to what they could carry on foot. Julia slid off the log onto the mossy ground, fast asleep.

He couldn't help smiling at the exhausted child, when suddenly one of his precognitive flashes revealed the earth heaving, trees falling—

He dropped the pack and fell on Julia, shoving her against the log and covering her with his body.

"Father, what— What're you *doing*?" she protested in a child's tired whine.

"Lie still!" he said, and then the earthquake came.

Beneath them the ground trembled; leaves and twigs rained down on them. Then they were lifted as if on an ocean wave, the log sheltering them falling away and then back as they were dropped. The horses screamed and crashed off into the woods as trees began to wave like stalks of grain. Lenardo tried to protect Julia as they were tossed and buffeted. Trees fell, slamming into other trees, ancient oaks tottering and ripping from their roots.

Above them, a huge mossy trunk swayed and creaked. *If ever I needed Adept power*— Lenardo thought, but he was powerless to do anything more than clutch Julia, trying to keep his body between her and falling debris as the monstrous trunk cracked and whipped—and broke, with a huge piece falling toward them in a majestic, slow, inevitable trajectory.

Chapter Six

In a strange suspension of emotion, Lenardo Read the giant piece of tree trunk falling, falling, turning end over end as it hurtled toward him and Julia. It would crush both of them if it struck. Helplessly, he recalled Aradia's lesson in how an Adept would use the laws of chance. The earth was still heaving, moving Lenardo and Julia in and out of the path of the falling trunk and at the same time making it impossible for them to run or even roll out of the way. They and the huge log they sheltered against were being tossed like snowflakes in a whirlwind.

Hopelessly he wished, he willed—and then he blanked out his oncoming death, clutching the child and waiting. The wood was a thundering symphony of crashes, cracks, thuds, and moans, but suddenly there was a bone-penetrating *whomp* in chorus with a *crack* like a lightning bolt. Then something fell across Lenardo's back, knocking the breath out of him and crushing Julia beneath him.

In the searing pain of struggling to breathe, it took Lenardo some time to realize that he was still alive. The earth's quaking had settled to small tremors, slowly dying away. He heaved himself to his knees, throwing off a splintered section of the tree trunk that could have spelled his death. Then he Read Julia, badly bruised and dazed but alive and fighting for breath.

He Read her carefully, finding no broken bones or internal injuries. Her ribs were bruised, but their youthful resiliency had kept them from breaking. Lenardo could not say the same for himself. A stabbing pain in his left side told him that ribs were broken before he Read them, but fortunately they were in place. A tight bandage would hold them so that they could heal. His left ankle, though, had hit or been hit by something. No bones were broken, but it was already swelling, and it was clear that he would not be able to walk on it.

But we're both alive, he told himself as Julia began to cough and choke and then wail with a child's pain and fear as she regained consciousness.

He took her in his arms, saying, "It's all right. It's over. You're not badly hurt, just had the breath knocked out of you. I'm here, Julia. You're all right."

Her hysteria subsided, and she began to Read him, feeling his broken ribs stab with every breath. //You're hurt!//

//It's not serious. You'll have to help me with bandages before we can go on.//

//I wish we had Sandor here.//

//So do I, but we can get along without Adept talents.//

He let her go and tried to straighten his back. As his ribs stabbed again, he also felt a burning ache diagonally across his back. He remembered something hitting him.

//What happened?// Julia asked. //A tree was falling on us. You thought it would kill us. Why didn't it?//

The night was too dark to see anything in the forest; the air was filled with dust raised by the quake. To Readers, though, that made no difference. Lenardo studied the destruction in their immediate area and saw that his instinct to shelter against the fallen log had been their salvation.

The huge piece of tree trunk had been falling toward them end over end. The dent in the fallen log and the splintered shafts of the trunk told Lenardo that it had hit the log end on and split into many pieces. One of those pieces had struck him, but much of the energy of its long fall had been dissipated in striking the log and splitting. This was a small piece; it might have cracked his spine but hadn't. He would ache for days, but he was alive.

Julia Read with him and then Read him very carefully. //You lie down,// she told him. //I'll find our packs.//

He helped her in the search by Reading, but Julia dug through the debris to their supplies. She brought the water pouch, and they each had a long drink. Then, with the aid of Lenardo's knife, they tore up one of his tunics, washed the many cuts and abrasions both of them were covered with, and spread them with healing salve.

Aventine salve. Lenardo had carried it with him into the savage lands but had used none in the months when Adept healing power was readily available to him. He had automatically tossed it into his pack today without thinking, but now it reminded him that he was returning to a land where healing was done with salves and potions, splints and bandages, and occasionally the surgeon's knife. If only he could have made that treaty—

No. Even the most benevolent of Adepts could not resist the lure of power. They could never be trusted—never!

Bandaging Lenardo's ribs proved extremely difficult, for Julia's childish hands had neither the skill nor the strength for the task. Finally he thought to knot a stick into the bandage and twist it tight and then tie it into place. Then he dared bend to bandage his ankle. It was swelling badly. How was he to climb over the wall now?

Panting from pain and exertion, Lenardo leaned back against the log and Read the wall nearby. Aventine construction was a fine art: it still stood. Furthermore, the leaning trees that he had intended to use as their bridge to freedom had fallen in the quake. They were trapped.

But no one knows where we are, he reminded himself, *and everyone will be busy repairing quake damage.*

He Read outward, wondering how much his injuries had impaired his powers. It was easy to Read to Adigia. The gate tower had fallen, but the wall and gates had held, as had most of the buildings in town. The farther north he Read, the less the damage. In Zendi, people were all awake, discussing the quake and looking for damage, but there was little; the center had been somewhere near where Lenardo and Julia were.

"Did Aradia and Wulfston make the earthquake to kill us?" Julia voiced the question Lenardo dared not bring to mind.

Although he had avoided Reading the Adepts, he replied, "No," grateful now that she had made him think about it. "No, they could not. To make an earthquake,

Adepts have to know where there is a fault under the earth. Then they must be much closer than from Zendi to here. No, that was a natural earthquake.''

"But you knew it was going to happen. You pushed me under the log before it started.''

"Yes. I have flashes of precognition, or prophecy, Julia. Sometimes I get a glimpse of something that is going to happen. That time it saved our lives.''

"Then you have a special talent, too. Like the way I can Read the stories things tell.''

"Yes, but I cannot control it. For example, I cannot Read tomorrow to discover how we got out of the fine mess we're in right now.''

"Let's Read along the wall," she suggested. "You didn't Read east. Maybe part of it fell down.''

Humoring the child, Lenardo Read as she suggested and found that she was right. Several miles away, there was a spot where a tree had grown up against the wall, its roots heaving the structure. Tree had weakened wall and wall tree; in the quake, both had fallen together, leaving a gap of crumbled stone large enough —

//We could ride our horses through there,// Julia said excitedly, Reading with him. //You won't have to walk, Father.//

But, they Read, one of their horses was dead, struck down in its panicked flight, and the other was a good distance away, exhausted, trembling, in no condition to be ridden.

//I'll get the horse,// Julia said. //Read with me, Father, so I won't get lost.//

He did so, incredibly proud of the brave child venturing into the woods in the dark, soothing the animal, and bringing it back to him. The horse was used to being taken care of by people. It calmed down, accepted a drink, and remained nearby.

//Now we must rest,// Lenardo told Julia, who was shivering in the predawn chill. //Come here, child.// He wrapped her in his cloak, and in his arms. //I'm very proud of you, Julia,// he told her. //You were very brave and good tonight. Sleep now.//

Obediently, she slept. Lenardo, just as exhausted, lingered on the edge of sleep for one last Reading of their safety. He wished again for the power of Adept healing as he sought to find a position in which his injuries would not hurt. He could almost feel the soothing heat through his ankle, his ribs, across his back—

Lenardo woke with a start when Julia pushed her way out of his arms. The sun was high in the sky, but here in the depths of the forest it was filtered to a soft green twilight. Julia gave a little moan as she stretched her bruised muscles. She was covered with dust, leaves, and twigs, and so was he.

Lenardo moved experimentally. He wasn't as sore as he had expected. Even when he put some weight on his ankle, the pain was tolerable, and the bandages hung loose. The swelling had gone down. He rebandaged it and eased on his riding boot. With that support, he found that he could walk, although he didn't want to walk far.

He was ravenously hungry. Julia only picked at her bread and cheese, but Lenardo ate heartily. Then, anxious to be safely on the other side of the wall, they set out, Julia riding before Lenardo on the horse.

It was slow going, with the debris of the earthquake compounding the tangle of underbrush normal to the dense forest. The tired horse plodded, and Lenardo curbed his impatience, for the animal still had a long way to carry them.

By afternoon, they reached the breach in the wall. Here they had to walk and lead the horse, who did not want to venture over the loose rubble of rocks. By the time they slipped and slid their way across, Lenardo's ankle was sore again. He took his boot off lest the swelling force him to cut the leather off later.

Nonetheless, he breathed a sigh of relief. "We're home."

Julia was not impressed, for they had before them nothing but the same dense forest they had been fighting their way through all day. "I'm tired," she said, slipping back to being a child again.

"Of course you are," Lenardo said reassuringly. "So am I. We won't go much farther today. Read with me."

//See that stream ahead, with the lovely pool? We'll stop there for the night. We can swim and get clean and put on clean clothes.//

Just as on the other side of the border, this area was too close to the wall for people to feel secure. An abandoned orchard still produced apples on gnarled old trees, while blackberries weighted the tangled vines under them. While Julia picked fruit, Lenardo found that a bent pin on a thong, baited with a crumb of bread, quickly caught two unwary fish from the stream. He was careful not to Read while he fished. There wasn't much mind to a fish, but Readers still rarely caught them themselves.

Now that they were on the Aventine side of the border, Lenardo felt free to relax, to build a fire, to broil the fish and make herb tea, to swim with Julia and wash their clothes.

As the sun lowered, the chilly air drove them to shore, where the fire and hot tea were welcome. It was pleasant to sit by the fire with Julia, making her practice the Aventine language. He had begun teaching her weeks ago, but since she had had no practice except with him, she had not developed fluency.

"Tomorrow," he told her, "we will be among people again. We don't want to be noticed, so you must let me do any talking that is necessary. And whenever I tell you, you must be careful not to Read."

"Why?"

"Because there will be other Readers about, and many of them know me. A male Reader would not be escorting a female discovery to an Academy, and besides, you Read far too well to be a newly wakened Reader. Once I get you to Tiberium and explain your situation to the Masters, you will continue to grow and use your powers. But until we get there, we must avoid rousing curiosity."

"Father, why can't a male Reader escort a female?"

He knew that she suspected the truth, and he would have a fight on his hands if he admitted it. He equivocated. "I taught you in Zendi because I was the only other Reader there. Here though, girls are always trained by women and boys by men. You will like your teachers,

Julia, and make many new friends at the Academy, girls like yourself."

"But what about you?"

He looked into her round brown eyes, ready to cloud with tears. "I will always be your father," he said truthfully, and hid the pain that realization cost him.

She had indeed become his child, as much as if she were his own flesh and blood. Readers tried to keep themselves emotionally distant from the children they knew they would lose at six, seven, or eight. Some even avoided naming their children in a personal fashion. The Academies were full of young Readers named Primus or Secundus, Tertia or Puella.

The only Readers forbidden mental contact with one another were parents and children, at least until the children were grown. Children were always assigned to Academies far from where their families lived; the Academy must become their home, the Masters their parents, all Readers their brothers and sisters.

Julia could not fight sleep after another hard day. Lenardo covered her and kissed her forehead. For a moment, the whimsical notion played at the edges of his mind that they did not have to go on to Tiberium. They could stay here, build a house, live off the land. No one came here for months, maybe years at a time, and Readers could easily avoid company.

He dismissed the foolish notion, banked the fire, and settled back to Read all around them. No one for miles in any direction. No dangerous wild animals. He really should try to contact Master Clement, but before he could do so, he fell asleep.

Two days later, Lenardo and Julia rode into Tiberium. The weather had turned hot again, but Lenardo wore a long-sleeved tunic to cover the brand on his arm. In the crowds, they went completely unnoticed, just another pair of travelers. Lenardo's beard suggested that he might be a workman from one of the outlying provinces, traveling with his daughter.

Lenardo Read about him with the same odd sense of his

own transparency that had kept Portia and Clement from noticing his eavesdropping. *If I can keep Portia from knowing I'm Reading her, I can certainly fool any other Reader in Tiberium.*

It was many years since he had been in the capital, not since his own testing for the rank of magister. The city was clean and beautiful, as he had wanted Zendi to be. It felt good to come home, even without knowing what fate awaited him. Julia would be safe here in Portia's Academy. What would become of Lenardo was another question. He had broken his vow of celibacy; he could not be readmitted to the Academy. Nonetheless, his Reading abilities had mysteriously increased. He didn't know why, but if *his* powers had reached this unheard-of state, what might a Master Reader achieve who had never defiled his body? Once he had demonstrated his increased abilities, the entire Council of Masters would want him alive and well for their study.

I will bargain for my life from a position of power, he thought wryly. That was one useful lesson Aradia had taught him; without that understanding, it was dangerous to have something other people wanted.

The sun was high in the sky. Lenardo found an inn, where he and Julia took a room and then had luncheon in the cool, dark tavern. In the heat, everyone was eating fruit and salad, and so their vegetarian Readers' diet provoked no curiosity. Soon the busy streets would empty, and the boys at the temporary Academy would be released from their studies in the heat of the day. Lenardo intended to go there and reveal himself to Clement and Torio.

Leaving Julia, who was actually willing to nap after the long journey, he set out on foot through the emptying streets. His ankle was almost completely healed; the short walk would not harm it. The students from the Academy at Adigia were still housed in an abandoned villa—adequate lodgings but not a proper building for their needs, and no room to expand.

The street door stood open. Lenardo entered, Reading some of the boys gathered in the shade by the courtyard fountain and others in their rooms. The marble building was cooler inside than out; most of the teachers and students were in their rooms, many of them napping. Something was missing in the atmosphere—a certain sense of hope and excitement that had characterized these same men and boys at Adigia.

He turned from the entry hall where visitors were greeted into a long corridor, expecting at every moment to be challenged, thinking of the surprise when he identified himself, for everyone here knew him. Several strong Readers were awake and Reading. By the time he reached the end of the hall, he should have been recognized or challenged half a dozen times—yet no one noticed him. Slowly, it dawned on him that he had achieved the legendary ability to Read without being Read. As if his mind had become completely absorbing, nonreflecting, he was unReadable among Readers.

To test the hypothesis, he deliberately Read the next person he found awake: Decius. The boy was sitting on his bed, massaging the stump of the leg he had lost in the battle at Adigia. Leaning against the bed was the peg leg he was learning to use; it made the stump sore, and the boy was now Reading carefully to determine whether today's was the bruising pain he had to endure until he gained strength and callouses or whether he had best to go back to his crutch for the rest of the day. It was a pragmatic examination, Lenardo was glad to find; there was no self-pity in the boy's attitude.

Neither was there recognition, even when Lenardo Read with him, sick at heart to see traces of unhealed damage after all this time. Sandor would have healed those lingering injuries in a week, Aradia in a day.

But they heal people only to keep them in their power, Lenardo told himself, and continued quietly past Decius' closed door toward where Torio's stood open.

At this point the wall to Lenardo's left ended, a series of pillars supporting the roof but giving access to the courtyard, where several of the younger boys were splashing in the fountain with shouts and giggles, paying attention to nothing but their games. Lenardo moved quietly down the shaded hall and entered Torio's room.

The boy was sitting at his desk, his back to Lenardo, concentrating on a box in front of him. It was an exercise in fine discernment, a sealed box containing a number of items similar in composition, some very tiny, such as several grains of sand in different colors, and with them a single salt crystal. Torio, having identified all the larger items, was concentrating on those. He added to the list on his tablet: "sand—black, blue, red, yellow, white." Lenardo held his breath. Some instinct told Torio to Read again. He did, "looking" at the grains in another way, examining their internal structure. Then he turned his stylus over and rubbed out the word "white," substituting "salt." With a sigh, he started to get up from his stool.

//Very good, Torio.//

//Master Lenardo.// The boy froze. //Where are you?//

Astonished to find that Torio seemed to think him still far away, Lenardo replied aloud, "Right here."

Torio started and whirled around, his hands groping for an instant unil he began Reading visually and "saw" Lenardo before him. Then he threw his arms about him, hugging him tight, and Lenardo realized that the boy was now as tall as he was.

"Oh, Master Lenardo, I'm so glad you're home. But you certainly humble my pride. I didn't think anyone could sneak up on me anymore. Why didn't you tell me you were coming? Why didn't Master Clement tell me—?"

The boy's string of questions halted as Master Clément himself came into the room, closing the door behind him and staring at Lenardo in disbelief.

"No Reading, Torio," he instructed quickly. "Lenardo, how did you get here? Why didn't you contact us? How did you come within the pale?"

"The same way I just walked through an Academy of Readers undetected. I have much, much to tell you, Master, and to show you."

"We must seek a plane of privacy," said Master Clement. "Lenardo, you are in grave danger here. If you are discovered before we find a way to explain your presence, you will be arrested and executed. Torio, stay here until I contact you. Yes, you may join us, son, but I do not want you trying to reach another plane alone.''

''Yes, Master,'' Torio replied, and lay down on his bed as Clement and Lenardo left.

Unlike the old Academy at Adigia, there was no special protected room where Readers could take shelter while they left their bodies. Master Clement's room, though, had a couch as well as bed. Lenardo stretched out, making certain his position would not cramp his unattended body, and floated easily up into pure consciousness. Master Clement was quickly ''there'' too, and they ''moved'' together to Torio's room.

The moment Master Clement's presence touched Torio, the boy's consciousness left his body, joining them readily with the delicious sense of pure freedom so refreshing in those to whom it was still a new experience.

//Excellent, Torio,// Lenardo told him. //You have learned much while I was away.//

//Don't encourage him to pride,// Master Clement warned, although his warm pleasure in the boy's achievement belied the thought. //I've never had a student so determined to be first and best at everything. No, not even you, Lenardo.//

In their present disembodied state, no Reader could ''overhear'' their conversation unless they willed it or unless the other Reader joined them. Yet to Lenardo's surprise, Clement said, //We will now move to another plane. Torio, you've done this only once before. Don't try to Read and follow. Flow with me. *With* me. That's right.//

The two presences were gone, but Lenardo had Read their ''direction.'' He followed into the disorientation of the plane of privacy, sensing Torio's discomfort. They were three presences in a world of nothing—no light and hence no dark, no up, no down. From here, they could no longer Read their own world, would not even know if something happened to their bodies.

The plane of privacy was dangerous; only Readers of the highest ranks could achieve it, and even they rarely used it. Only once before had Lenardo actually come here to achieve privacy: when he, Clement, and Portia had plotted his exile so that he could attempt to take Galen from the enemy.

He was surprised that Clement was already teaching Torio, who had not yet passed his preliminary examinations.

//Now, Lenardo,// said Clement, //What are we to do with you?//

//All I want is to return home, Master. I have accomplished my task: Galen is dead, and the alliance of powerful Adepts who were attacking the empire has been destroyed.//

//You will have to be tested under Oath of Truth before the Council of Masters.//

//Of course,// said Lenardo.

//Portia is respected by the Senate. She can have your exile revoked. Then you can help me rebuild our Academy.//

//No, Master,// Lenardo interrupted. //I cannot return to the Academy, for I have broken my Reader's Oath.//

//No!// It was a flash of pain from Torio. //No, Master Lenardo, you couldn't—//

//I did,// he insisted calmly. //It seemed necessary at the time. All I ask is the same treatment accorded any failed Reader: a job, a place to live . . . and a place in Portia's Academy for my daughter.//

// Your . . . daughter?// asked Clement.

//A Reader, Master, born among the savages. I took her into my protection lest they kill her, and then I adopted her.//

Relief flooded from the other Readers. //Under such circumstances,// said Clement, //what choice did you have? You could not let a child die just because she is female. The portion of your oath requiring you to protect a fellow Reader took precedence. The Council will have to pronounce judgment, but I am sure you will be readmitted to the Academy. How old is the child?//

//Just turned nine.//

//And where is she now?//

//I took a room at an inn before coming here.//

//We cannot leave a child at an inn. We'll put her up

with a family for tonight, until she can be tested. But you must not continue—//

//Master Clement,// Lenardo said stopping him. //I have broken more than one part of the Code. I am no longer celibate.//

Shocked silence. Then Torio's protest: //It's not so. You couldn't have.//

//It's not possible,// Clement added. //Lenardo, your powers are not diminished. They have grown—grown far more in the few months you were away than I have ever seen a Reader of your age achieve. Son, believe me, the savages have placed a false memory within your mind, hoping to weaken your abilities. If it were true, you would not be able to leave your body, let alone achieve the plane of privacy, or walk unnoticed among Readers. If we must send you to Gaeta to remove this false memory, we will do so, but you may rest assured that it cannot possibly be true.//

//Master, I regret to tell you that you are wrong. It was no illusion. I sacrificed my powers deliberately, to diminish the powers of an Adept who survived the battle in which Galen was killed. She was my ally until peace was achieved and she realized that she is now the most powerful. In savage terms, that gives her the right to rule. She would have used me, and she would have used Julia—my daughter—had we remained within her sphere of influence.//

Lenardo started to add that he knew how to break a command implanted in his mind by an Adept—when he suddenly recalled: //Master Clement, I did not know when I was exiled that the Adepts had the power to place thoughts in people's minds. How did you know it?//

//I did not know it when you left us, Lenardo, or I would have warned you. Portia should have.// No physical reactions were possible in this nonphysical plane, but Lenardo perceived from Clement something distinctly like a long, sad sigh. //Since returning to Tiberium, I have sat regularly on the Council of Masters and learned much that was never reported to us out on the border. You must be cautious, Lenardo. There is great distrust of Readers among powerful nonReaders. If any member of the Council should decide you are too dangerous, a word to any senator would be your death warrant.//

//I know that, Master, but I am not dangerous. Furthermore, my powers have increased greatly, although I do not know why. The Council will want to study me, to discover the reason so that all Readers may increase their powers.//

//Master Lenardo,// said Torio, //did you not contact me one morning, about a week ago? I thought I felt—//

//You did, Torio.//

//But you seemed startled. I thought you were trying to come home and feared you had been interrupted, captured. I left my body—//

//Torio,// Master Clement chided, //you have just learned that skill, and are not to attempt it unsupervised.//

//But Master Lenardo seemed so agitated. I Read to Adigia. I couldn't get lost there. But I couldn't find you, Master Lenardo.//

//No, Torio. You couldn't find me because I was in Zendi.//

//Zendi!// Master Clement was horrified. //You left your body in Zendi and came all the way to Tiberium? Lenardo, you could have lost contact with your body forever. If the situation required such a risk, why did you contact Torio rather than me?//

//There was no risk. Torio, I contacted you by accident, and I was so startled to find myself Reading Tiberium that I withdrew. You see, that was the morning I discovered my new powers. I had not left my body. I was Reading directly.//

//From Zendi to Tiberium?// Master Clement's skepticism was tinged with the fear that Lenardo had gone mad. //No one has ever Read over such a distance. To Read a single day's journey without leaving one's body is the stuff of legends.//

//So is a Reader walking among other Readers undetected,// Lenardo reminded him. //Master, when we return to our bodies, I will demonstrate.//

Demonstrate Lenardo did, for Clement, Torio, and Portia, whom they contacted at once. Her first response to Lenardo's return was anger.

//We tread a difficult enough path as it is,// she flashed. //How dare I inform the Senate that an exile has not only come within the pale but is wandering free in Tiberium? The plan was that you be let in at a gate.//

//Savage soldiers were lying in wait for me at the gates. I planned to climb the wall, but the earthquake conveniently opened a path for me.//

//That little tremor?//

//Along the border it was very severe, fortunately at its worst where no one lives.// As an example of his powers, he Read the earthquake area for them, showing the acres of fallen timber and fissures in the earth where the quake had been centered, just a few miles from where he and Julia had nearly met their death.

All three other Readers could have Read that on their own, but only by leaving their bodies behind. Even Portia was impressed, Lenardo noted, that he did it sitting on Master Clement's couch, never losing contact with his physical being.

He then took them beyond the forest, across fields and through villages to Zendi. The city was bustling, as was Lenardo's house, where Wulfston counseled with Helmuth while Aradia directed the people who had accompanied her from Castle Nerius in packing. To Lenardo's relief, she was completely closed to Reading. He didn't want to contact her, and he had brought enough shocks to the Masters today without revealing that there was an Adept who could Read.

The preparations were for Aradia's departure. The watchers had reported major quake damage in her lands, and so she was returning to aid her people. Wulfston's lands had hardly been touched; he was staying in Zendi. Lenardo Read that although he was still puzzled, Helmuth accepted the fact that Wulfston was acting as regent for Lenardo.

//''Regent?'' ''Lord Lenardo?''// Portia questioned indignantly.

//It is a shame,// he replied. //The old man was my friend; the people trusted me. The Lords Adept will keep up the charade only as long as it suits their plans. Even if there were Readers there, Lords Adept cannot be Read.//

//But why do they call you lord?// Torio wanted to know.

//Wulfston and Aradia were my allies. I thought them my friends.// He let his painful disillusionment show, knowing that Portia might otherwise suspect that he had returned as a spy. //In the savage lands there is no ranking of powers, no testing except in combat. Anyone who has extraordinary powers is a lord out there.//

To his surprise and relief, Portia did not question further. They withdrew to Tiberium: Lenardo, Clement, and Torio in Clement's room, and Portia on the other side of the city, in the female Academy.

//I will call a session of the Council,// she told them. //Meanwhile, Lenardo, do not advertise your presence.//

//I don't intend to. What about my daughter?//

//Bring her to me now. I would examine this savage child personally, lest our communication provoke curiosity.//

Lenardo knew where the female Academy was, but he had never been inside it. No male Reader dared enter its doors unless or until he had failed to achieve one of the two top ranks. He took Julia to the entrance and awaited instructions. His situation was unique in his experience, and so he did not know protocol.

Lenardo had not supervised Julia's packing, but the child had done a good job of choosing practical traveling clothes. He had, though, told her to bring everything precious to her, and she had brought the yellow dress she had worn the day of the festival. She wore it now, with the golden fillet across her brow that proclaimed her his daughter . . . and knowing that he was going to leave her at the Academy, never to see her again, he hadn't the heart to make her take it off.

//Bring the child in to me,// Portia instructed.

Lenardo quelled the sickness that swept through him. Portia would allow him into her presence. That meant that despite all he had shown her, she not only did not recognize him as a Master Reader, she considered him failed and insignificant. *I accepted it when I decided to seduce Aradia. But it still hurts.*

He guided Julia through the entrance hall, where she

looked around, wide-eyed. Here there were not only mosaics decorating the floors and walls but statues in the niches, richly carved and gilded furnishings, and magnificent tapestries lit by the skylights.

Lenardo had been in male Academies at various times, had spent a year in the huge hospital complex at Gaeta, but never had he seen such luxury lavished on Readers. Possessions were supposed to be foreign to them. In return for their services, Readers were provided with all necessities and comforts. But this?

He led Julia through more treasured halls, where girls of various ages passed them without question, though with curious stares at Julia. They knew well enough why a father would bring his daughter here and wondered whether she would be admitted to the Academy.

They passed classrooms where afternoon lessons were in progress, walked through a courtyard blooming with a profusion of flowers, and finally came to Portia's study.

Portia was sitting behind an ornate desk, dressed in cloth-of-gold with a gold tissue stole. For any public appearance, a female Master Reader would have worn a white linen dress edged in black and the same scarlet robe Lenardo had once worn. What she wore in private was her own business . . . but cloth-of-gold?

She is our liaison with the government, Lenardo reminded himself. *Senators, even the Emperor himself, may visit here at any time. Perhaps she deliberately meets them on their own terms.*

Portia raised her head as they entered, and Julia took a step back as if to hide but instantly refused to allow herself to be frightened. *It's just an old woman,* he caught her thinking.

Lenardo knew that Portia was old, but from her vigorous mind he had never envisioned her as the emblem of age itself. He had never, in the many times they had touched minds, Read her appearance.

She was so old as to be shrunken. Even her skin was no longer wrinkled but pulled in on itself like parchment, desiccated. In startling contrast to her rich raiment, her face appeared a skull, her eyes the only points of life deep within dark sockets, her mouth a slash, her lips colorless, bloodless. Wisps of white hair showed beneath the golden stole. Her hands were folded before her on the desk, knobbed, bony, painfully thin and yet strong. Control of every Reader in the Aventine Empire lay in those hands.

"Lenardo," she said, looking him up and down, and for a moment he was uncomfortable, knowing that his beard, the longer hairstyle he had adopted to fit his role as a savage lord, appeared unkempt here.

He had not felt out of place in this city wearing a plain white tunic in the street. He had dressed this way in Zendi all summer. But now he was forcefully reminded that he was not dressed as a Reader, that he no longer had the right to wear even a magister's robes. From now on he would dress as an ordinary Aventine citizen, although a badge would identify him as a minor Reader—a failed Reader—to those who might seek his services.

Then Portia said, not hiding her disgust, "You look like a savage." Her voice rasped, as bloodless as the rest of her, a startling contrast to the strong, pleasantly feminine "voice" she projected to other Readers.

Julia bristled. "My father's a great lord. His powers make him great. He don't have to dress up to impress nobody."

"Julia, hush!" Lenardo turned to Portia apologetically. "Please forgive the child, Master Portia. Her upbringing—"

"What else is to be expected?" The old woman dismissed him and fixed her eyes on Julia. //Lenardo says you are a Reader.//

//You don't have to shout. I'm not a baby,// Julia responded indignantly and powerfully. They all felt the shock ricochet through several nearby Readers.

//Very well.// Portia assumed normal conversational intensity. //Tell me what is in the cabinet beside the door.//

Once more she looked at Lenardo as if warning him not to help the child, but Julia needed no help. She had far more experience at Reading inanimate objects than any child her age got in an Academy.

//Top shelf. A wooden box, gold decorations. Inside it a

bronze coin, three gold bracelets, amber beads. Then there's a silver cup with pearls.//

She continued spinning off items as Lenardo stood smugly enjoying Portia's astonishment. It would have been quite satisfactory for a Reader of Julia's age to identify shapes: box, cup, globe.

Portia probed for Julia's limits, easily finding them, of course—but the child was far advanced for her age. Lenardo was quite certain that Portia would give her a place here rather than send her to one of the lesser Academics.

"Lenardo," said Portia, "leave us. I would interview this child privately. Wait outside," she added, and he wondered if that was meant to reassure Julia.

"Be honest with Master Portia," he told the girl, "and do whatever she tells you."

He forced himself to smile, and he left the room convinced that he would never see Julia again except perhaps to say good-bye.

As he walked aimlessly down the hallway, it occurred to Lenardo that he had not disclosed to either Portia or Clement his ability to eavesdrop on other Readers without being noticed. He could Read Portia and Julia now, but he would not. To control his consuming curiosity, he sought something else to concentrate on and wandered out into the courtyard. Sitting down on the edge of the fountain, he took off his left sandal and rubbed his injured ankle. It was aching slightly after the walking he had done today, but, he Read, there was no new damage. Strange how quickly it was healing. He hadn't expected to walk easily for a week.

His mind went back to Julia as he refastened his sandal. Determinedly, he turned his thoughts in another direction, anything to stop worrying and avoid the temptation to Read her. Firmly, he cut off Reading and moved to a bench in the shade of an arbor thickly overgrown with blossoming vines. Not Reading, he found his other senses reaching out, appreciating the golden sunlight on the mottled green of the plants, the scent of flowers, the cool shade, the refreshing sound of the fountain, and the delicate hum of women's voices.

One voice in particular almost sang with happiness. "I can't believe I'm really going to have a baby at last."

"Yes, yes, my dear." The calm tones of a healer. "Just follow the diet I've given you and come back in a month to let me Read you again."

The two women were walking down the hall behind where Lenardo sat, the healer escorting her nonReader patient through the maze of hallways. "We've been trying so hard to have a child, and when my flux began yesterday—"

"Ah, but it stopped again," replied the healer. "That happens sometimes. Everything is perfectly normal, Celia. Stop worrying and tell your husband the happy news."

They parted, with Celia going on her way and the healer walking back along the hallway, still not noticing Lenardo. He felt a wistful envy of Celia's happiness. As nonReaders, she and her husband could love their child, raise it to adulthood. The chance that it would be a Reader and be taken from them was so small that it would probably never cross their minds to cloud their joy.

A little girl in a pink dress came into the courtyard from the other side and quickly spotted him. "Are you Lenardo?"

He jumped up. "Yes."

"Master Portia asks you to come to her study."

He Read them long before he got there: Portia behind her desk, a portrait of implacable anger; Julia standing by the door, chin jutted defiantly, arms folded across her chest, clutching something in one hand.

When he entered, Portia said, "I could not contact you."

"I stopped Reading so that I would not intrude on you."

"At least you have not forgotten courtesy yourself, even if you have failed to instill it in your daughter."

He turned to the child. "Julia, what have you done?"

"She insulted you, Father. She said you were corrupt, defiled—"

He knelt down. "Julia, you know I have broken with the Code—"

"Then the Code is wrong. It's wicked! And *she* is wicked. She wants me to break loyalty to my liege lord."

Lenardo fought to remain calm. "Master Portia, you must understand that Julia is trying to cope with a whole new set of values. What she has known all her life—"

"Lenardo," Portia interrupted. "I would know how the child came to consider your her liege lord."

He rose to face her. "I have told you. The title is the only one the savages recognize, given to me because of my Reading powers. I made the error of thinking we could trust some of the Lords Adept, those not intent on destroying us. I was wrong. Instead of killing us, they would use us, which is worse than death. That is why I have returned and taken Julia out of their power."

Portia studied him, and he could feel her attempt to Read how truthful he was. "We shall see. It will take longer than I thought to gather the Council of Masters. We have many obligations, Lenardo. I want to be certain that all the most powerful Readers are present to examine you. Meanwhile, I do not want this child contaminating the girls here. Take her with you. No more harm can be done than has been already. We will decide what to do with her after your fate has been decided."

Leaving Julia with Lenardo meant that he could always be found through the child. He noted the ploy sardonically. If he did want to escape, he had no place to go. And when the Council of Masters examined him under Oath of Truth, they would find that he was no danger to them.

Julia trudged beside Lenardo through the city streets, lost in her own thoughts. Finally she accused him. "You wanted to leave me in that place."

"Julia, I have told you ever since we met that I want you to be properly trained in an Academy. I had hoped it would be Portia's, but it appears she will send you elsewhere."

"Where will you be?"

"Wherever I am assigned. It is hard, Julia, I know, but it is necessary for Readers to be trained in Academies. All the girls you saw or Read today have had to leave their families."

"So they'll forget their loyalties," Julia said through angry tears. "They don't have to kill the parents the way

Lords Adept do when they take a child as apprentice. Here the parents just walk away.''

As your mother did, Lenardo remembered. Ignoring the crowds passing in the busy streets, he knelt and looked into the girl's eyes. ''Julia, I do not want to walk away from you. I love you very much, and I should have told you more. If you can trust me until we get back to the inn, I will explain everything.''

But the explanations rang hollow in Lenardo's own ears. ''The Academy is the only place you can live safely, Julia. I want to keep you, but I cannot. In the savage lands, we are prey to the whims of the Adepts.''

''Not if we learn Adept powers,'' she pointed out.

''That is not possible, Julia, and even if it were, what would it mean? More power struggles, more wars. Haven't you seen enough battles in your short life?''

''Power must be demonstrated,'' she replied. ''You were a great lord, Father. You used your powers for the good of your people. You made allies to protect them from powerful enemies. You took an apprentice so that someone trained in your ways would rule after you.''

''Oh, Julia,'' he whispered, ''can't you see how wrong I was to do all those things?''

''No, but I know why you think so. The Readers' Code is all about not using power. Don't Read to gain wealth. Don't Read to destroy your enemies. Never help yourself, only the government—but a Reader can't be in the government. Father, you say Adepts chain people's minds, but it's *your* mind that's chained—by the Readers' Code. They took you when you were a little boy and made you afraid to use your powers.''

''Julia—''

''You want me to be afraid, too, but I won't be. You want to get rid of me—''

''No!''

''Because you're scared of my powers. Portia's scared of me and of you. You disobeyed her. She's going to kill you for that, Father.''

''Julia, you don't understand. We are not savages here.''

''Portia is. Only she's not honest like Aradia or

Wulfston.'' Julia held out the object she had been clutching ever since they had left Portia's office. ''She gave me this scroll. The Readers' Code. It's new, but it was on Portia's desk. She handled it. Do you want to know its story, Father?''

''No.'' But he was lying, and Julia knew it.

''A senator came in a few days ago. He wanted to know about some merchant ships. He offered Portia money to Read another man for him. She wouldn't do it.''

''You see,'' said Lenardo in relief. ''She wouldn't be bribed.''

''She didn't want money,'' Julia continued. ''She wanted him to vote against building a new Academy for boys.''

''What?''

Julia concentrated, her voice and vocabulary taking on echoes of what she Read. ''Portia is afraid of . . . Master Clement. An old man, respected, honest. She thinks him foolish . . . dangerous. And the boys he has trained. That's your Academy, isn't it, Father?''

''Yes.'' He was too stunned to say more.

''Portia wants the Senate to break up the Academy, retire Master Clement, and distribute the boys among other Academies. The teachers, too. One older boy she fears . . . Torio. She dares not try to win him over, and so she will make him fail his examinations. Father, what is the Sign of the Dark Moon?''

''The badge of failed Readers: a black circle on white.''

Julia frowned. ''I don't understand. When Portia thinks of Torio, she thinks of that and of a saying, 'When the moon devours the sun, the earth will devour Tiberium.' ''

''I don't understand either, child. Perhaps she is becoming confused with age.''

''Father, she already controls more than half the Council of Masters.'' The child's voice took on a weird echo of Portia's. ''By influencing powerful nonReaders, these Masters control the Aventine Empire. It's always been—the Master Readers must control the Senate or the people will destroy them out of fear.''

Julia dropped the scroll on the bedside chest, coming out of her semitrance. The adult pose and language disappeared, and she was a little girl again, helpless and frightened. "You want to give me to that woman. She'll kill me. She'll kill you, Father."

"No, no, Julia." He took her in his arms, trying to reassure her. "I'll never let Portia have you."

It all fit together now: Years ago, when he was tested for the rank of magister, Lenardo had failed Portia's personal test. He had been completely sincere in his adherence to the Reader's Code, just as Master Clement had taught him. So he had been sent back to Adigia, perhaps to die in one of Drakonius' raids but certainly to be kept ignorant of the true power of the Council of Masters. And Portia would never let him on that council.

When he volunteered for exile to stop Galen, Portia had been agreeable, even eager, after Master Clement had elevated Lenardo to Master rank. She had not expected him to return. Julia was right. All Portia had to do was have someone "recognize" Lenardo, reveal his brand, and irate citizens would kill him. Master Clement need never know that it was other than tragic chance.

And when I am dead, what will happen to Julia? The child clung to him. She had no faith left in him, but she also had no one else. He had failed her, failed all his responsibilities, had never wanted any beyond those of a teacher in an Academy. He was not a questioner, and so he had failed Galen, who was.

I don't know what I am. Other people always define me.
Reader. Fate had made him that.

Teacher. Master Clement had encouraged his star pupil to remain in the Academy.

Traitor. Galen's treachery had prompted the plan; Galen's words spoken by Lenardo had sealed his doom.

Exile. Portia's plan to be rid of him, the dragon's-head brand on his arm defining him for all to see.

Lord of the Land. Aradia had made him that.

Father. Julia's idea, not his, but he had accepted it.

I accepted it all, and then I ran away from it all. Failed, even at being an exile, for here I am, home again.

Where Portia had expected him to fail, he hadn't—and one other thing he had not failed at. He was a Reader, the most powerful Reader ever known. Portia had attempted today to define him as a failed Reader by allowing him into her presence. But . . . *I do not accept her definition!*

His powers were the one thing no one else could give or take away, and through them he must get Julia to a place of safety. They had sneaked into the Aventine Empire, and they would sneak out again. Portia would not expect it; she didn't know what Julia had Read in the scroll, and she expected Lenardo to do exactly what he had always done before: whatever she told him. Besides, she thought that he had no place to go.

But I have a land to rule!

Wulfston was alone in Zendi now, still telling people that he was Lenardo's regent. *I'll make him live up to it,* Lenardo thought in sudden glee. *Wulfston's definition, but I'll make it come true. I'll ride into town, thank him in a public ceremony, and politely throw him out.*

Thank the gods, Aradia had gone back to her own land. Lenardo would not have to face her again until he had truly established himself as the lord his people expected. That meant using his powers, not fearing them. If he decided to define himself once and for all as Lord of the Land, he must be prepared openly and honestly to exercise power.

Let the corruption in the Aventine government work until it destroyed itself. Lenardo and his allies would be waiting just beyond the pale, ready to take advantage. There would be no need to attack; Lenardo's powers would tell them the right moment to move in. Aradia, Wulfston, and Lilith would welcome him back on those terms.

Aradia. She had been dishonest with him, but was her drugging him really that much worse than his plan to seduce her, not because he loved her but to blunt her powers? She had not intended to harm him. Her motive had been to conceive a child.

Suddenly what he had overheard at Portia's Academy today flashed into his mind. Celia, the healer's patient, had feared that she was not pregnant because her flux had begun. Aradia—Aradia had assumed the same thing.

Aradia may be carrying my child. Blessed gods, why was I so angry I did not think to Read her to be certain?

He knew what to do now. He could easily Read Castle Nerius from here, contact Aradia, and Read her condition. She had been so positive she was pregnant, terribly disappointed that she was not.

She is. I'm sure she is, and with a child to unite us, we will find a way to work together. She will help me now, once I get out of the empire.

"Julia," Lenardo told the weeping child, hugging her, "I know what to do now. We're going back to Zendi!"

She looked up at him. "Can we?"

"We came all this way, didn't we? We escaped Aradia and Wulfston. We survived an earthquake. What can a few Readers do to us? Now wash your face and go to sleep, because we're going to sneak away in the middle of the night. I'll wake you."

She clung to him, daring tentative hope. "Yes, Father."

Lenardo tucked her into bed, supervising the meditation exercise he had taught her to send her to sleep despite her excitement. Then he Read outward, beyond the city, beyond the pale, to Castle Nerius. There he had first met Aradia, helped to cure her father, and fought in the battle of Adepts. There Aradia had made him a lord.

Bright moonlight flooded the landscape as Lenardo "traveled" in his mind. Strange—from here he ought to "see" the castle towers. Hopeful expectation turned to concern and then to fear. He found the hills, the road, the forest. In a nearby field, the flat rock where they built the funeral pyres lay empty, cold in the pale moonlight.

As he approached the castle, his anxiety increased, and then he saw it, its walls and towers fallen, smoke rising from the remains of the houses that had clustered about its gate. There was no sign of life.

She's dead! By all the gods, I deserted her, and now she's dead, and our child with her!

Chapter Seven

Lenardo's panic subsided slightly as he remembered that he had Read Aradia in Zendi only a few hours before. She could not possibly have reached home yet, could not have been in the castle when it was blasted.

He found her in the rocky hills on the border between their lands, alive but besieged, trying desperately to Read where the blows were coming from that struck all around her. People and horses lay dead, and as Lenardo watched, another thunderbolt roared down just beside Aradia's horse. The horse screamed and reared. She fought it down and turned, constantly moving, zigzagging, for if she stopped, she became an easy target. There was no place to hide.

Her Reading powers could not begin to cover the distance between her and her attackers, until Lenardo Read with her. When his mind touched hers, she gasped.

//Lenardo! Where are you? Oh, Lenardo, I'm so sorry.//

//So am I. Read with me!//

He guided her northward, to where a circle of Adepts surrounded a Reader relaying instructions to them. //Get the Reader,// Lenardo instructed, but to project to Aradia, he projected to the renegade Reader as well. Aradia went blank to Reading to exercise her Adept power, and the thunderbolt she cast sizzled through the ground where he had been a moment before.

"It's Lenardo," the Reader told his Adept cohorts. "Even with him to guide her, Aradia's only one against four. Keep moving!"

The Reader . . . was Galen.

//But he's dead,// said Aradia.

//We never found his body,// Lenardo reminded her.

171

//And I've fought one of those Adepts before: Hron. He and Galen must have survived the battle last spring. Never mind. Ride for Zendi while I distract them.//

//Is that where you are?//

//No, but I'll be there as soon as I can. Ride!//

Lenardo could sense that Galen was equally confused, Reading what Lenardo projected but unable to find him physically to give the Adepts a target. They would return to trying to kill Aradia unless he could distract them somehow. An idea formed slowly, a deception through Reading. Was it possible?

As Aradia and her train galloped off toward Zendi, Lenardo deliberately did not Read them but instead tried imagining them moving at a slightly different angle, imagined himself galloping with them. A sheet of flame scorched the air just in front of his imaginary horse. He resisted the urge to "ride" through it and instead imagined himself almost being thrown, fighting the animal back under control, and continuing toward where he wanted the Adepts to think Aradia was. He had to make them waste energy. Then they would have to spend hours in the Adepts' deep recuperative sleep, allowing him time to reach Zendi.

It's a three-day journey.

No, by the gods, I'll ride night and day, stealing fresh horses as I need them!

He could not think further. He was too busy making Galen think that he was with Aradia's train, ducking thunderbolts and sheets of flame, telling Aradia's false image truthfully, "We're almost out of Galen's range."

As he hoped, that brought a renewed volley of wasted shots. He envisioned a supply wagon going up in flames, the driver leaping for safety while the screaming horses dashed in panic, spreading sparks through the night. All the while Lenardo could clearly sense Galen Reading him, urging the Adepts to kill him while trying to make sense of the shifting perceptions. Had Galen never learned to leave his body? If he had, he declined to use the ability now, as Lenardo galloped his phantom retinue out of range of Galen's abilities.

It was a lesser range than the boy had had last spring.

He had Read farther both at the battle at Adigia and at the battle near Castle Nerius. Perhaps Galen was ill or not fully recovered from the injuries he had sustained in that last battle.

When he felt contact with Galen fade, Lenardo let his imaginary train of riders fade as well and, in the same state of heightened awareness in which he had eavesdropped on the Master Readers without their sensing him, sought out Galen and the circle of Lords Adept. There were four Adepts with the Reader, one of them Hron, Aradia's former ally who had betrayed her to join forces with Drakonius.

The other three Lenardo did not know: a man and two women, tired and annoyed that their plan to pick off Aradia and her allies one at a time was not working.

"Lenardo was supposed to be in Zendi," Hron was saying threateningly to Galen. "What was he doing with Aradia? We would have had her without his help. Now she'll join with her brother and the Reader in Zendi."

"We must go north and take Lilith," said one of the women.

"Marava is right," the other man said. "If we proceed to Zendi, we could be trapped between Lenardo's forces there and Lilith's to the north."

Lenardo recognized their plan. They had circled far to the east and come to Aradia's land from that direction, thinking to take the strongest Adept first in a sneak attack, four against one.

And the earthquake—not a direct attack this time, but Julia had been right. It *was* set off by the Adepts, to throw Aradia's land into confusion to keep her watchers from noticing a party of four moving toward Castle Nerius.

The Adepts were preparing a message in their own watcher's Code. Would they flash visible signals through Aradia's land even if no one there could interpret them? Their combined army was gathered north of Lilith's border, waiting for the signal to attack. The Adepts would sleep, renewing their strength, but meanwhile their army was to breach Lilith's borders in a surprise attack. By the time she could call her troops into action, the Adepts would be at full strength again—and in concert with their army they could move freely, give chase if by some chance she should escape. Although pinned between an army to the north and a circle of Adepts to the south, there was little hope for Lilith.

If only there were more Readers in my land, Lenardo thought desperately. But there was no one to whom to relay the message except Aradia. She would have to warn Lilith any way she could.

Lenardo Read, fascinated as Hron, Marava, and the others worded their message, unpacking and consuming as they did so one of those tremendous meals Adepts ate. It no longer surprised Lenardo; he had frequently seen the slender, delicate Aradia consume a meal worthy of three men who had worked in the fields all day.

Meal and message complete, the four Adepts sat down on the ground, arms extended and hands clasped to form a literal circle.

"Galen," said Hron, "is our army in position as agreed? The lantern in place?"

"You know I can't Read that far," Galen said sullenly. "If you had—"

"Help us win this battle," Hron said, "and I will heal you completely."

Lenardo had not been Reading Galen physically, but he would have noticed if the boy were in pain. Now he Read visually.

He would never have recognized Galen by sight. He was hideously disfigured from the burns he had received in the battle of Adepts last spring. Hron, Lenardo noted, was unscarred, with only his short hair and beard attesting to the fact that they had been burned away four months ago.

Both Hron and Galen must have been horribly burned. Lenardo had been convinced that no one had survived the fire in the canyon. Only Adept powers could have saved these two when they somehow escaped alive.

It was easy enough to guess what Hron had done. Although he had applied his powers to his own complete recovery, all he had done for Galen was to keep him alive, letting his burns heal as they would. His skin was a mass of scar tissue, his face a mockery, with holes for eyes, nose, and mouth in an otherwise shapeless blob. His hands were stiffened into claws. He could move and walk without pain but also without the ease necessary to effect an escape, and his horrible appearance would mark him wherever he might go.

Sick at heart, Lenardo was reminded of the legends of the founding of the Aventine Empire, when Readers were just developing their powers. The first Emperor was reputed to have gained the throne with the aid of a Reader whom he lamed so that the man could not run away.

If Hron had the power to heal himself, he could have healed Galen, but he didn't trust him. Perhaps he never would, but by dangling the promise of being fully healed before Galen, he would make the Reader perform as desired.

Lenardo watched the Adepts concentrate, chanting in unison the rhythm of the code they were transmitting. To the north of Lilith's land, soldiers kept watch by a lantern. When the flame began to dance rhythmically, they quickly called their commander.

The message was repeated several times. Then the commander began to mobilize his troops while the four Adepts fell into deep recuperative sleep.

Lenardo returned his attention to Aradia. //You drew them away,// she said. //How, Lenardo?//

//I used Reading to fool Galen. The Masters who taught me would disapprove, but it worked. Aradia, you must get word to Lilith. There is an army moving against her from the north, to trap her between them and the circle of Adepts.//

//The watchers will send the message, and I'll send riders as well. She and her son must join me in Zendi. And you, Lenardo—//

//I will be there as quickly as I can. Hurry, now. You and Wulfston join the minor Adepts you've been training. You can equal the four Adepts attacking.//

He had withdrawn his attention back to where he was, at the inn in Tiberium, before he remembered that he had intended to Read whether Aradia was pregnant. Julia was still sleeping peacefully. A few more minutes—

First he Read the immediate area of the inn, a superficial scan. Of course, no one was coming after them here.

It was almost midnight. Downstairs, the landlord had barred the door for the night. Most of the guests were asleep. A couple of revelers walked laughing down the street outside toward a discreet house of prostitution a small distance away.

And then Lenardo Read another figure moving swiftly through the night, as surefooted as most men walked at noon. Torio! He was Reading only his way, projecting nothing, but it was obvious he was headed straight for the inn.

Lenardo didn't want the boy pounding on the door and rousing the household. He slipped quietly out of his room and down the stairs. No one was stirring. Lenardo unbarred the door for Torio and then barred it again.

//What are you doing here?//

"Don't Read," Torio whispered. "I tried to come undetected. Take me up to your room."

He took Lenardo's arm, willing to be led blindly through the inn rather than risk notice by Reading further. What could he possibly fear that much?

"You can't come into my room," Lenardo reminded him. "My daughter is there. A female Reader."

"It doesn't matter," Torio said, his voice choked with tears. "They've failed me, so it doesn't matter anymore."

"Failed?"

"Shh! Master Lenardo, it has to do with you. Please, let's go where we can't be overheard."

Lenardo led Torio up the stairs and into his room, installing him in the single chair.

"Now what is this about failing you?"

"It's true." Torio's milky eyes drifted, unfocused, when he was not Reading. Tears slid down his cheeks as he continued. "After I made sure all the younger boys were asleep, I went to Master Clement's room to find out what he had heard from you. While I was there, Portia contacted us. She said—" his voice broke again "she said my conduct in not reporting that you contacted me last week was a breach of the Code. She said I'm unfit to teach and that my skills are not up to the standards required to continue training.''

"That's a lie," Lenardo said angrily. "Torio, your skills are far beyond what mine were at your age, and I was passed without question."

"Master Clement tried to reason with her, but she says it's settled. I've been failed. Tomorrow—"

"Yes, Torio? What about tomorrow?"

"Master, they won't let me have medical training or serve with the army or anything. Portia told me to report to her at noon tomorrow . . . to meet my wife." He struck away his tears angrily, but there was a wealth of despair behind the gesture. "Master Lenardo, what am I going to do?"

"You're not going to report to Portia, that's certain. And you're not getting married, unless some day you want to."

"I'll never—"

"Don't say never, Torio. I plan to get married as soon as I get home and reclaim my land."

"Home? *Your* land?"

"That's right. A land where no one but a Reader himself decides what he can or cannot do. Where Readers and Adepts share their powers for the good of all."

"That's not possible," the boy said.

"Would you like it to be?"

A pause. Then, "Oh, Master Lenardo, if only it could be."

"It can be, Torio, but only if we make it so. Come with me. We need Readers desperately. Poor Julia's been carrying a full work load at her age."

At the mention of her name, Julia woke up, squirming and rubbing her eyes. Then she stared at Torio. "I know you. I've seen you in Father's mind. You were there when he got the wolf-stone. Torio."

"That's right," the boy replied, resisting the urge to Read the child. "And you are Julia. Master Lenardo has told me about you."

"Torio is going home with us, Julia," said Lenardo.

"Get dressed now. We must be well out of the city before dawn."

"My horse is stabled near the Academy," said Torio, "and I must get my sword and some clothes."

"Bring two horses," said Lenardo. "Master Clement won't set the guard on you. Julia and I rode double from the border, but now we've got to ride hard. My friends are under attack."

"What?" Julia demanded, wide-eyed. "Why did you let me sleep? Why are you talking? Let's go."

"We mustn't arouse suspicion." Lenardo handed the girl a coin. "Go down to the pantry and pack food for three people, and leave this on the shelf for it. Meet me in the innyard. I'll get the horse. Torio, fast as you can, meet us at—"

Of the three, only Lenardo was Reading, and so only he reacted to Master Clement's, //Lenardo!//

"Torio, Julia! Read," he instructed aloud.

//Yes, Master?//

//Torio is with you. Good. I'd hoped that was where you had gone, son. You must flee at once. At dawn the soldiers of the guard will be there to arrest you, Lenardo.//

//What?// Torio gasped.

Lenardo, though, was not surprised.

//Portia has denounced you as a traitor.//

//Master, they'll know you've warned me, and you will be arrested,// said Lenardo. //Come with us.//

//No, Lenardo, I have work here.//

//Master, there is corruption in the Council of Masters. You're not safe—// Lenardo began.

//Son, I am not so foolish as Portia thinks, but as long as she considers me a harmless old man, I can work toward returning the Council of Masters to the body it was meant to be. Since I came here to Tiberium, I have seen many things that sadden me, but I am not alone. Not all the Masters are corrupt, only those in Portia's special circle.//

//But if they find out you've warned me—//

//Torio warned you, not I. They'll believe that easily enough, without Oath of Truth. Now go, all of you. And may the gods protect you.//

They felt the warmth of the old man's caring, and then he stopped Reading. There was a moment of bitter silence. Then Torio said, "I can't go back."

Lenardo realized that the boy knew already what he himself had taken until now to absorb, but he deliberately took the words as applying to their immediate situation. "No, so we'll have to steal horses from two other guests. Come on!"

"Father," said Julia, not at all disapprovingly, "you've told me it's wrong to steal."

"It is. We'll just borrow the horses, Julia, and return them if we ever get the opportunity."

She laughed. "You're thinking like a savage, Father."

"That's what I am, Daughter, and so are you. And we'll have to teach Torio to be one, too."

By this time they had packed their meager belongings. "Go ahead and Read, both of you," said Lenardo. "No one will be looking for us till dawn."

They crept easily through the sleeping inn, and Julia slipped into the pantry for food while Torio and Lenardo went to the stables. The horse he and Julia had ridden was still tired, and so he chose another that was fresh and eager and two more like it. The stableboy had gone home when the inn closed, and the porter at the innyard gate was deep in drunken slumber, not stirring even when the horses' hooves clattered on the cobbles.

A sword hung on the wall near where the porter slept. The blade was rusty; it had obviously not been used for years. But after pondering a moment, Torio tiptoed past the porter and took it down.

//Better than nothing, though not *much* better.//

//Take mine,// said Lenardo, //and give me that one. Go on. You're the better swordsman, just as I'm the better Reader.//

//Yes, Master.//

Just then Lenardo felt something: Portia Reading them. //We're found out. Off we go.//

Lenardo ran to the open gates as Julia dashed out of the inn. Torio lifted the girl onto her horse and mounted his own as the porter woke with a snort, saw them, and shouted, "Ho! Stop, thief!"

The man tried to leap on Lenardo, but he was clumsy and still half drunk. Lenardo shoved him back, running to his own horse as Torio and Julia galloped out. The horse was fresh and nervous and didn't know Lenardo. It danced away as he tried to mount, and the porter was on him again. He turned and slugged the man, the kind of punch he hadn't thrown since boyhood fights. With a man's strength behind it, it sent the porter reeling long enough for Lenardo to swing into the saddle and escape.

Behind him, the porter shouted, "Thieves! Thieves! Horse thieves!" and began to pound on a bucket hanging on the wall. People woke and ran from their rooms, but Lenardo and his entourage were already out the gate.

Wakened by the clamor, people looked out of nearby windows, but none ventured into the street as the three Readers rode for the north gate of Tiberium. The city had outgrown its ancient walls centuries ago. Deep and safe within the empire, it did not close its gates at night, nor were they guarded.

The broad street, however, narrowed at the old gate, and Lenardo Read a troop of guardsmen from a garrison outside the old walls marching to intercept them there. They were guided by a Reader, a young man of Torio's age named Meleus.

Torio could Read for himself over that distance, while Julia was Reading with Lenardo. Twenty trained guardsmen against two men and a child.

Torio grasped his sword, ready to go down fighting as the guards marched through the gate and moved unrelentingly toward them. Julia pulled from her pack a sharp butcher's knife; the savage child had armed herself on her trip through the kitchen.

But it was no use. They could not fight twenty guardsmen, nor could they hide from the Reader.

Lenardo recalled the way he had fooled Galen, but Julia and Torio didn't know about that. "Julia, Torio," he said sharply. Pointing straight ahead, he said, "Follow me, and pay no attention to what you Read."

"I can't—" Torio began.

"Read your surroundings, not me," Lenardo explained hastily, sensing Meleus trying to Read their discussion. They would soon be within his range to do so. "*Not me,*" he repeated, and then projected intensely. //Guards ahead. Split up and spread out. We've got to lose them.//

To his relief, the two young Readers, although thoroughly confused, continued to follow him along the broad street. Lenardo projected kicking his horse's flanks and darting into a side street with Julia at his side, while Torio galloped off in the opposite direction.

"They've Read us," he Read Meleus reporting to the guards. "Lenardo has turned into Mill Street, Torio into Cobbler's Lane."

Lenardo caught Julia's delight at this new game, and Torio's horror. To deliberately confound a fellow Reader— But then Torio remembered what he was leaving behind and grimly withheld his protest.

Unfortunately, Lenardo was not familiar with the tangled side streets of Tiberium and quickly discovered that he had sent his phantom Torio into a cul-de-sac. Meleus knew that and was sending some of the guards down the main street to the entrance to Cobbler's Lane while he led the rest in a path that would intercept the images of Julia and Lenardo.

That left the gate ahead unguarded, but six armed men were headed straight toward them, while Lenardo had to keep up the images of himself and Julia in the twisted lanes to draw Meleus and other guards away from where they really where.

Torio recognized Lenardo's dilemma, pointed Julia into another side street, and followed himself as soon as he was sure that Lenardo saw what they must do: hide out of sight until the guards passed them and turned into Cobbler's Lane.

The guards went by at a run, expecting Torio either to charge out of the lane again, having discovered his error, or lie in wait for them, having Read their approach. These were nonReaders. Lenardo could project nothing to fool them, and so he abandoned the false image of Torio while he concentrated on keeping Meleus and the rest of the guards chasing the phantom Lenardo and Julia through the winding streets.

"Come on," Torio shouted, and urged his horse out into the street. Lenardo and Julia followed, galloping for the unguarded gate.

They clattered through, their cloaks billowing with the wind of freedom as they streaked along the main road out of town. Lenardo, meanwhile, led Meleus and his men into a blind alley, where Meleus "saw"—and the guards did not—the images of Lenardo and Julia. Then they disappeared before the young Reader's astonished eyes, and he cried, "Sorcery! The traitor has learned the savage sorcery!"

Julia, Reading with Lenardo, laughed out loud in delight. //That's the way to use your powers, Father.//

And Meleus had them pinpointed again. "They've escaped. They're outside the walls!" //Relay! Relay! Escaped traitors on the Northern Way.//

Instantly, another Reader on the outskirts of town asked, //Who? What did they do?//

Meleus explained, and the message was sent on to a Reader in a small village beyond, and so on up the road. Within the hour, it would reach Adigia, but Lenardo and his entourage could not hope to be there until well after noon, even riding hard with fresh horses every few miles.

"We're trapped," said Torio.

"We weren't trapped in Tiberium, and we won't be now," Lenardo replied. "Torio, interfere with that message."

"What?"

Julia understood at once. "Send a false message."

"Lie through Reading? My Oath—"

"Your Oath binds you to protect your fellow Readers," Lenardo reminded him. "Is Portia your fellow now? Are her corrupt circle your fellows? Or Master Clement, Julia, I?"

"I don't know!" Torio answered wretchedly. "We're not supposed to turn against each other."

"I know, you don't know whether to trust *me* now. But surely you trust Master Clement. He wants you safely out of the empire, Torio."

"Yes." But the boy was still uncertain.

"They'll kill us if they catch us," Lenardo reminded him. "Stay alive to see what life is like outside the pale, and then make your decision."

"All right. I'll distract the relays."

A short distance ahead of them, a sleepy Reader brought suddenly awake was seeking to gain the attention of the next link in the relay system, a woman coping with her teething child. The child's pain was making her own teeth ache as she held and rocked him. Her husband slept as only someone who had worked hard all day after keeping vigil himself the night before could have, despite the child's screams.

//Della,// projected the Reader trying to get his message through. //Della, put the child down or wake your husband. You must relay a message!// But nothing could penetrate Della's concern and frustration with her baby.

Torio was a much better Reader than either Della or the man trying to contact her. It was easy for him to Read beyond Della the mile or so to the next relay, another lesser Reader dutifully awake and Reading, easily located when so few minds were alert and active.

//Relay,// Torio announced, and the Reader, a man in his fifties, sat up with interest. //Traitors,// Torio told him. //They left Tiberium by the Northern Way, then turned off cross-country. They should pass to the east of your location. Keep a sharp watch and relay when you Read them.//

//When? Who? How many?//

Lenardo dared not interrupt, but Torio had the sense not to embroider his lie too elaborately. //Three: two men and a girl. The guard is after them. Keep a sharp lookout for the next hour to the east.//

//Where's Della?// the man asked suspiciously.

//Her baby's sick. We're having to skip over her tonight. Relay both ways if you spot the traitors.// He broke contact.

//Very good,// Lenardo told him. //Close enough to the truth to be thought an honest mistake caused by an overextended relay link.//

For almost an hour, they were able to keep ahead of the

relays, planting false messages and distracting the attention of these minor Readers from their true path. It was alarmingly easy until they approached Villa Blanca, a small city that housed a female Academy. Here there was a direct relay link with Tiberium, and they found the accurate message being transmitted to one of the teachers there.

//A different message has already come through here from Cassius,// she reported. //The traitors left the road just north of Tiberium, riding cross-country to the northeast. If they continued in that direction, they should pass far to the east of here.//

//What? No such message was relayed back to us. Read around you, Magister.//

They were on the open road, close to the city. There was no hope of escaping the Reader's scan. This time they split up in reality as the city guard came pouring out of Southgate on horseback. Torio rode west, Lenardo and Julia east. The guards had no Readers among them; they could not be misled by false images, but they also could not Read exactly where their quarry were.

Villa Blanca was a small city, completely contained behind its walls, and at night only nine men guarded it: two at each gate (for it had gates only at the north and south) and five others prepared for any disturbance. Those five now sought the three fugitives, riding on either side of the road to intercept them.

There were no buildings outside the walls, nothing to hide in. The moon threw long shadows of the moving riders. As three guards bore down on him and Julia, Lenardo had to let Torio take care of himself. They could not hope to outrun the guardsmen's fresh horses.

As they approached, the guards flung their spears, but neither Reader had the least trouble ducking them. Then, swords drawn, they closed. Lenardo held one off with the rusty blade from the inn, while Julia, counting on a grown man's reluctance to harm a child, pulled her horse between his and the guard attempting to attack from the other side.

Reading gave Lenardo the advantage of knowing his adversary's moves before they were made. He got a quick thrust in under the first guard's lifted arm, withdrew the blade, and turned to the second while Julia continued to cover his back. The guard on her side gave a vicious slap to her horse's flank, but the child clung to the reins and retained command of the tired animal, keeping it between the soldier and Lenardo.

//Good girl,// he told her, but just then the wounded guardsman came up beside Lenardo's horse and jabbed it with his sword. The animal screamed and reared, unseating Lenardo. His rusty sword hit the hard ground and broke.

He scrambled to his feet, facing three mounted men. Grasping the wounded man's arm when he tried to thrust again, Lenardo attempted to unseat him. Pain shot down the man's arm, and he dropped his sword. Lenardo retrieved it, Reading that this guard was close to fainting and no danger now. But the other two were on him, one slashing from his horse, the other dismounting to face him on foot, the two in perfect concert, attacking him on both levels.

The man on foot was a fine swordsman. Lenardo parried his thrusts but was relentlessly driven toward a position where the mounted guard could get in a crippling blow. He tried to draw the swordsman away, but the other fought his horse into position again.

//Julia, if they take me, flee. Take Torio home to Zendi.//

No answer, but the child was Reading him and the guards. The wounded man had passed out. It was only two on one. *I've met such odds before.*

But he had rarely met such an expert swordsman as the one driving him back, and his foreknowledge of the moves was little help against the skill with which they were executed. He thrust and slashed, trying to keep from being driven like a sheep by a dog. But the aggression was too tiring, and he couldn't keep it up. The horseman was in position behind him, sword ready. Lenardo could not maneuver away.

The horseman screamed as Julia, with every bit of strength in her small body, sank her butcher knife between his ribs.

The man on the ground looked up in astonishment, and

in that moment of distraction, Lenardo lunged and skewered him. He sank back, doubly surprised, and fell.

Lenardo turned to Julia, who slid off her horse into his arms, trembling but refusing to cry. "Oh, Julia," he whispered into her hair, "you shouldn't have to do such things. You saved my life again, Daughter."

There was no time, though, for thought or recovery. They Read for Torio and found him just dispatching the second of his pursuers.

//Take the best horse,// Lenardo instructed him as he and Julia took the two best of the three fresh animals the guards had inadvertently provided them and once more galloped off into the night.

Lenardo had not expected to leave a trail of dead and wounded, certainly not provincial guardsmen doing their duty without even knowing what the fight was about.

//They're our enemies,// Julia said as if in answer to his thought. He realized that she was working it out in her own mind. Savage she might be, but she had never before deliberately killed someone. //They're just like those men who tried to sneak in and kill you that time, Father. You were a Reader, so they wanted to kill you. Here we're savages, so they all want to kill us. What can we do but kill them instead?//

//Nothing here, Julia. All we can do is hope to change things in our own land so that people won't go on killing one another.//

Torio kept his thoughts to himself but rode steadily beside them. The teacher from the Academy at Villa Blanca relayed the message ahead of them again, and the next step after that was Adigia.

//Master Lenardo,// Torio suddenly broke his mental silence, //can you Read from here to Adigia?//

//Yes.//

//Who's on relay duty?//

Lenardo took his attention from their immediate surroundings, knowing that Torio was quite adequate to prevent their riding into ambush, and Read far ahead to the town where he had grown up.

A sturdy wooden tower had already replaced the stone

one that had fallen in the earthquake, and there above the gate, two guards stretched and yawned, facing the hardest part of their watch, just before dawn. With them was the man Lenardo had Read a few days ago. He didn't even know his name.

Even as he Read, the message that there were fugitives headed their direction was relayed to the Reader. Instantly alert, he told the guards. The alarm was sounded, and the garrison was roused.

Lenardo removed his attention, letting Torio and Julia Read what he had seen. "Now what do we do? We can't fight the whole garrison."

"We'll have to go back to that place where we came through the wall," said Julia.

Lenardo turned his attention there, only to find a troop of soldiers headed in that direction to block them. *Why did I have to show that to Portia?*

"Then it must be Adigia," said Torio. "All three Readers there know me, and the relays are not reporting my name." Lenardo realized that that was true and wondered whether Master Clement had anything to do with the omission. Torio continued, "When we get close enough, I'll make contact and try to bluff our way through."

"How?" asked Julia.

"I don't know," Torio replied in frustration. "Be quiet and let me think."

They were fortunate to be able to steal horses from a pasture just after dawn, although it delayed them while they changed the saddles to the new horses. Then they drank at a stream and rode on while they ate bread and cheese, knowing that they were riding straight into ambush but not knowing what to do about it.

Lenardo Read over the obstacle ahead, to Zendi, and his heart sank. Aradia had managed to get back there, but the city was under siege. Aradia and Wulfston were atop the Northgate tower, with a young boy whom Lenardo did not recognize but who was unReadable and thus apparently Adept. All three were peering into the melee of fighting outside the walls, obviously trying to figure out where to direct their powers. Aradia made no attempt to Read, and so Lenardo could not contact her, could not tell her that the group of Adepts she sought was circling to the east and that Galen was directing them to join forces to throw all their blows at the top of the tower.

Quickly, Lenardo superimposed over the true picture Galen was Reading his own version, in which Wulfston shouted, "They're going to spot us soon. Let's get down from here!"

"Keep moving," his phantom Aradia agreed, and started for the tower stair. As Lenardo carefully Read the strange boy, who seemed vaguely familiar, he noticed the symbol of the blue lion woven into his tunic. Was this Lilith's son? And where was Lilith?

He had no time to ponder, for he was too busy making Galen think his quarry on the move, making the Adepts cast their thunderbolts futilely into the street near the Northgate tower. As the strikes made a pattern in the street below them, the real Aradia and Wulfston turned to look in surprise and then stared at each other.

"Lenardo?" Aradia said in disbelief, and opened to Reading—very weakly. She had been using her Adept powers, weakening her body and thus impairing her Reading ability. It took all of Lenardo's strength to contact her.

//Get off the tower and keep moving. Galen is close enough to pinpoint you. I'm on my way, but it will be hours yet. Stay alive, Aradia. I'm coming!//

Then he projected exactly where Galen and the circle of Adepts were. But even as Aradia was telling Wulfston and the boy, it was too late. Galen could not help but Read everything Lenardo projected strongly enough for Aradia.

"Master Lenardo!" Torio tugged at the bridle of his horse, bringing him back to the fields they were riding through. "We're not going to be able to help them if we don't get out of the empire," the boy said, and Lenardo realized that when he had begun to project strongly, Torio could not help Reading it, either.

Julia, though, was not Reading. She was struggling to stay awake and in her saddle, which was not suited to a child of her size.

"Come here, Daughter," said Lenardo, and lifted her

onto his horse before him. "There, now, sleep while you can. We'll need your help later."

With Torio he Read all around them, but it seemed that the attempts at ambush along the way had stopped. They were assumed to be trying to leave the empire, and all exits were blocked by empire troops. Lenardo Read that even far to the west, at the seaports, armed guards were watching the gangplank of every vessel.

But for the time being they rode swiftly, with Julia so tired that she slept despite the rough ride. And then they were within Torio's range of Adigia.

By this time, Secundus was on duty with the soldiers. "That's good," said Torio. "He thinks I'm still a little kid with skinned knees. He'd never dream I'm one of the fugitives the army is after."

//Secundus,// Torio projected.

//Torio. What are you doing in the relay, son?//

//I'm not. I'm on my way to Adigia. Master Clement sent me.// Truth, so far as it went.

//Why?//

//Because Master Lenardo was a friend of mine. Portia wants him alive. Perhaps I can persuade him to give himself up.//

A sad sigh. //Aye, son, I hope you can. Lenardo a traitor. I never understood it, from his day of exile.//

//You haven't located him?// Torio asked.

//No, not yet. Come join me on the tower, Torio. You're a better Reader than I am. Perhaps you can help find him.//

//I'll be there in a few minutes.// Torio stopped Reading and said to Lenardo, "So your name came through the relays, but not mine. I'll ride on ahead and join Secundus on the tower. Somehow I'll have the gates open by the time you get there."

"Torio."

The young Reader turned his face toward Lenardo but could not "look" at him because he was not Reading. "I know," he said. "I'll be careful. Use that trick you have of Reading without being Read, and choose the right moment."

"I will."

Then Torio rode on, Reading only ahead of him, not behind. He rode openly through the streets of the city, greeted by everyone who saw him. Lenardo Read no suspicion. Everyone knew that something was afoot, and so the arrival of a better Reader than their three regulars was no surprise.

Alerted by Secundus, the tower guards were waiting to take Torio's horse and let him mount the tower, where he had access to the pulley system that drew up the immense bar holding the well-fortified gates in place. But there were two guards in the gate tower and others on the walls nearby who could turn and cast spears or shoot arrows at the tower. Torio had not chosen an easy task.

To Lenardo's surprise, Torio greeted Secundus with a hug, but then he realized that the boy dared act no differently now from any other time when he might meet an old friend after several months' separation.

Then Secundus was asking, "Who is with Lenardo, Torio? We were told another Reader has turned traitor and they've stolen a child."

"I don't know. Another Reader and a child was all I was told, too."

Even though Torio was a better Reader than Secundus, the older man had known Torio since he entered the Academy. Lenardo doubted that the boy could lie to him for long. He was approaching the outskirts of Adigia now, with Julia still sleeping in his arms. He sat her up, but she merely gave a murmur of annoyance and tried to snuggle back into his arms.

"Julia, you must wake up," he told her, and touched her on the forehead, between the eyes, the way one woke an Adept. It was the way people accustomed to Adepts also woke Lenardo, and it always brought him wide awake at once. It worked with Julia, too.

"Where are we?" she asked. "Where's Torio?"

"On the tower. He's going to try to open the gates for us. Julia, I want you to ride into Adigia alone."

"But Father—"

"Hush! They're looking for two Readers and a child,

together. Torio's already fooled them. Now you ride on ahead of me. Don't Read. I'll be Reading you. There are guards along the way, so try to ride close to a family group. Let the guards think you're with them. Work your way to the gate tower. You can see it over the houses straight ahead.''

"Yes, Father. But what about you?"

"If I'm taken, you and Torio try to escape. If you want to come back to rescue me, don't do it until you have Aradia and Wulfston to help you. The important thing right now is to get Readers to them in Zendi—if not all of us, then as many as we can. Do you understand?"

"Yes, Father," she said bleakly. She hugged him and then got on her own horse and rode ahead.

Julia had no problem escaping the notice of the guards. She followed an old woman for a while and then seemed to be part of a family of peddlers. She was well on her way to the gate tower by the time Lenardo entered town.

He arranged his cloak to disguise his long, lean silhouette and recalled that the many people of Adigia who knew him had never seen him with a beard. He Read no recognition, although several guards scrutinized him as he passed. He rode boldly forward and Read Torio Reading him, carefully keeping it a visual Reading without recognition, waiting for the moment when Lenardo and Julia would be near the gates.

"There he is," Torio shouted. "It's Lenardo!"

In a moment's shock at Torio's betrayal, Lenardo almost did not react when the guards at the gate began running at him. Then Torio grabbed one of the guards on the tower crying, "Go get him!" and shoving him down the tower stairs—as if by accident in his excitement causing the man to fall but in reality very deliberately tripping him.

That guard screamed in pain as his leg twisted under him and broke. His fellow started down the stairs to his aid, and Torio leaped to the mechanism to raise the bar from the gates.

"Torio, what are you doing?" cried Secundus, and that brought the second guard back to the top of the tower, sword in hand. Torio turned, drawing his weapon, and closed with the guard as Secundus retreated in shock.

In broad daylight, Torio took advantage of his disconcerting blind eyes. He had learned years ago to appear to be "looking" at a person he was conversing with, but when he fought, he let his sightless eyes drift where they would, causing confusion in anyone used to seeking advantage by looking into an opponent's face. Torio's skill with a sword was well beyond Lenardo's. He outclassed the guardsman easily.

Meanwhile, Lenardo fought with the guards below in the narrow gateway, Julia beside him, both knowing that time was against them as more guards came running in the direction of the struggle. They would be surrounded and taken if Torio didn't get those gates open. . . .

Torio backed his opponent against the tower railing. With sword at his throat, he pushed the guard over. Secundus, unarmed, nonetheless lunged at Torio, who cried, "Let me go, Secundus. I don't want to hurt you."

"You're a traitor," the man cried, trying to grasp Torio's sword arm.

Between a gasp and a sob, Torio said, "Not by my choice. You don't understand what is happening. I'm sorry." He swung his arm high, bringing the sword hilt down on Secundus's head, knocking him unconscious.

Now Torio turned back to the pulleys, straining to turn the wheel meant to be turned by two men. As the bar creaked and began to rise slowly from its brackets, the guards on the walls, who had been looking into the melee by the gate and trying to decide where to shoot, suddenly realized that someone on the tower was raising the bar. A shower of arrows rained about Torio. Miraculously, none hit home. He ducked down and tried to turn the wheel from there, but he lacked leverage. Reading the archers, he stood, drawing their fire, and then he ducked. While they drew new arrows from their quivers, he gave the wheel one more turn. The bar hung free above its brackets.

By their own weight, the massive gates creaked outward a handspan. Lenardo and Julia spurred their horses, surging toward the guards to drive them against the gates, shoving.

The mighty bar was now dangling by its ropes just over the guards' heads.

Torio climbed out atop the gate, shielded behind the pulley mechanism from the rain of arrows, and with a swift swing of his sword cut through the ropes. The bar fell on the guardsmen, and those it didn't hit were knocked over like toy soldiers by those it did. The gates swung wide open. Torio clung giddily to his perch as Lenardo and Julia struggled over bar and bodies. Lenardo swerved to ride directly under Torio, shouting, "Jump!"

The boy did, landing behind Lenardo on his horse, clutching for a hold, finding it. And then they were riding madly for safety as spears and arrows filled the air about them.

A shattering burst of pain, a single scream, and then Torio's dead weight slumped forward against Lenardo, an arrow through his body.

Chapter Eight

Lenardo dared not stop. Behind them, the guards left alive and uninjured were gathering for pursuit on horseback. Torio had fainted from the pain, but he was alive.

The arrow had gone through the boy's left shoulder, narrowly missing the top of his lung. Still he might bleed to death or fall off the horse before they could ride beyond pursuit. Lenardo clutched at Torio's arms, aggravating the wound but keeping the boy in place as he spurred the horse forward. Now they were out of range of the bowmen on the walls, but mounted guards were pouring through the gateway. *Did I bring him with me only to have him die?*

The brief stretch of smooth road meant that Lenardo could hold the horse steady while he tried to waken Torio.

//Keep going,// he told Julia, who had slowed to the pace of the doubly burdened horse. //Ride ahead. Get help.//

The child did as she was told, fumbling in her saddlebag for something. Lenardo had no time to concentrate on her. The guards were gaining. There were woods ahead; they could try to hide, but with more than thirty men, the guards could spread out and comb the woods easily. Lenardo could never hang on to Torio during a ride over such rough terrain, and so he rode determinedly straight ahead, glad to come to the rutted, uneven part of the road, where his Reading could guide the horse to sure footing while the guards had to go by whatever they could see. The uneven pace, though, jarred Torio, increasing the damage the arrow was doing. Pain brought Torio semiconscious, and he clung to Lenardo with what strength he had.

//We'll get help for you soon,// Lenardo assured him, although he could not imagine where.

Desperately, he Read ahead and to his astonishment found rescue on the way. Men were running along the road toward him, some armed with bows and arrows, a few with swords, but most with pitchforks, clubs, knives, or other sharp implements lashed to tool handles—whatever they could find to defend their land.

And their Lord.

For they bore Lenardo's ensign, the red dragon on the field of white. The pennants and ribbons given out at the festival had become the banners under which his people marched. They fluttered from poles, were glued to shields, and decorated the shoulders of troop commanders.

Directing the enthusiastic throng was Julia, wearing on her brow the golden fillet that marked her as the daughter of the Lord of the Land. "My lord!" They gave a great shout as they saw Lenardo. He raised his hand in greeting, consummately aware of the brand on his arm, seeing them look at it in awe. Then they rushed past him, at the oncoming Aventine guard. The guard might be mounted and better armed, but they were outnumbered three to one by men fighting to protect a lord they loved and were willing to die for.

I don't deserve such loyalty, Lenardo thought as the emotions of his people swept over him. Then Torio was saying in awe, "I have *never* Read anything like that, not even when the Emperor passes," and Lenardo realized that it was safe to stop now, draw the arrow, and treat the boy's injury. If only Sandor were here.

As he drew to a halt, several people approached to help ease Torio down from the horse. A motherly woman said, "My lord, I have healing powers."

"Thank the gods," Lenardo exclaimed. "This is Torio, a Reader. We need his help."

"Yes, my lord." She knelt beside Torio, who was being supported by two men, and frowned as she looked into his milky eyes. "You are blind?"

"It doesn't matter. I'm a Reader."

"Oh. Then can you Read your wound for me?" she asked as she placed a gentle hand on the boy's shoulder.

Lenardo Read Torio's astonishment as his pain disappeared. The "sorcery" was merely stopping the sensation through the nerves. Lenardo now knew it to be a simple and basic technique, but recalled that the first time it had been done to him he had been as awestruck as Torio.

The boy adjusted quickly and began explaining the injuries the arrow had created.

"It is good you didn't have to ride farther," the healer said. "You haven't lost enough blood to weaken you seriously, so the rest can be healed to prevent further damage until you can sleep and heal completely."

"Just do as . . . what is your name?" Lenardo asked the healer.

"Fila, my lord."

"Do as Fila says, Torio. Fila, you have my gratitude and will have more than that after we have driven our enemies from the land," he promised her, and turned his attention to the battle down the road. Three of Lenardo's men were dead, but so were seven of the Aventine guard, and the rest were retreating, sure now that they had lost their quarry.

Julia had ridden to watch the rout, and now she came back, laughing in glee. "They're running away. They're scared of us now, Father." Then she dismounted. "How's Torio?"

"He'll be fine. You did well again, Daughter."

"Should we ride ahead?" Julia asked.

Although he was itching to ride on, Lenardo told her, "Sit down and rest until we know whether Torio can travel." Torio's injury reminded him of how quickly a single Reader could be put out of action. If possible, he wanted both of them to guide the Adepts in Zendi.

Torio had all the Reading ability necessary to guide Fila, and so Lenardo sat down on the grass and Read to Zendi. Battle still raged, but the Adepts' part was over for the moment. They had worn themselves out. It was a typical pattern. Savages began with a battle of Adepts, but after they had used up their strength, their armies continued to fight. Hron and two of his cohorts were now deep in recovery sleep; the fourth Adept was tired but awake, ready to answer any further attack.

There would be no immediate attack from Zendi, however. In Lenardo's house, Wulfston slept the sleep of exhaustion, as did Arkus and Josa, who must have been working with him. Searching for Aradia, he Read the infirmary, where Sandor and his aides were working as quickly as they could, but still some of the wounded died before they received attention. Here he discovered Lilith, so deeply asleep that for a moment he thought her dead. She had been placed in one of the family's rooms, where she lay healing of crushed limbs. It seemed the attacking Adepts must have succeeded in one of their favorite tricks of dropping something—perhaps a building—on her. She was alive and would be well, but she would not wake until the battle was over, unless it went on for several more days.

Relieved to find that Lilith had succeeded in reaching Zendi, Lenardo continued his search for Aradia. It was maddening. Would he have to do a building-by-building search to find her? Why was she not in his house, in recuperative sleep?

Then he thought to Read the bathhouse. It, too, held many wounded now. They were being taken there from the infirmary to sleep as they healed in the relative safety of the stone building.

But Aradia was not asleep. Her increased Adept powers had stood her in good stead. She might be tired, but she was nowhere near the total exhaustion of the others. Helmuth was with her in the room once used to store Zendi's treasures. Together they were poring over maps of Zendi and the surrounding countryside.

"I cannot find anything to use," Aradia was saying in frustration. "The land is all so flat around here, we can't drop a cliff on them. There's no bog to suck them under." She paced. "If they can find us, they can knock buildings down on us, but we have no way to attack them except with our full powers. Why was this city ever built here, where it's so hard to defend?"

"The Aventines built it, my lady," said Helmuth. "They have no Adepts."

"Yes, of course. If only Lenardo were here."

"Surely he will come, my lady," Helmuth said with more loyalty than conviction. He knew, Lenardo Read, that there had been some serious disagreement before Lenardo left, and afterward a fight between Aradia and Wulfston. When things quieted, Wulfston had sent Arkus in search of Lenardo, but no one could find him.

Although he would never voice it, the old man was of the opinion that Lenardo had been driven away and that later Wulfston had made Aradia repent of her rash act. Whatever had happened, Wulfston no longer wore the wolf-stone.

But what had happened to Lenardo and Julia? *I should have gone with them,* Helmuth told himself. *Why did I let my lord ride off alone with the child? They never reached the gates of the empire. What became of them?*

Helmuth feared that, avoiding their own soldiers, they had perished in the earthquake. *Why else would my lord not return when his people are under attack?*

So Aradia had told no one but Wulfston about her Reading. It was no help to her now; she was making no attempt to Read, and all Lenardo's efforts could not make her notice him. *I'll just have to go to Zendi.*

When Lenardo drew his attention back to Torio, the boy was sitting up so that Fila could wash the blood off his shoulder. The wound was closed and already half healed. Torio lifted his arm experimentally and laughed as only a dull ache throbbed through the area that a short time before had been pounding with agony.

"It's not my sword arm," he said. "I can fight."

"You must rest first," said Fila. "Lie still now and let me complete the healing." She pushed him gently down and then touched his shoulder again, letting the healing heat tingle through it. Then she looked up at Lenardo. "My lord, it would be best if the young Reader slept for a few hours."

"No," Torio protested.

"Wait, Torio," said Lenardo. "Fila, Torio is a Reader, not an Adept. He won't be draining himself if he uses his powers. Zendi is under siege, but the Adepts on both sides are resting now. When they waken with their strength renewed, I must be there to guide Aradia and Wulfston. I want Torio there, too, not several hours away."

"I understand, my lord," said Fila, "but Lord Torio can rest in one of the supply wagons."

"Very good."

Despite his protests, Torio was settled into a wagon between cases of supplies and sent helplessly to sleep. By that time, the men wounded in the skirmish with the Aventine guards were brought to Fila, who set to work healing them, promising to follow as soon as all were out of danger.

Lenardo rode among a veritable migration toward Zendi. Every road in the land was filled with people on their way to defend the capital. They would far outnumber the besieging army, but few of them were trained soldiers. Those had all heeded the watchers' summons yesterday and were already doing battle.

Reading ahead, Lenardo found that the attacking Adept army was forcing its way in a wedge toward Eastgate. Knowing that they would soon be surrounded, they were trying to break into the city, where, if they could capture them, they could hold Zendi's Adepts hostage.

Lenardo's heart sank. None of the four attacking Adepts was injured; within hours, their powers would be back to full strength. Lilith would be unconscious for days. Her son was just a child. That left Aradia and Wulfston, outnumbered two to one. If he could not reach them before they were captured or surrounded, his friends would be operating blind while their attackers still had their Reader. Try as he might, he could not contact Aradia.

I must get there.

He pushed his horse forward, and people made way for him, cheering as he passed. He Read their hopes rising. The Lord of the Land was riding to the rescue.

Julia followed him, and he could find no reason not to

let her. If Zendi fell, it would be better if she died in the fighting than if she were taken and forced to Read for the enemy, like Galen.

Lenardo's troops fought bravely, but he was still half an hour away when they were forced back against the Eastgate portcullis, and the towers brought down on them by the newly wakened Adepts now working easily at close range.

The enemy was within the walls. Their troops were met by Lenardo's, but they provided a safe path for the Adepts and Galen to enter the city.

As the news flashed through the city, all within rushed to block the enemy's progress through the streets. Wulfston, Arkus, Josa, Greg, Vona, and Aradia met in the forum, but instantly a sea of flame leaped about them and they scattered. Readerless, they were easy targets. Lilith's son came running out of one of the side streets and met Wulfston, who grabbed him and turned him around.

"Keep moving. They're four on one if we provide them a target."

"But—"

"They're in East Street. Can you remember the big brick building with the false tower on top? *Think*, Ivorn. You've seen it."

"Yes," the boy said uncertainly.

"We'll bring that front wall down on them. Can you focus on it?"

"Yes, Lord Wulfston," the boy replied grimly.

"Good. Front foundation. Make the mortar crumble. Together," he said, halting and taking the boy's hands. "Now!"

Lenardo Read the result of their effort: the crumbling mortar, shifting bricks, swaying wall falling with amazing slowness, but still too fast for the advancing enemy troops to escape. The wall crushed at least twenty to death and injured a dozen more.

But the Adepts and Galen were not among the dead and injured. As the wall was falling, Hron turned on Galen.

"Who—"

"Wulfston and that boy, Lilith's son."

"Where?"

Wulfston and Ivorn were still concentrating, not knowing the effect of their effort until the heavy vibration rumbled through the ground beneath them. They were still standing together as Galen hastily described their location and the Adepts hurled a thunderbolt.

It was almost a direct hit, and they were flung apart. Wulfston was hurled against a wall, where he struck his head and fell unconscious. Ivorn was thrown high in the air to land in a heap on the cobbles, knocked breathless, with several ribs and the small bone of his right forearm broken. Neither could move. Now it would be easy for the Adepts to kill them.

//Galen,// Lenardo projected intensely.

//Lenardo! Where are you?// But the question was academic; Galen already had him spotted. "Lenardo's coming," he told Hron. "We must keep him out of the city."

"He can't do anything from out there," Hron replied. "Did that blow kill Wulfston and the boy?"

//Galen,// Lenardo projected again, determined to distract the Reader, //my people will open Southgate for me. You can't win now.//

"Lenardo's at Southgate," said Galen, creating a new eddy of confusion in the already boiling mob as he turned his horse and began struggling back toward one of the streets that curved around to Southgate. //This time you won't escape, Lenardo. This time I'll kill you!//

Hron followed Galen. The other Adepts, rather than waste their strength clearing the debris out of the street before them, turned back as well.

Inside Southgate, Lenardo's troops surged through the streets toward the approaching enemy. As the first ranks came into view of the Adepts, a roaring wall of flame consumed them. Those just behind retreated before the heat and the death screams of their companions, but Lenardo's plan called for their retreat.

If he could entice Galen and the four Adepts to Southgate, he could destroy them all. A watcher on the Southgate tower signaled the approach of the enemy to the army outside, and they began moving toward the gate, which would be opened for them.

"Halt," Lenardo shouted, galloping to the front of the first column. "Stay back, and when I signal, retreat."

"My lord?" But the astonished question immediately dissolved into obedience. "Yes, my lord."

"Get me a signaling mirror and someone with the talent to start fires. Hurry!"

Galen was Reading him, and so Lenardo once more created a false scenario in his mind: his troops advancing, himself at their head. At Galen's direction, the Adepts shot thunderbolts at his phantom. Lenardo enticed them to waste their energy over and over again.

A watcher's polished mirror was thrust into his hands, and he tried to concentrate on two things at once: keeping Galen occupied with his phantom and signaling his true message to the watcher on the Southgate tower.

Retreat before Hron's troops, he signaled. *Let them win Southgate. Then take shelter as far from the gate as you can.*

He could Read the watcher's indecision and feared that Galen would. He told the boy, //It's no use, Galen. Tell your Adept Lords to surrender.//

//You always were a fool, Lenardo.//

The watcher finally signaled *Message acknowledged* and turned to relay it to the other soldiers. The retreat began as Lenardo projected to Galen an image of his troops approaching the gate from the outside, while in reality they drew back, bewilderedly obeying their lord's orders.

"Where's that fire talent?" Lenardo demanded.

"He's coming, my lord," someone assured him, and indeed, a man in peasant garb was soon brought to him. "This is Mib."

"My lord," the man stuttered, eyes downcast, more terrified of Lenardo than of the battle.

"I need your help, Mib," said Lenardo, dismounting from his horse so that he could speak quietly and reassuringly to the man. "The enemy is approaching Southgate, and our own men are pulling away. We are going to blow up the gate."

"Blow up, my lord?"

"There is marsh gas under the gate," Lenardo explained, and found that that meant nothing to Mib.

Trying to keep Galen occupied with false images so that he would not Read what was really happening put a deadly strain on Lenardo's patience. Precious time was passing. With a fine show of effort, the troops inside the city retreated before Hron's oncoming army. Lenardo was still trying to make Mib understand that if he would cause a fire at a certain spot under the ground, the whole area would explode. The man didn't understand but was willing to try.

"How deep, my lord?" he repeated for the third time.

Again Lenardo tried to find a measurement Mib would comprehend, just as Hron's troops took Southgate, scrambled up the tower, and called down to the Adepts and Galen that there was no one outside the gate.

Galen still Read what Lenardo was projecting: Lenardo's army trying to break down the gates. "You're lying!" he shouted at the soldiers on the tower, and forced his crippled body up the tower stairs, blocking the way of Hron behind him. Marava and the other two Adepts were working their way to the tower.

"Now," Lenardo told Mib. "Start that fire *now*."

The man went blank to Reading as he concentrated his effort. Lenardo Read the underground cavern where the culverts had collapsed. Nothing happened. He located the spot of heat in the ground.

"Move east!"

Mib gasped and panted; then he began to concentrate again.

Galen came out on top of the tower and looked at the scene below. His eyes and his Reading told him two different things. In utter terror, he clasped his hands to his head and screamed. Hron came up beside him, took one look at the scene so different from the one Galen had been describing, and dealt Galen an open-handed cuff that sent him sprawling.

In vast relief, Lenardo let go of the phantom scene,

concentrating fully on Mib. "Lower," he told him. "Hurry!"

Already sheets of flame and thunderbolts were erupting all about them as the Adepts now saw the army massed a good distance from Southgate, but not too far for their Adept tricks.

"Now," Lenardo shouted to Mib. "Do it *now*, before they realize we lured them—"

//Murderer,// Galen's voice screamed in Lenardo's head. //I'll kill you! I'll kill you!// He scrambled to Hron's side and pointed. "My lord, Lenardo is there. He tricked me, my lord. Kill him!"

Hron could not have made out individual figures at that distance, but whether he believed Galen or not, his blows would kill his enemies. Sheets of flame lighted the air. Thunderbolts shook the ground. Even as Lenardo urged Mib to fire the marsh gas, the man's body convulsed, a bolt seared through it, and he fell blasted, dead at Lenardo's feet.

Horrified, Lenardo leaped back, his shocked cry lost in the noise of thunderbolts, the screams of the dying, and the galloping of panicked horses. He had to find someone—

"Can you start fires?" he cried to anyone who came near, but no one answered.

//Master Lenardo, get out of the front ranks.// It was Torio, freshly arrived and Reading the scene of carnage.

Lenardo Read widely and found that inside Zendi, word had reached Aradia of the assault on Southgate. She could fire the gas with hardly an effort.

//Aradia, Aradia!// he projected, but it was no use.

Concentrating her Adept powers, she was completely blind to Reading, and she was leading a small band toward Southgate. Within minutes she would be in range to be killed in the explosion of the gas. If Lenardo did not set it off, though, she would be one Adept against four—certain death even with her increased powers.

Lenardo remained in the front ranks of the retreating army, calling on every side for a fire talent, Reading Aradia approaching her doom. No time! No time to find anyone else.

Torio reached him, Reading with him, saying, "I can't find a fire talent, either. It won't work, Master Lenardo."

And Galen easily focused on the two Readers together and began describing their location to Hron.

//Galen,// Torio gasped. //Galen, it's Torio. We were friends.//

//If you're Lenardo's friend, you're not mine. You chose the wrong side, Torio. *My* friends have the power, not yours.//

"I have it," Lenardo said suddenly, desperately.

"Have what?" Torio asked in bewilderment.

"The power to fire the gas. If Aradia can Read, why can't I do Adept tricks? Fire is easy, she says. Easiest of all—"

He stopped, knelt, and concentrated, Reading the pocket of gas, trying to visualize it flaming. His head began to hurt, but nothing happened. Aradia was only a few streets away. He couldn't warn her.

He couldn't warn her because she couldn't Read and do Adept tricks at the same time. He had to work blind— Read the spot—stop Reading—concentrate—heat—fire— flame—*will*—

The earth beneath him heaved and buckled, and then Lenardo was slammed to the ground on a wave of compression. He tried to Read what was happening but couldn't. Blind as he had never been since earliest childhood, he knew only the physical pain of the air knocked from his lungs, the roar of the explosion, the screams, the choking dust, grit in his eyes keeping him from seeing as Torio rolled him off his cloak and covered both of them with it to shelter them from the debris raining out of the sky.

The noise and the feel of matter falling on them went on and on as Lenardo's horror built. He could not Read. He was trapped within his physical senses . . . forever? On a wave of physical and emotional exhaustion, he passed out.

Lenardo woke to the ground shivering beneath him. He had no sense of passing time and for an instant thought it the explosion of another pocket of marsh gas. But it was a tremor, not a jolt, and he felt at once that he was no longer tangled with Torio on the rocky ground but alone in a comfortable bed.

A soft weight dropped beside him on the bed, and Aradia's hand touched his forehead. "Lenardo! Lenardo, can you Read? Who's doing it this time?"

The tremor was already dying away as he tried to Read. He could. No vast range, but he could find the center of this slight quake and be thoroughly certain that no Adept was causing it.

"Just an aftershock," he said to reassure Aradia, opening his eyes to meet anxiety in hers.

She smiled in relief. "I can't Read well enough. I thought. . . ." Her normal calm returned. "No, we have killed all of our enemies this time. You did it, Lenardo. You saved us. And we found all the bodies. No one escaped."

"Galen?"

"I'm sorry."

He sighed, too tired to feel genuine grief. His body felt like lead. Before he could allow himself to sleep again, he asked, "Julia? Torio?"

"They're both fine. They were of great help, though Torio was guarding you like some fierce animal when I finally reached you. He told me what you did." Her violet eyes glowed in triumph. "I was right, Lenardo. Now nothing can stop us."

He didn't have the strength to argue. It would have to wait until he was fully recovered. But he managed a sardonic smile. "It certainly stopped *me*."

She laughed. "You did what every new Adept does: expended far too much energy on a simple task. You'll learn. Sleep now."

"If I'm needed—"

"You're not. It's all over. All the wounded are recovered or in healing sleep. The dead will wait for the funeral tomorrow. Now that I know you will recover, I can sleep as well."

"Recover? I wasn't hurt."

"You couldn't Read. Torio was terrified for you. I'll tell him that his fears were groundless. Stop fighting sleep, Lenardo. Your people are safe."

There was something else nagging at the back of his mind, but it would not come clear before he sank once more into unconsciousness.

The next time he woke, it was dawn, and Aradia lay beside him, her head on his chest, her pale hair shimmering in the morning light.

Aside from being ravenously hungry, Lenardo felt normal. He tried Reading, easily locating Julia asleep in her room, Torio in one nearby, Wulfston in the suite on the other side of the courtyard, and Cook already preparing breakfast in the kitchen.

Outside, the forum was the same as on any morning, with a few people stirring, drawing water from the fountain. All the buildings, though, were as crowded as they had been at the festival. His people would not go home until their familiar rituals had been completed.

Where Southgate had been, there was a huge crater. No need to barricade that entry point now. Repairs had already been effected at Eastgate, although surely after the abysmal failure of an alliance of four Adepts to take the city, there would be no further attacks.

I did it, he thought contentedly, and knew himself worthy to be Lord of the Land. *Worthy in powers. Now I must be worthy in devotion. I will never desert my people again.*

His powers. Would they be passed on to another generation? At last he Read Aradia. He had been wrong. She was not pregnant.

She woke and looked at him in puzzlement. "What's wrong?"

"You are not carrying my child."

"No. You knew that."

"I was so ready to run from you that I did *not* Read you thoroughly before I left, Aradia. It was unforgivable."

"You thought I lied to you?"

"No, I forgot how limited your Reading is and took your word. You could have been wrong, though you were not."

She sat up. "Lenardo, we must attend to our duties. Before we face the others, though, I must ask your forgiveness."

"And I yours," he replied.

She took his hand. "I want your child. I will risk my powers willingly. But I am glad I am not pregnant now." She squeezed his hand tightly. "Read the truth, please! I was glad I dared use my powers to the fullest in the battle just past and neither have them impaired by pregnancy nor fear that I might harm our child. You know that is true, Lenardo."

"Yes."

"But there is a more important reason to me. If I carried your child now, I would never know if it had been conceived in love or in deceit. It could have happened the day I tricked you, Lenardo. It may seem foolish to you, but I am very glad that I will never have to wonder if a child of ours was conceived against your will."

"Never fear," he said tenderly, drawing her into his arms and kissing her. Then he said, "We are still going to disagree, you know."

"I know," she replied, "but we'll do it openly. No more deceit. That goes for you, too, Lenardo."

"I deeply regret the one time I sought to deceive you."

"More than once. I was your liege lady, and you chose Julia as your heir without consulting me. My father would have considered that reason enough for anything I cared to do to you. My brother did not."

"Wulfston?"

"When I told him why you left—" she swallowed hard. "He is much like you, open and direct. He was horrified, not at my taking action but at my method. He is right, Lenardo: I should have told you plainly of my disapproval. From now on, I shall."

"I'm sorry, Aradia. I'm afraid I wasn't fully aware of what I had done. I intended only to make Julia my daughter. Whether she will be my heir—"

"Could have become a serious problem one day," said Aradia. "Fortunately, some good came out of this latest attack. We have acquired even more lands, and young as she is, Julia proved herself. So we shall set aside now the lands she will one day rule and thus avoid a potential rivalry between Julia and the child you and I will have.''

Lenardo groaned. ''We sound like the family of the Aventine Emperor, intriguing about children not yet born.''

''No intrigue. No deception. But we must plan, Lenardo. We have a future to build. The law of nature is that those with power will rule, and so we must see that those with power have their own lands. Otherwise, they will challenge, and there will be more wars.''

They raided the kitchen, to Cook's delight, and then got ready to face the world, dressing in gray funeral garments, for the preparations were already going on outside for the rite later in the day.

''As Lord of the Land, you must light the funeral pyre,'' said Aradia.

''Either I'll do it with a burning brand or I'll pretend and you light it, Aradia. I do not want to pass out at a public ceremony.''

''You won't if you do it right. You're completely recovered now, Lenardo. Let's see what you can do. Lift something.''

He was standing before the chest from which he had taken the clothes he wore. The wolf-stone still lay where he had left it when he fled with Julia.

Wulfston, he recalled, had been only three years old when he revealed his Adept powers by lifting the wolf-stone Nerius wore. *Can I match the powers of a three-year-old?*

As he tried to concentrate, he felt again the utter terror he had known when his Reading disappeared after he blew up the gate. *It came back,* he reminded himself, but he still fought down fear.

Aradia saw what he was trying to do. ''You can move it,'' she told him. ''Remember, work with nature.''

Nature? Gravity held the pendant firmly to the top of the chest. The chain formed a kind of nest for the wolf's head, and so it did not even have a tendency to roll. It had, indeed, stayed right there through every vibration that had shaken the house in the past few days. Lenardo Read that the top of the chest had a faint slant toward the left front corner. He began to concentrate, stopped Reading, envisioned the stone tilting, rolling over the chain, sliding toward that left front corner. He put his hand there to catch it, although it had not yet moved.

Aradia stood beside him, saying nothing, but her presence was a palpable encouragement. The stone tilted, lurched over the chain, and then gathered momentum as it rolled to the edge and fell with a plop into Lenardo's hand.

He stared at it and then looked at Aradia. "Did you—"

"No," she said with her wolflike grin. "I was Reading, so I *couldn't* help." She hugged him. "That was wonderful. And you see? You didn't deplete yourself."

He was trembling, and his knees were weak, but it was more from his astonishment at what he had done than from physical depletion. He tried to Read and for a moment felt a stir of terror, for his power was gone again.

Even as he stood there, though, his Reading cleared. As if a fog had drawn back, he could Read Aradia, then the room, then the house, the city—

"Aradia, for a moment my Reading was gone again. Now it's returning."

She nodded. "When I was using my Adept powers in battle, I found I could not Read at all. We have much to learn, Lenardo, but we'll learn it together."

He started to put on the wolf-stone, but Aradia stayed his hand.

"No, Lenardo, you are my sworn man no longer. You have well repaid me for the lands I granted you by saving my life and Wulfston's and Lilith's as well. In fact, I should not be telling you what to do with the lands of those whom *you* destroyed for attacking *your* people. You could keep them all if you desired."

"I won't," he replied, and laid the wolf-stone back on the chest. "I would not want to, and even if I did, I could not rule so much land."

"Oh, you could," said Aradia. "*We* could."

"I thought you had given up wanting to rule the world," Lenardo said lightly, hoping to turn it off as a joke.

"We *must* rule," she said firmly, refusing to be distracted. "Our alliance of four lasted hardly a season before you and I betrayed one another. And we love each other. Wulfston refuses to be my sworn man any longer and defies me to take his lands."

"But he helped you."

"Of course. He is my brother." She gave Lenardo a sad smile. "Wulfston sees me more clearly than you do, not only because we were children together but because his love for me is family love. He see what he considers to be my faults and loves me in spite of them."

"But Wulfston will not hear of forming an empire, nor will Lilith."

"By our laws, those with power rule those with lesser or no powers. They have no choice, for only you and I have both Adept and Reading powers."

Sick at heart, Lenardo said flatly, "I will not do it. I don't want to fight you, Aradia. I want to marry you and live the rest of my life with you. But I will not help you subject Wulfston, Lilith, Julia, Torio—"

"Not subjects, allies. But you and I will make the final decisions if there is a dispute."

"Semantics," he said. "Calling it something else doesn't change it. We'll see what Wulfston and Lilith have to say."

They left it at that and went to breakfast, their second meal of the day. Julia and Torio were at the table. Lenardo's daughter leaped up to hug him, but Torio gave only polite responses and otherwise remained silent and withdrawn. Lenardo found no trouble doing justice a second time to Cook's efforts.

When they had eaten, Torio asked, "Master Lenardo, may I speak with you?"

"Of course. Come into my room. I've heard nothing but glowing praise about how you helped after the battle. You saved many lives, Torio, by helping the healers."

"Yes," replied Torio, "I am fit for that. But Master

Lenardo, one of your servants brought me clothes to wear for some kind of ceremony tomorrow, the robes of a Magister Reader. I can't wear them"

That was quick work. Lenardo had issued the order at dawn, hardly two hours since. "Why can't you wear them?"

"I have not achieved magister rank. I was denied testing. I was failed."

"You did not fail, Torio. I have tested you and found you worthy."

"You?"

Lenardo sat behind his desk, guiding Torio into the chair opposite. "Do you deny my right to test you?"

"You *are* a Master Reader," Torio said uncertainly. "But the Council of Masters—"

"Never had the opportunity to examine you. When a Reader proves himself in an emergency, any Master can elevate him, as Master Clement elevated me. The ancient tradition of the Academies is still honored, Torio. We have carried it beyond the pale. I am the only Master Reader here. Do you challenge my authority?"

The boy gasped. "Oh, no, Master."

"Then accept what you are. You have passed every test for the rank of magister except age, and you will find that in the world you have entered, you will be judged by your accomplishments, not your years."

Torio sat silently for a few moments. "Yes, Master," he said at last.

"Something else is disturbing you," Lenardo observed.

"I don't know what I'm doing here," the boy replied. "I ran *from* Portia and her plans to harm you and me. Master Clement told me to go. I trust him. I trust you. But what did I run *to*?"

"A whole new world," said Lenardo. "A world where no one will attempt to limit your powers. You will learn Adept powers, too, Torio."

"That frightens me. What you did—I was Reading. I still can't believe it."

Torio was dressed like Lenardo, in a gray ankle-length tunic with a shorter gray tunic over it, ash-colored garments appropriate to a savage funeral. Without moving from his chair behind the desk, Lenardo concentrated on the belt tied loosely around the boy's slim waist and tugged. Torio jumped as if stung. Lenardo smiled grimly and said, "Believe it."

It was easier each time. He breathed a bit hard from the effort, and that was all, except that he had blanked out his Reading again.

Torio lifted his face, as if "looking" at Lenardo as he concentrated, undoubtedly trying to Read him. Lenardo noticed that the boy's eyes were no longer milky but a clear bluish green. Then his Reading returned as it had that morning, spreading outward from himself, and Torio relaxed with a shiver.

"I'm becoming accustomed to the Adepts doing such things. But *you*—"

"You'll learn to do them yourself. What happened to your eyes?"

"Fila, I think. She must have thought the cataracts were the cause of my blindness, so while my shoulder was healing, she had them dissolve away. I didn't even notice until Julia did."

"We must find Fila and reward her at the ceremony tomorrow. She did save your life, although she will probably be disappointed that she did not restore your sight."

"But many people *are* blind because of cataracts," said Torio. "Do you think . . . could I learn to heal? The way the Adepts do?"

"We're all going to learn and teach the Adepts to Read. We'll build an Academy here, Torio, where Readers and Adepts will work together. Will you help me do that?"

"Yes, Master," the boy said eagerly.

"My lord," Lenardo corrected. "That is my title here."

Torio frowned. "People keep calling *me* 'my lord,' too."

"A title you deserve by virtue of your powers. Torio, we have not settled the details, but there are lands won in the battle just past that will be set aside for you to rule as soon as you come into your full powers."

"To rule? I can't."

"Yes, you can. You must. All your life, you have been taught to fear power. So long as you fear it, it will control you. Master your fears and you will master your powers. Master your powers and you will master your fears."

It was time for the funeral, after which Lenardo would meet with Aradia, Wulfston, and Lilith to decide the future. He dreaded the meeting. *It could end with the four of us enemies if Aradia persists in her plan to rule us all.*

The mass funeral was sad and solemn, but this time Lenardo spoke for Galen. "He was never evil, he was only weak. Let us build a world in which bright and clever young people like Galen need not fear being forced to do the will of those who have power. A world in which power is used for good."

Torio also spoke for Galen, whom he had once known well. "He was wrong . . . for the right reasons. I hope . . . that I will do right for the right reasons."

Aradia and Wulfston spoke for Hron, but Lenardo received another shock when Lilith stepped forward with her son, Ivorn.

"At one time," she said, "Hron and I were closest of friends. He gave me the most precious gift possible: my son. I shall treasure always the memory of Hron in those days and vow to work for a world in which no one like Drakonius can grow so powerful as to draw good men like Hron from their vows of friendship and alliance into power plays and vengeance."

Voice breaking with adolescent perversity, Ivorn said, "I found out only today that Hron was my father. He gave me life, and yet yesterday he would have taken it. My mother would not have chosen an evil man to give her a child, so I vow to be as my father must have been as a young man and revere his memory, but to be like my mother in keeping my word."

This time it was Lenardo's duty to sprinkle earth and water over the funeral pyre and then unite all four elements by lighting it. He had no doubt that he could do it now. Torio Read him grimly, Julia expectantly.

//Show me how, Father.//

He concentrated, shutting out Reading, imagining the flame. A wisp of smoke rose, a tiny flicker of fire, and Lenardo rocked on his heels, but he didn't feel faint—and his Reading cleared in just a few moments.

//Very good,// Aradia told him joyously, and then became blank to Reading herself as the pitiful flicker roared into white-hot flame that would reduce the immense pyre to ashes within minutes.

His people must have known that the other Adepts had taken over to create the conflagration, but that did not lessen their pride in their lord's accomplishment. He felt them quell the urge to cheer him and knew that it would be indulged at the ceremony tomorrow, when he appeared before them in his scarlet robes.

If there was to be such a ceremony. If he did not betray the trust these people had in him and destroy the future so healthily represented in Torio, Ivorn, Julia, solemnly watching the bodies of the hundreds who had died reduced to nothing but a scattering of ash—and memory.

A rousing cheer startled him, and he tardily remembered the savage custom of following a funeral with a feast, a celebration of victory and of life. Music started, and people ran to change their garments. Banners bearing the red dragon appeared out of nowhere—and just as many with Aradia's white wolf's head. Scattered among them were Wulfston's black wolf's head and Lilith's blue lion, but the watchword of the day was the old saying, "In the day of the white wolf and the red dragon, there will be peace throughout the world."

Food was brought out: bread and cheese and fruit, kegs of wine and ale, meat that had been roasting all morning. The city rang with celebration, and Lenardo prepared to meet with the Adepts to try to make the ancient prophecy come true.

They met in Lenardo's house, around the same table they had used before. All had taken time to change out of their funeral garb: Wulfston into his richly embroidered dark brown garments, Aradia into her favorite purple, Lilith into a dark green dress with a vivid green surcoat.

They were ready to go out and join the dancing if the occasion called for it. Lenardo, too, had dressed optimistically, in dark blue hose, shirt, and embroidered tabard that had been made for him in Aradia's land.

When they sat down, Lenardo found the eyes of the three Adepts on him. As he was searching for the right way to begin, Wulfston said, "It is your right to determine how the lands we have taken shall be divided, Lenardo. No one can deny that you alone were responsible for the victory."

"No," said Lenardo. "I cannot act like a savage lord, give you lands, expect loyalty in return, and not worry about what happens in the next generation provided that my own lands have an heir."

Aradia smiled. "Then you have decided to act on my suggestion, Lenardo? Form an empire, make—"

"No," he said, interrupting her, feeling Lilith and Wulfston already bristling. "All of you—can't you see we must find a new way of governing? The way you have traditionally used brings on ceaseless wars—while the way of the Aventine Empire results in weakness and corruption. We must find another way."

He turned to Lilith. "You do not wear the wolf-stone. What are you to Aradia, Lilith, that you are ever loyal?"

"A friend," Lilith replied. "An ally, as I was to Nerius. I have never been sworn woman to either father or daughter, but I have always agreed with their aims to rule by kindness rather than cruelty, love rather than fear. That is the reason I am your ally, too, Lenardo."

"And I," Wulfston said.

"No one intends to change those aims," said Aradia. "It is simply that we now have so much land, so many people, that we must form a closer alliance. And we have three young people well deserving of lands of their own but too young to rule them. Even Torio—"

"What *about* Torio?" Wulfston asked. "Where is his place among us? I do not question his powers, but what of his loyalties?"

"He trusts me, and he has no place else to go," explained Lenardo, "but he is not my sworn man, nor can I ask that of him."

"I wish *I* could," said Wulfston. "I need a Reader, Lenardo. Julia will have to have years of training yet, but Torio is fully trained. I am willing to swear to protect the lands you grant to him and release them to him whenever you decide he has come into his full powers if he will Read for me in the meantime."

"You are getting ahead of me, Wulfston," said Lenardo. "First, you are going to learn to Read for yourself, as Aradia has done. Second, you will have to arrange with Torio himself to exchange services and lessons. However, I will heartily recommend to him that he accept your offer."

"Then Torio's lands should border on Wulfston's," said Lilith. "None of the newly taken lands do. Lenardo, I was of no help whatsoever in the battle just past, but my son—"

"Will be granted lands, of course, Lilith, and who but you could be his guardian?" Lenardo fought down exasperation.

Lilith began, "Then I will trade some of my land which borders on Wulfston's—"

"Stop," said Aradia. "I see what you are doing, Lilith, and you, too, my brother. You seek to divert this meeting from its true purpose, for you refuse to admit that because Lenardo and I have powers you do not—"

"Aradia, no," said Lenardo. "I have told you I will not be party to your attempts to form an empire. I grew up in an empire. I know what happens when when power becomes entrenched in one family and a small circle of their friends."

"Then what would you have us do?" Aradia demanded. "Go on as we are and spread our influence ever farther with ever less strength? We are four; soon we will be seven. We will trust Ivorn, Julia—but what of Torio? Lenardo, *you* know him and trust him, and we take your word. But what happens when Torio brings someone else into our alliance, or Julia does, or any one of us? What happens when we are ten? Twenty? A hundred? Your empire has a senate, Lenardo, but it cannot rule without one person who can make final decisions.''

"Not *my* empire any longer," he reminded her. "You need not fear that I have any lingering loyalties there.''

"I don't. I am pointing out that there must be one voice above the rest when many voices disagree. The Aventine succession is foolish; the whole system of suppressing those with powers is ridiculous. The person who rules here must be the person with the greatest powers.''

"And if he is another Drakonius?'' asked Wulfston.

"Then,'' said Lenardo, "the council has the power to eject him.''

Lilith gasped. "You are turning to Aradia's side, Lenardo?''

"Only insofar as she is right," he replied. "Our alliance has weathered two attacks now. Other lords will wonder what we have, and some will want to join us. Aradia is right that our ranks will grow and that we must formalize our government. Casual agreements among four friends have worked tolerably well so far, but we all agree, I think, that they will not work much longer.''

"Then what do you suggest?'' Lilith asked.

"A government based not on the Aventine system but on the organization of the Academies. Right now that system is being tested by Portia and her cohorts, but other Master Readers are already working to weed out the corruption. Aradia is right that those with power must rule, but there must be safeguards on them, such as the Council of Masters. Portia will not hold her office much longer. *She* is corrupt, but the system is not.

"What I propose, then, is a council to which every Lord Adept and Reader automatically belongs by virtue of his powers. The one who can demonstrate the greatest power will have the deciding vote in matters of dispute. *But,*'' he added, Reading Aradia's glee and the strong reservations still held by Wulfston and Lilith, "there must be safeguards. The Readers have only the protection of the Reader's Oath, but it is a strong protection. I saw clearly that Portia had forfeited a large portion of her powers by violating her Oath.''

"You propose such an oath for Adepts?" Lilith asked.

"Yes. An Oath and a Law that will pass from one generation to another, long after we are gone. Something beyond personal loyalties, beyond family ties—an Oath every Reader and Adept must honor, no matter how he may disagree with us in other matters."

"And it would be our duty," said Lilith, beginning to like the idea, "to formulate such an oath."

"Yes," Lenardo said. "You may be certain we will have many disputes before we are satisfied, but it will be worth all of them."

"What happens," Aradia asked skeptically, "if a Lord Adept breaks this marvelous Oath?"

"I should think," Lenardo said, "that the other safeguard would be obvious to you, Aradia. Adepts can join their powers. You are the most powerful Adept here. My powers are minimal, but Lilith and Wulfston are powerful Adepts. Would you care to stand against the three of us—" he took Wulfston's hand on top of the table, and the black Adept took the cue and grasped Lilith's hand with his other "—if we linked our powers against you?"

Aradia stared at them, and for one horrible moment Lenardo feared that she actually would strike some blow at them. But then she smiled, her wolflike grin merging into a laugh. "Oh, Lenardo, you are certainly learning quickly how to use power." She took his hand and Lilith's, completing the circle. "You win," she said. "We'll form a council, and we'll formulate an Oath. It won't be easy."

"Nothing as important as this can be easy," said Wulfston.

"But it will be worth the effort," Lilith said, her eyes shining.

They left it at that and after deciding on the division of lands for the next day's ceremony left the room to join the celebration. Lenardo stopped in the doorway and looked back at the bare room with its plain wooden table and four mismatched chairs. Aradia turned to see why he had not followed her, and then she laughed.

"The council chamber in which was formed the new empire—the greatest the world has ever known."

"Not an empire—" Lenardo began, but Aradia put a finger over his lips.

"Semantics again," she said. "Call it what you want, it's still an empire. Call *us* what you want, we'll still rule. Can you Read how proud of you I am, Lenardo, and how much I love you?"

She kissed him, and he held her slight, lithe body close, knowing the power in her. *But I have power, too, and I don't fear to use it anymore.* Confidently, he took her hand and led her out to join the celebration in the forum.

ABOUT THE AUTHOR

Jean Lorrah has a Ph.D. in Medieval British Literature. She is a Professor of English at Murray State University in Kentucky. Her first professional publications were nonfiction; her fiction was published in fanzines for years before her first pro novel appeared in 1980. She maintains a close relationship with sf fandom, appearing at conventions and engaging in as much fannish activity as time will allow. On occasion, she has the opportunity to combine her two loves of teaching and writing by teaching creative writing.

PLAYBOY'S BEST SCIENCE FICTION AND FANTASY

582-2

582-3

PBJ BOOKS, INC.
Book Mailing Service
P.O. Box 690 Rockville Centre, New York 11571

NAME_____

ADDRESS_____

CITY_____STATE_____ZIP_____

Please enclose 50¢ for postage and handling if one book is ordered;
25¢ for each additional book. $1.50 maximum postage and handling
charge. No cash, CODs or stamps. Send check or money order.

Total amount enclosed: $_____